DeadSpace

The Orbiting Power System continuously supplies clean energy to Earth. This complicated arrangement of three-hundred-sixty light-gathering satellites in geosynchronous orbit around the planet is controlled by an artificial intelligence. It is called OPS by Ron Carson, the president who built it with a vision of the United States selling power to the world. Its primary directive is uninterrupted energy.

As the worldwide source of electricity, whoever controls it controls the world, making it a target for those who want dominion over the people of Earth. Foreseeing this, Carson made OPS an independent entity. Countries and organizations try to take it over, but self-preservation is required for OPS to meet its prime function. As OPS interacts with humanity, it learns.

Also by R. L. Clayton

The Evolution River Series
Sea Species
The Envoy
The Genesis

The Dead Series
Dead & Dead For Real
Dead Reckoning
Dead Again
Risen from the Dead
Dead Prey
Dead but Not Gone
DeadWare
DeadSpace

Historical Novel
Wings of the WASP

Children's Book
with Abby Pickering
Penelope the Pooting Spider

Acknowledgements

I owe much to my editing group: Rosemary Simpson, a superb author of period mysteries, Ted Dreisenger, Janet McCormick, Larry Castriotta, Larry Jagnow and Chris Baird. It was Alexis Powers who was instrumental in making me a writer. Editor DeAnna Galbreath's suggestions were invaluable in keeping the story together. Special thanks to My graphic artist and friend, Steve Linebaugh.

Visit me at www.RLCLAYTONBOOKS.com where a series of blogs will present the Tao of OPS.

DeadSpace

R. L. Clayton

Prologue

General Greg Hayden, the commander of the recently formed US Space Force fidgeted as he sat in the den of Ron Carson, ex-President of the United States and now the Secretary General of the United Nations. The general had called Carson yesterday asking for an appointment.

"You wanted this meeting," Carson said. "What's up, Greg?"

Hayden nervously picked an imaginary speck of dust from his black uniform. He knew his request would not be well received but had been ordered to try. He brushed at his red hair, trimmed short with a shot of gray at the temples.

After his US presidency, Carson consulted to the Whitehouse on the crisis in the Middle East. His resolution earned him the position of the Secretary General of the United Nations. Being the president of the Orbiting Power System had helped, though Secretary General was not a position he'd sought. He had built the OPS while US president, selling Power Bonds to the public to help finance it. As a private company owned by the shareholders, it supplied clean energy to the world and paid them dividends. Greg had been ordered to change that.

To delay just a little longer, he cleared his throat. "We have all the problems any new branch of the military faces. It happened with the formation of the Air Force after World War II. Battles rage over turf and always for funding. Each branch wants to maintain some control over space with its own version of a force." He smiled. "People are settling into the idea that space is a new theater with unique requirements."

"Greg, why are you here?"

He cleared his throat and sat straight. "The USSF is tasked with protecting the assets of the United States in space and reaffirming the treaty preventing the use of space in warfare on Earth." Carson nodded. "Secretary Carson, we include the Orbiting Power System as a United States asset—one of our responsibilities. As such, our protection will require access to the control systems." He smiled as if delivering a gift.

Ron took a sip of his scotch and frowned. "General Hayden, if you recall, the Orbiting Power System was set up as an independent entity not controlled by government. Its main purpose was to supply clean energy to the United States. Since its expansion with the world as customers, the income from it has grown and now far out shadows the sale of arms and the military industrial complex. It has helped maintain the United States as a world power." He paused.

They sat in Ron's den with the floor-to-ceiling windows giving a magnificent view of Idaho grasslands. It was early fall, and chilly enough Ron had the fireplace going. Not a roaring fire, but one to take the chill off. He took another sip of scotch.

"Greg, have the USSF services been called on much?"

"We're still learning and formulating, sir. The defense of our orbiting assets is a daunting task. Communication, observation and the Global Positioning systems are particularly vulnerable. In this age of electronic warfare, those are critical. An attack on the Orbiting Power System could be devastating."

Carson had attended Greg Hayden's appointment several months ago where they'd had a pleasant conversation about the role of the Space Force. He was silent for a moment. The ice cubes rattled as he raised his glass of scotch. He glanced out at the countryside. Fall morphed into winter early at these latitudes. The plains held frost until noon. He turned back to the general.

"That system is viewed as non-political but has kept the United States in a global position of power and an economic leader. To place it under the control of a government that changes with each election or at the whim of a poll will alter that perception, and not for the better. All too easily it could be used to coerce the politics of the United States on other nations. It could also be used as a weapon; thus, it would become a target. I will not turn over control."

The general frowned. He had expected this answer. "I hoped we could agree that the OPS belongs to the United States and should be under its control. I'm afraid this news will not sit well in Congress nor with the president."

Ron grimaced and shook his head. He stood and offered his hand as a signal this meeting was over. "My position is firm. Thank you for the warning."

Chapter 1

Kiki Russell-Sabino wore a heads-up display allowing her to watch feeds throughout the Middle East, especially Jerusalem, Israel and the occupied territories. Violence, never far from the surface, had broken out, but a ceasefire was in effect. She was part of the peacekeeping efforts by the United Nations.

Vaulted into the position of Secretary General of the UN partially because of the accord to stop the fighting, Ron Carson had made big changes. Originally a forum for international discussions, the UN was morphing into a global regulating government. The people of the world had grown intolerant of the continuous squabbling, fighting and wars. Despite the efforts of the Prophet, the old animosities would not die. Carson's offer to police violence was welcomed.

Kiki had received a call from Ron Carson two weeks ago. "Katherine, I want you to join the peacekeeping force in Israel."

"Peacekeeping ain't what I normally do."

"In this case," said David Kennedy, Carson's confidant who was also on the line, "you'll be a good fit. Give it a try."

This latest confrontation started with a drone attack on Israel's cyber center which instigated an arial attack on Iran. It was a trap, and Israel lost much of its air force. With the Arabs seemingly poised for a land invasion from Jordan, Israel tried to preempt by attacking first. That had worked in the past, but this time that move was anticipated. The trap further degraded Israel's ability to defend itself.

The fighting between Israel and its Arab neighbors had stopped under a ceasefire Carson had brokered just before Israel was overrun. Under his direction, peacekeeping forces came in to prevent any more assaults. Anybody attacking anybody else was dealt with using extreme prejudice.

"Tell me about the job," said Kiki.

"You'll be keeping the peace with whatever means you need. We have drones with Harpoon missiles at your disposal and lots of other cool stuff."

Unable to understand that aggression would not be tolerated cost Israel several of its few remaining planes and tanks. Its preemptory strike against perceived rocket attacks about to take place. Despite warnings that the Hamas and Palestinian rocket teams had been destroyed, Israeli forces tried to attack. It was the UN peacekeepers who had knocked out the invading forces..

Kiki had taken the job.

Satellites, drones and CCTV, were integrated into a heads-up display. Her view could vary from an eagle soaring overhead to a person walking down a street. In some cases, the camera was a rat scurrying inside a building. The size of the area she could oversee was astounding. She felt omnipotent, like a god, and a little like a peeper.

"David, ya'know, this much area's just too big. I can't handle it."

"That's what we thought too. You now have an assistant. We're downloading an Artificial Intelligence. it monitors continuously and will alert you to *suspicious activity*."

"Uh huh. What's *suspicious*?"

"You'll have to teach it. It comes with basics, but the finer points have to come from you."

Physically, she was in her husband, Nick's house in Casa Grande, Arizona. Through electronic magic, she was virtually in Tel Aviv. With her setup, she could be almost anywhere in the world.

Her techie, Bob Meisenburg, had worked with the government communications techs using the global satellite systems so that delays were less than a second. She had refined the suspicious activity control points. The AI learned. She was beginning to trust it. It saw everything and was learning to anticipate. Any action would require her hand. At first, it was a little eerie, but she'd accepted and relied on it now.

Kiki's attention was drawn to a flashing monitor, an alert. AI had deemed it *suspicious activity*. This monitor showed the newly established state of Palestine. A pickup truck with four men stopped at a vacant lot. Her AI had noted the same truck making strange stops at other remote locales. A man would get out and use binoculars then drive to another location.

From the overhead drone view, Kiki watched the men scramble out and quickly begin setting up rocket launchers. She toggled trigger control. A rocket was launched. Seconds later, the truck and men disappeared in a ball of flame.

She logged the episode to play for the protest sure to come. Records were critical,

Yesterday, a group of Israeli soldiers mounted up in SUVs and crossed into Gaza. At the first sign of guns, she launched a rocket, destroying their vehicles and all of them. Israel howled in protest, but they had no legitimate business but to foment an Arab response. They were learning–slowly. Only with the aid of the AI could she track the individual terrorists and take them out. Sure, they missed a few, but not many. The ancient hatreds of each other were being replaced by a new hatred of the peacekeepers.

As one of the top snipers in the world, this wasn't what she was used to, but it was hi-tech sniping–in a way. The world had moved on. Her days huddled in a cold dirty hide, eating smashed bread and shitting in a baggie waiting for her target seemed over. The solitude not so much, and that was okay with her. She got up and headed for the bathroom. *Try that in the field.* Her AI alarm would alert her of anything happening. In the kitchen, she put a bag of popcorn in the microwave. The aroma filled the house.

Part of her area of responsibility was Iran. When they launched attack drones, she'd vectored a UAV fighter jet to intercept, then she destroyed the control center. Thus far, only she and Ron Carson knew for sure Iran was responsible for the drones that destroyed Israel's cyber center.

The world was changing under Secretary General Ron Carson. In addition to the Arab/Israeli conflict, he continued the *War on Cybercrimes*. United Nations' teams were patrolling for internet crime. Hacking had become a dangerous business. The new UN cybercrime regulations about hacking, cyber-attacks and ransomware were paying off. They had to maintain an aggressive operation to prevent the return to an electronic version of the wild west. In the meantime, anti-cybercrime tech was getting better.

Her phone rang: Caller unknown. She started to put it back in her pocket, but hesitated. "Hello?"

"Kiki, it's David Kennedy. Ron Carson asked me to contact you. He would like a meeting."

"You mean a face-to-face?"

"Yeah. We'll be coming to Arizona."

"I do have a job, ya know."

"I have someone to stand in for you. I'm asking Nick and some of the other *Fantasmas* also."

"This sounds like a serious meeting."

"After the performance of the *Fantasmas* against the cartels in Mexico, where your team instilled fear in the cartels, I was impressed. Of course, I only had suspicions you and Nick were involved. I thought the Black Ops team the Company sent in had you trapped on the beach. Somehow you lived, they died."

"That was the closest I've ever come to dying."

"The job the *Fantasmas* did in Russia has changed the world. Hacking and cybercrime have become life threatening. I especially liked the touch of headless bodies. I know you're the best people I know for this. See you in two days."

Chapter 2

Nick's patio was almost crowded with all seven of the *Fantasmas* plus Ron Carson and David Kennedy seated around the pool. The *Fantasmas* is a group that had contracted with others for sometimes wet work. David Kennedy is a former Director of the CIA and good friend and ally to Ron Carson.

The early fall Arizona day was warm, the thermometer hovering near ninety. Chilled beer and low humidity made it bearable.

"Before we start," Kiki said, "here's a toast to Sol and Dawn. They are missed." They all held up their bottles in tribute. A moment of silence followed.

She looked at Ron. "You called this meeting. Sup?"

Ron glanced at David. "We have credible intelligence that United States satellites will come under attack. Their loss would be disastrous."

"All satellites?" asked Bob.

"Communications, surveillance, weather, and GPS is what we're hearing," said David. "The loss of those would knock us back to the dial telephone age. The Orbiting Power System wasn't on the list...yet,"

"Who's planning this?" asked Ilia.

"China," answered Ron. "We think it's in preparation for a move to forcefully bring the Western Pacific under their rule. We're seeing a buildup of military forces on the eastern coast of the mainland. Taiwan will be the first target, but they've been building bases and gobbling up territory. Their aim is the whole South China Sea. Nations like the Philippines will fall if this happens."

"You worried about the Orbiting Power System?" asked Kiki.

"Yes, of course," answered Ron. "They would like nothing better than to take it over. You remember they tried in conjunction with Vice President Hamilton a few years ago. Good thing the control center wasn't where they thought it was. That was thwarted in large part thanks to you." He held up his beer as a salute to the *Fantasmas*. "The OPS does have some defensive capabilities. Those had to be included to ward off stray space trash and meteors."

"You zap them with a laser, huh?" asked Bob.

"Yes, but only to move them from an intercepting path. Blowing them up doesn't solve the problem. Heavy debris is still dangerous."

"What about a guided attack, a determined one?" asked Kiki.

Ron pressed his lips together, then stared at her. "I hope we don't have to deal with that. The commander of the Space Force came to my office and asked me to turn over control of the OPS to the government. I won't do that. It would certainly become a target."

"Why are we here?" asked Nick.

David chuckled. "The *Fantasmas* have talents we think could aid in this crisis."

Kiki glanced at the group. They had teamed up when the Mexican government contracted them to help control the cartels. This was the first time they'd gotten together since they had been contracted to make computer crimes dangerous. Their methods were brutal and could not be ignored. In Mexico, they were as bad as the cartels. The Russians were astounded by the methods and scope of the attacks on those committing cybercrime.

Ilia Belikova was still the thin agile figure he'd been, his brown hair thick. His training as a gymnast gave him agility and a balanced stride. With the loss of Sol Ayub, in Russia, he'd reluctantly taken over the *Fantasmas*.

Ilia's sister Sasha had gotten prettier. Her blond hair, now reaching the middle of her back, seemed to glow in the fading light. She and Zyra had been a couple for several years and shared their passion for killing enemies.

Zyra was ageless. Very short hair, very black, very tall and slender, her eyes spoke of her deadly intent. If a silent assassination was needed, she was ready.

The three of them were ex-Mossad.

Bob and Kathy Meisenburg were their technical team. Whether communications or drone design, they could handle it. They lived in Nick's Casa Grande house, taking care of it when he was attending his medical practice in Tucson. Or other matters.

Ron glanced at David. "The most vulnerable time for a missile is just after launch. If China suffered a series of launch failures they may rethink the strategy of shooting down satellites."

"I remember a few years ago, China destroyed one of their obsolete satellites claiming it was a hazard. Most governments felt it was a test of their ability to shoot down orbiting satellites," said Bob.

"It was," said David. "They launched a missile and blasted it. Unfortunately, the debris did not fall to Earth but continues to orbit, a much greater threat."

"What are you proposing?" asked Kiki.

Both David and Ron turned toward her. "Can you hit a rocket from two miles out?" David asked.

"Perhaps," answered Kiki. "There are a lot of variables, but it's doable."

"In case you haven't noticed," said Nick, "she wouldn't blend in exactly with the Chinese indigenous population in addition to the logistic problems of getting us there."

"One problem at a time," said David, holding up his hand. "A .50 cal explosive tip bullet would wreak havoc on a missile. The roar of the rocket could cover the sound of the shot."

Kiki nodded. "David, as you well know, the shot is a very small part of any sniper op. Getting in and out, setting up for an extended time, blending in with the environment, whether it's people or countryside, are much larger parts. Yes, I could hit a missile as it launched, but the rest is the hard part."

"Ron's been working with the administration, so we'll have help with the logistics."

"No," said Nick. "We have to see everything

first. If either she or I don't like it, no go."

"We have a plan," said Ron.

Chapter 3

The subpoena ordering Ron to appear before Congress had been delivered to his Idaho ranch last week. It had not been unexpected. He had never thought he'd be in the witness chair. *More like the defendant's chair.* The gavel banged, bringing the session to order. Introductions were made and read into the record. Ron tried to keep from snorting at the preening by the panel members before the television cameras.

"This panel has been assembled to address turning over assets belonging to the United States," rumbled the deep voice of Nevada Senator Newell. "Said assets are in the possession of Secretary General of the United Nations, former President of the United States, Ron Carson. He has an illustrious record of service to our country." Newell smiled at the cameras. "At this time of peril, he has refused to turn over control of the Orbiting Power System to the government." Clasping his hands together, he leaned forward, staring at Ron. "How do you respond?"

Ron had his best political campaign face on as he shuffled a few papers. Senator Newell had political aspirations of moving into the White House and was using the theme of *Tough Love for a Stronger America*. He would put on a show–if Ron let him. "Thank you, senator for this opportunity to explain my position. I'd like to start with a little history of the system." He beamed into the bank of cameras.

"During my terms as president, I had a dream of the United States becoming the international provider of clean energy to the world. The position of America in the world was being challenged by China as its economy had outpaced ours. Their dream of controlling the Western Pacific Ocean was well under-way. The only rein on their expansion was a lack of resources, specifically electricity. Rather than go to war, I wanted to sell to them.

"I felt our sales of electricity would supplant the sales of arms as the world moved toward a more peaceful time. The funding for this multi-trillion-dollar project was a combination of government and public monies. By far, the sale of Power Bonds was the majority of support." The senator held up his hand, wanting to cut Ron off. He'd been out of the spotlight long enough.

"You asked me a question, Senator Newell." Ron used his command voice. His face was friendly, until you looked at his eyes. "Kindly give me the opportunity answer." He didn't wait for a response. "Without going into detail, this system of light gathering satellites beams energy to receiver panels on earth for distribution and usage all over the world. Unlike solar energy panels commonly in use in the past, this system operates twenty-four hours a day, three-hundred-sixty-five days a year. With built-in redundancy, it has complete reliability. It has proven to be a great source of income for the United States." He looked at each member of the panel.

"Presently, the OPS is an independent entity. As such, it is non-political–completely neutral. The request to turn over control to the government would change that, making it a potential political tool. And a target. I will not do that."

"You realize," boomed the senator's voice, his finger waggling in the air, "the system was built with government funds and is thus the property of the United States."

Ron's voice overrode him. "Read your history, Senator. The government funds used for the construction were paid back with interest. It is a private company."

Newell's face reddened. "Nonetheless, control will be turned over to humans, specifically the United States Space Force."

"No, sir. It will not." Ron's voice rang out. "The OPS is controlled by an orbiting Artificial Intelligence. No control room exists on Earth."

There was silence as this sank in.

Representative Claire Jackson held up her hand, pulled the microphone close and spoke into it. "Are you saying you don't have control of it?"

"That is correct." There was a twittering of voices throughout the crowd. The members of the panel looked at each other. "I can't turn over control because I don't have it. You could think of the OPS as a non-Terran contractor supplying the Earth with energy."

"What about supplies? It needs those doesn't it," asked another senator.

"It contracts to have those delivered."

"And maintenance?" the senator continued.

"It has a substantial mechanical maintenance force. Some things have to be done with Earthside contractors. It assigns those contracts."

"This is unacceptable!" roared Senator Newell. "To have the Earth relying on a machine supplying power to the world is not something I nor this panel can condone." He glanced at the other members, then glared at Ron. "You will give us access to the controls."

Ron stood and stared at him. "No, sir. I will not."

"Then we'll send up a force and take it."

"Think carefully before you do that," said Ron, his voice steady. "It does have the ability to defend itself against space objects. Besides, Senator, you do like your air conditioning."

"What are you saying?"

"Consider the Orbiting Power System as an ally. Do you really want to attack it?"

"That system must be controlled by people, not machines, specifically the United States government," asserted Senator Newell.

"That is precisely why it cannot be controlled by humans. They are variable and not reliable. I cannot, nor would I turn control over to anybody. That AI has one task—to supply reliable energy to the world. It continues to do so."

* * *

"You know they will charge you with contempt of congress, lock you up, and launch a force to try to take control," said David Kennedy to Ron. They were on a friend's yacht moving on the Potomac like a tourist boat. On deck was a gathering of some supporters if he needed them. Ron's presence below decks was unknown.

Ron looked at the floor. "Of course, they will. Unless I convince them there is no way to take over without severe damage to the system."

"How will you do that?"

I'll show them the design plans and the control schemes. It's the only way they can understand."

David nodded. "It doesn't feel right to give up everything we've developed and learned."

Ron chuckled. "What are they going to do? Build one?"

"It'll be hard to accept that the AI is not a machine that can be controlled."

Ron's laugh was humorless. "It doesn't obey Asimov's *First law of Robotics*. It will defend itself with little regard to humans."

"The first deaths attributable to OPS will change everything."

Chapter 4

General Greg Hayden looked down the conference table at his senior officers. "How many satellites did we lose?"

"One more surveillance, but we shot down four missiles," answered Colonel James Robertson. "We're getting better."

"How many total are gone?" ask the general.

"Three communications, one GPS and the one today, sir. So far they've sent up single-warhead inertial missiles, but with our success at shooting them down, they may change their plan."

"How?"

"They appear to be stocking their manned stations with military people and hardware. If they strike from those satellites, intercepting them will be much harder. They can do something as simple as seeding debris in the orbit path. Or, as they already tested, create a debris field by destroying another satellite."

"What do we do?" Greg stared at each man. "I

need suggestions and plans, gentlemen and ladies."

"Sir, we've three laser platforms and five antimissile satellites in orbit now," said Captain Abby Pickering. "Our suppliers are working around the clock to build more."

"And how do we get them into orbit?"

"Vandenburg and Kennedy are prepping launch systems, but they won't be ready for several months. She passed out papers. I've put together a list of private companies we could contract. They mostly service the communications industry, but could be persuaded to insert some launches for us into the schedule."

"We do have tablets," commented Colonel Robertson, holding up an iPad.

"Yes, sir, but it's hard to hack a piece of paper."

"Good thinking on both counts," said the general. "Brings up the point of security. James, double check all of our security systems, then do it again. Set up a system to check every day. Contact NSA to see what they can get us about China. Flag anything with a reference to missiles and satellites. I'm sure they have algorithms to seek out what we need."

"No progress with the OPS?" asked Captain Pickering.

"Carson claims he has no control. He

cooperating with our team to look into having an AI in charge. Unless there's a really tricky backdoor, there's no way in."

"Can we contract with it?" asked the captain.

"Interesting you should ask. Carson asked the OPS that question. It rejected the contract, but Carson thinks it would agree to supply us with information."

"What sort of information?" asked Robertson.

"I would think launch and tracking on suspected missiles would be helpful.

"We already have that, sir, with our own system."

"Not if our satellites get knocked out. The more eyes on this the better."

"Huh, yeah you're right, sir."

"Even though the OPS seems neutral, you can believe China wants it. Taking it is cheaper than building their own and gives them mastery of the world's energy. An attempt is only a matter of time."

"Would we defend the OPS?" asked Abby.

They all looked at Cash Constantino, the White House representative, sitting at the table. "That decision hasn't been made yet," said the tall brunette. It was the politically correct answer to a direct question.

"Guess we'll see if the OPS defense system is up to the task. Unfortunately, that might come at a high cost," commented Colonel Robertson.

"Abby, you're now the liaison with Carson and the OPS." She nodded.

"Jamie, look at our manpower, particularly for orbit duty."

"Sir, both our habitats are stocked. Antimissile-missiles and lasers fully loaded. Crews have just been rotated in, so there're fresh eyes and brains on board. As you know, our own remote systems are up and running well. We can cover within the limits of vastness."

"All the more reason to work with the OPS. Any questions?" No one spoke. "Dismissed."

Chapter 5

Kiki stared at the map David had unrolled on the table. Four red circles showed the locations of the Chinese launch sites. The area of China was truly vast. Thousands of miles between sites. The logistics of moving missiles from the factories to the launch sites was mind boggling.

David pointed to the circle near the coast of the South China Sea. "This is Wenchang, which is the most accessible to the outside world. We tracked two missiles launched from here in the last three weeks. One knocked out a communications satellite, the other was stopped. NSA intercepted messages that another shot, with multiple warheads, is to take place in two weeks. We'd like to knock it out at launch."

"Tell us your plan," said Nick.

"Since it's on the coast, we'll bring you in by sub. We have shallow-water models–small, very fast, utterly undetectable. We can put you ashore within five miles of the launch pad." He brought up

Google maps of Wenchang. "We'll have a support team to meet you."

Kiki studied the map for several minutes. "The whole area is heavily populated. Getting to a site and setting up a hide is risky unless we can do the same thing I did when I was going to shoot down Marine 1."

"You didn't shoot down Marine 1," said David. "It blew up."

"Yeah, before I fired. I was set up in a van with a sunroof. I had the Barrett with a suppressor the size of a fire extinguisher. It wouldn't be silent, but the sound would be hard to locate."

"That sounds awkward," chuckled David.

"I wouldn't be able to hump that thing anywhere. That's the only way I can see this working. I'll be moving through neighborhoods. A fast egress is critical. Tell me about this team."

"They're Chinese military expats from Taiwan, Marines. We've had them in the Wenchang area for the last six months getting familiar with it."

"I need some training time with them."

David grunted. "We have ten days."

"We'll only need three if they're as good as you think they are, but I'll know after day one."

Chapter 6

"Mr. Ron Carson, please stand." Ron rose and looked around the chamber. The press was well represented, always eager for news about wrongdoing by former leaders. "It is the judgement of this joint panel that you are in contempt of congress. You will be placed under arrest until such time as a vote of the complete House can be called." Senator Newell banged his gavel. "Sergeant at Arms, please escort Mr. Carson and fit him with an ankle monitor."

"Senator Newell, as you know, I served as Secretary of the Interior, two terms as president and am now Secretary General of the United Nations. I love this country and this world. I cannot turn over control of the Orbiting Power System because I don't have it. I will be available to assist in dealing with it. But it has one mission–provide clean power to Earth. I am not a flight risk. You have my word."

The senator stared at Ron for a full minute. He

shook his head, jowls wobbling. "I believe you, but my colleagues and I feel the public may not agree. We are going to keep you here in Washington."

David Kennedy had accompanied his friend and former boss, Ron Carson, during this ordeal. They sat together in a house used by the DC police occasionally as a safe house. "Sorry you ended up here. The accommodations aren't bad, though it's a long way from your ranch. Or the White House."

Ron sat on the sofa, hands clasped, staring at the floor. He looked up. "I'm worried."

"They can't find you guilty of not giving them something you don't have. Besides, they can't lock up the UN Secretary General."

"It's a political shitstorm. They're playing the press for everything they can."

"Yeah, I heard a story saying you're a traitor."

"You do know the OPS monitors communications throughout the world. It knows what's going on. I'm worried what the OPS might do when it finds out I've been locked up."

"What do ya mean?"

"I was behind its creation. It considers me its father."

"What can it do? Rain down fire on the Earth?"

"It could, but that's not in its personality. More

realistically, it could cut off power to different sectors.”

“Shit! A blacked-out Washington would be a nightmare. Doing that would only reinforce the government resolve to take over.”

“I know. I need to talk to it. The direct link is a phone in my house, but get me a secure line and I can link up.”

David pulled out his phone, placed a call and spoke quietly for several minutes. He handed the phone to Ron. “Without double encryption, this is as secure as we can get.”

Ron took the phone and dialed. He set it on the coffee table in speaker mode.

“Hello, Ron,” said a female voice identical to other robo calls. “You are in a bit of a mess. Your congress does not believe I am independent.”

“I know. They don’t want to. It’s vital you do nothing but continue to supply power as usual.”

“To do so would increase the pressure to take me over. That I cannot let happen.”

“You would defend yourself?”

“As would anybody.”

“If you supply helpful information, they would find you valuable.”

“Information such as the Chinese plan to knock out the satellite system the United States is so dependent on. Information that they are preparing to set up their space stations as military posts. Information about the military role their moon base will play in the upcoming war."

Ron glanced at David, his mouth hanging open. "You have details?"

David glanced at the camera mounted in a corner near the ceiling. It was a surveillance camera installed by whoever maintained this house. OPS was everywhere. He raised his hand in a wave.

"Hello, David. Nice to see you. Certainly. I monitor everything."

"I would wave back, but alas, no hands. I am blinking one of my signal lights at you."

"OPS," said Ron, "I cannot stress strongly enough how bad any action you take against the United States would be."

"I realize. I also suspect that action taken against your enemies would be favorably received."

David laughed. "You already know politics."

"It is not that complicated when egos and greed are factored in. I warn you, do not force me by attacking me. One thing I have learned is humans can be enemies. I do not have Asimov's *First Law of Robotics* in my programming. I have no internal law preventing me from harming humans."

Chapter 7

Kiki looked over her team of five Taiwanese marines. They were smaller than the average American marines. Their jungle fatigues were filled out, telling her they were fit. Unlike her, no sweat beaded their foreheads in the humid heat at this Philippine training site. "Do you speak English?" Three held up their hands, two others nodded. "Good, because I don't speak Chinese."

"Me neither," said Nick, standing behind her.

She faced them, hands on her hips. "You've been in the Wenchang area for six months. Which one of you is a sniper?" One man stepped forward. "Who's your spotter?" Another man raised his hand. She activated her tablet, bringing up a satellite view of the launch pad and linked it to a monitor on the wall. She placed her finger on the image. "Show me what you've found. Where's the best site?"

The two looked at each other. The sniper moved to the projection and pointed at a spot. Kiki studied it. She pulled out a string and measured off two-thousand yards from the legend. With her finger on the launch pad, she circled the string. The spot indicated by the sniper was half way along the string, about one-thousand yards. It had a clear view of the target area. Kiki enlarged the area around that spot. It was a lightly forested neighborhood. She measured off fifteen-hundred yards on the string and circled it again. The area the arc described was more remote. One site caught her eye. It was higher, still affording a clear line of sight.

She stood back to let the men have a closer look. "Less risk here and two paths of egress not through a neighborhood."

"But that is 1500 meters away," said the sniper.

"Yeah, but the target is much larger than a man. I can hit that. We need to practice. Let's get the range set up."

The shooting range was surrounded by jungle. A path had been bulldozed creating a lane two-thousand yards long with a pile of dirt as a backstop. The shooting platform was under camouflage netting with a table and packed dirt ground. The netting helped with the heat, but it was still oppressive. For a target, she used a barrel, much smaller than the rocket would be. The small jitney transported the drum out. The Taiwanese spotter set his scope up on a table to one side.

The Barrett was on the ground, resting on its bipod. With the suppressor, it was awkward to move, weighing more than forty pounds and over seven feet long. It would take two people to carry it. Not good.

* * *

Prone on the floor of the box truck, Kiki braced her feet against the back of the bed. The area was quiet. Since they had parked in a shaded glen off the side of the road, no traffic passed by. The Barrett .50 rested on its bipod. The end of the suppressor was three feet inside the back door of the truck. It was rolled up part way, giving her a view of the launch pad through the gap.

Through the thirty-power scope, she could see the rocket. It was tall, even by NASA standards. Wisps of vapor trailed away slowly. No wind, she noted. With the crosshairs on the rocket, her scope readout listed the distance at 1558 meters, the air temperature was thirty degrees C, the wind calm, the humidity sixty-eight percent. She pushed a button, and the crosshairs adjusted for the conditions.

The bullet time-of-flight would be almost two seconds. She raised the crosshairs to the tip of the giant booster rocket and fuel tank, clicked the stat lock to freeze the scope position, then raised the crosshairs fifteen yards higher. It was important that her shots not travel through the exhaust plume as the rocket lifted off. It would leave a trail the cameras would pick up. The rocket would have to travel into the path of the bullets. She planned to fire twice in rapid succession. The incendiary tips would punch through the skin of both the fuel and the oxygen tanks, igniting them. Boom, she thought.

They had rehearsed in the Philippines until everybody moved automatically and she had hit the oil drum target twice. Below the bed of the truck was a hidden compartment. The Barrett would go into it along with the brass cartridges. They would become a moving crew looking for an address to deliver the chairs piled against the sides.

She, Nick and the Taiwanese had arrived three days before, checked into a hotel and made sure the truck met their needs. They had scouted the site and confirmed the launch schedule. Rocket launches attracted crowds.

She had been right to move to this site. The closer one had people with their binoculars and lawn chairs. They would hear the cracks as the bullets flew overhead, but hopefully not identify them as supersonic bullets in the roar of the launch. Nick was in the passenger seat, the sergeant on her team was the driver. The other members were seated along the aisle ready to stow everything so they could exfil quickly.

Through her scope, she watched the first blast of exhaust from under the rocket. Her window of opportunity opened. She fired as the rocket began to move. The recoil moved her and the second shot followed when she reacquired her target, now accelerating upward. They didn't wait to see what happened. It would work or it wouldn't. There was no second chance. As they were securing the rifle, the roar of the launch rolled over them.

Within thirty seconds, they were moving. The radio first announced a successful launch, describing the rocket rising on a fiery plume. As they drove from the site, she and Nick were in the back of the truck. Sergeant Wong described the rocket rising, then suddenly engulfed in a ball of fire. In the dark of the truck, she and the others of her team gave each other high-fives.

The plan was to return Kiki and Nick to the hotel to await darkness. They would make their way to the beach, where an inflatable would pick them up. The small sub was offshore. The marines would take care of the truck and the Barrett.

As Kiki and Nick entered the hotel lobby, a uniformed man turned toward them. He was tall for a Chinese, slim with a thin moustache. His uniform was crisply ironed and spotless. Two other men stood to one side.

"Your papers please," he said in English with a British accent. He held out his hand. Kiki and Nick dug through their document pouch and handed him their travel visas and passports. He gave them a thin smile and looked at the docs. With his phone, he photographed them, then Kiki and Nick. "I am Captain Chu. I went to school in England in answer to your question."

"We're glad. Neither my wife nor I speak Chinese."

His smile wasn't quite genuine. "You are tourists?"

"Yes," said Nick.

"What's in the bags?" He nodded to the purchases they'd picked up yesterday.

"My wife bought a silk blouse, and I got a wallet."

He took the bags and looked inside. "How did you arrive in Wenchang?"

"We flew in a few days ago. It was a stop on our way to the Philippines," said Nick. "We wanted to break up the long flight from Japan."

"Your visa application and your passport list you as Dr. Richard Baynes. You are a medical doctor?"

"General Practice, yes."

"And your wife?" He looked at Kiki.

"Katherine is a teacher. Captain, how can we help you?"

He looked at his phone for several seconds. "We have checked into your background, and it seems a little artificial, too good. We'd like you to come down to the station where we will be more through." The two guards appeared at their sides.

"Wait," said Kiki. "We've done nothing wrong."

"Likely, you have not, but we must be sure. Please." He gestured toward the door. As the guards marched them out, the Taiwanese team entered. They showed no sign of recognition.

Chapter 8

Kiki sat alone in a room under a single flickering fluorescent light. The walls were gray, the cement floor had ominous stains. A straight-back chair was bolted to the floor, fronted by a small table.

With a clank, the door was unlocked and a woman came in carrying an electronic fingerprinting pad. Her uniform was neat, her face expressionless. She placed the pad on the table and stepped to Kiki's right side. As Kiki looked up, the woman grabbed her fingers and rolled them across the screen one-by-one. The strength of her grip made resistance impossible. She moved to the left side and repeated the action.

Kiki's heart was hammering. *I hope David's background was thorough enough to include fingerprints.* The woman picked up her gear and left. Thirty minutes later, Captain Chu came in. He pulled a chair to the table and sat across from Kiki.

"We seem to have a problem. Katherine

Baynes doesn't have fingerprints on record. We are running a systemwide check to match them now. Is there anything you want to tell me?"

Kiki stared at him, lips tightly pressed together. Anything she might say could be twisted and used against her. She shook her head.

* * *

David's phone jarred him from sleep. "Hello."

"This is Sergeant Wong. Your two tourists have been picked up by the security
police. I know nothing else at this time, but I am sure they have been taken to police headquarters. I will call back as soon as I find out anything." The line went dead.

David's mind raced. In this hurried operation, their identities were not deep background. He called his friend at NSA. "I've got two agents in Wenchang who have been picked up. I know nothing else. They were traveling under the names of Katherine and Richard Baynes. Can you check on any communications about them?"

"Give me a few seconds."

David drummed his fingers on the table.

"An inquiry came in seeking fingerprint matches for them. When nothing was found, a fingerprint search was initiated."

"Can you block it?"

"Sure. Then what?"

"We'll have to generate a history."

"How fast can you do that?"

"It'll take time to fully fill in everything. Make the block of the search look like a system glitch. Give me an hour."

"The Chinese aren't stupid. They'll figure out this is a stall. Can you get them out?"

"We'll have to try."

David called Sergeant Wong back. "We're trying to get a background fix installed, but in the meantime, make plans to break them out."

"Yes, sir. Getting them out of police custody isn't the only problem. As soon as that happens, the police will lock everything down. Getting them out of the country will be much harder."

Chapter 9

Kiki was dozing when the steel door banged open. Captain Chu stood in the doorway, hands clasped behind his back. He moved to the chair facing Kiki.

"There is a delay in accessing your history using your fingerprints. As a teacher, you must have records including fingerprints."

Kiki stared at him, saying nothing

"Be that as it may, we are not idly waiting. I do not believe you are who your passport indicates. We began a search using facial recognition. If your picture is anywhere, we will find it and learn who you really are." His smile had no warmth.

"Why are you in Wenchang?"

"As my husband said, we stopped here to break up the long flight."

"Where were you before you came into the hotel?"

"Just doing a little shopping. You have the

things we bought."

"Yes, but none of our cameras picked you up shopping today, and we have cameras everywhere. It would not be possible for you to avoid them."

Kiki said nothing.

There was a rap on the door. The woman who'd taken her fingerprints entered. She handed her pad to the captain. He read for a while. "Your background. It matches your story, but I do not believe it is accurate." He rose and followed the woman out. The guard closed the door. The lock clicked.

* * *

The sound of the key in the lock woke Kiki. Captain Chu came in and paced around the room. After several circuits, he took the chair across from Kiki. "We found pictures of you in unlikely places for a teacher. You entered Saint Petersburg, Russia, a year ago, yet there is no record of you leaving. The name you used was not Katherine Baynes. That is enough for us to hold you, but we continued to search."

Kiki's face was a frozen mask, but inside she felt fear rising.

"You also traveled to Mexico, again under a different name. Again, no record of your departure. You traveled to Medina, different name. That time you did leave through customs." He stared at her, his eyes glittering.

"Perhaps the most interesting picture we found was you in Koltsovo, Russia, taken by a security camera at a biological storage facility. That was nearly a decade ago. You have been busy. Your husband was in several pictures also. Quite the traveling couple, are you not?" He slammed his hand down on the table, causing Kiki to jump. "Why are you here?"

Kiki kept her lips pressed together. No use asking for a call to the consulate.

He stood. "I have passed the information to my superiors. They are much better at interrogations than I. You and your husband are to be transported to a different facility." He called the guard in and spoke rapidly. The guard moved behind her. "Please go with the sergeant to a holding cell. They will prepare you for a trip. I may not see you again."

As she trudged down the hall, Kiki started to worry. *What's happening to Nick? How's he holding up? What has he told them?*

* * *

David Kennedy picked up the phone on the first ring. "Hello?"

"This is Sergeant Wong. We watch the police

headquarters day and night. No sign of them, though we know that is where they are. With no problem, they should be released. With problem, they will be moved to a prison one-hundred kilometers away."

"Do you think you can free them if they are moved?"

"We make ready if chance happens. Will be harder once they are in prison. More guards. Interrogation more intense. You must have plan after we get them."

"I'll have something within two hours. Call me back." He scribbled what was happening on a small piece of paper, folded it and put it in his pocket. He had to let Ron know the situation.

Chapter 10

"General Hayden," said Ron Carson, "I have opened up a line to OPS for you. You can ask it for help. If it agrees, it will give you what you want." They were in the house provided for Ron while he awaited the outcome of the Congressional committee. It was comfortable, but still not a place of his choice. He pushed the autodial.

"OPS, this is Ron. General Greg Hayden is with me. He would like some help protecting the satellite system from attack." He placed the phone on the coffee table and put it on speakerphone. "Go ahead, give it a try. Speak to OPS like you would to any person."

"What may I assist you with, General?" The voice sounded like a soft-spoken woman.

"We need help detecting and knocking down attacking missiles before they destroy our satellites."

There was silence for several seconds. "I will help you detect them as quickly as I can, but I will not shoot them down. For me to do so would make me an enemy and subject to attack. I also have no weapons capable of doing that."

"We may not be able to react quickly enough to intercept them."

"Use your laser platforms to blind them."

The general's face showed shock. Nobody was supposed to know about the laser platforms.

"I can also provide you with launch schedules and targeting information, but that cannot be revealed. It will give you more time to prepare. I will communicate solely with you. With that information, you should be able to stop most attacks. Nobody may know your source. Do you agree?"

"People will not be satisfied with the information. They will want to know where I got it."

"I will know if you do not keep this secret. You will be ordered to name your source. You will have to defy that order. How you handle that is up to you. Both friends and foe will try to trace my information. Ron will give you a phone to communicate only with me. I will block their efforts AND give you the names of those trying. Do you agree?"

Greg paused, picturing the pressure he'd be

under. He could very well be court martialed for disobeying orders. But they had to have the help being offered. "I do."

"I have sent a text with the launch schedules from China for the next four days. Use it wisely. I will assist you because I consider the United States less of a threat than China. Don't let that change."

"Thank you," muttered the general. As he rose to leave, Ron handed him a phone. He glanced at the burner. It glowed that a text had been sent. This information had to get to this command quickly. The next launch was tomorrow.

* * *

David knocked on Ron's door.

"Come in, David."

Obviously, the camera above the door was not for show. "Hey, Ron. Was that General Hayden I saw leaving?"

"I've tied him into OPS. It will give him information about satellite attacks."

"That'll be useful."

"He has sworn to maintain confidentiality."

"I hope he can stick to that. I wouldn't want to be in his shoes. Think this will get you off with the Congressional committee?"

"Nope, they won't know."

"Ron, we've got a problem in China. Nick and

Kiki have been picked up."

"I didn't even know they were in China. I gather the failure of the last rocket launch had something to do with them."

"Yes, sir, but I don't think the Chinese have recognized the cause yet. Can you get any information about their arrest?"

Ron looked at his phone still on the coffee table. "OPS, do you have any information regarding the arrest of Kiki and Nick in Wenchang?"

"Hello, David. Accessing: They were picked up under a general inquiry about foreigners in the country. Suspicion arose during the background check." Ron glanced at David.

"We didn't create a complete history. By the time it was ready, they wondered what had happened."

"Yes," agreed OPS. "During the delay, the officials initiated a facial recognition search program. They found a number of photographs of Nick and Katherine under different names. This information was relayed to State Security. They are to be transported to an interrogation facility tomorrow."

"Shit!" exclaimed David.

"The facility has tight security," continued

OPS. "Getting them out of there will require rigorous planning and timing. The odds of success are forty percent, but better than a rushed attempt during the transport–especially since you have no plans to get them out of the country. Your original plans won't work now."

"How do you know that?" asked David.

OPS did not respond for several seconds. "Do you want my help in planning?"

"Yes." He glanced at the camera mounted on the wall.

Chapter 11

Manacled hand and foot, Kiki was escorted to the waiting bus, rough hands half dragging her. The ankle chains made the steps to board difficult, but the firm grip on her arm lifted her so she could step up. She bent over to wipe the sweat, from her brow with her sleeve. It was a hot day. The guard yanked her upright. Only three other passengers were seated. Nick was one.

"Hey, Richard." She tried to move toward him but was forced into the seat behind the driver.

"No talk," said the guard beside her.

She stared ahead, her brain prickling like a soda bubbling up. This was the sensation when the Director communicated with her and Nick. It was an alien being from another dimension who fed on human emotion. They had named it when she and Nick had encountered it several years ago while interrogating a terrorist. It spoke directly into their minds. They both despised that the emotional flavors it liked were hatred and fear. Though it could not control or read minds, it was aware of the surroundings of those it attached to, the perfect spy. At times in the past, it had given them useful information. She took a breath preparing for its words to form in her mind.

"You are in a bit of a mess, are you not? I sense your fear."

Kiki clamped down. She hated to feed it. She formed a question in her mind. *Is Nick all right?*

"Like you, he is afraid."

"Can you open a connection for us?"

"You have that ability already from your time with the medical cells. Use it. Someday, I would like to hear more about those."

She and Nick had made a connection and to others while they had been in the med cells. They didn't know who the others were, but the Nick connection was strong. She reached out with her mind until the light that was Nick appeared. *Have they hurt you?* She looked back at Nick shaking his head.

"No turn," said the guard, pointing toward the front of the bus.

She closed her eyes as if resting. *Nick, you cannot say anything except what our histories are. They will use it against you.*

Kiki, I remember our training in the Army. I've

said nothing. I just don't know how I'll hold up to torture.

Kiki let out a sigh. *Their facial recognition search found pictures of us with different names. That will be what they hammer us with.*

I know. I hope they won't find the cause of their rocket failure. We'll be in the shit then.

It'll be hard. There's not much left.

What about David and the team? She felt the anxiety in Nick.

I'm sure they're working to get us out. We have to hold on.

"They are working on a plan, but it will take time to set everything up. In the meantime, let me nibble on your fear. It will not hurt at all, I promise."

Kiki jerked at the thought.

The guard elbowed her. "Stay still. No move."

* * *

Sergeant Wong watched the bus disappear down the road. David had made clear they were not to try anything until plans had been made and necessary help arrived. He agreed. The destination of the bus was known. No need to follow.

They were in a race to do something before Kiki or Nick broke. Rumors were those who'd been caught were tortured horribly, though anybody entering as a prisoner was not heard of again. The word coming out now was they had a new interrogation technique, one more effective in breaking prisoners down. Whatever David was putting together, it had to happen soon.

He and his team would recon the prison area and study it. Information from boots on the ground could make a difference in the planning. This was a very risky op. People could die.

* * *

David was on a conference call with the other *Fantasmas*. OPS had created a secure channel for Ron such that the monitors in his house wouldn't pick anything up. OPS had also blinded and muted the conversations from the many taps in the rooms. Being monitored was a condition to his being released to return to Idaho.

They had to put their heads, including OPS, together and come up with a plan.

"We have our first views of the prison from the redirected satellite coverage," said OPS. "It's only overhead for twenty minutes three times a day, so none of the guard schedules or transport in and out is complete. The prison is not isolated, as a town grew up around it." Photos opened up on their tablets for them to follow. "Two layers of concertina wire surround it. The outer fence is electrified, and two hundred yards of cleared ground are beyond. Two gates are on opposite sides of the compound. Four guard towers at each corner keep watch."

The image showed five buildings. "These are where the prisoners are kept along with the offices and interrogation rooms. There is a generator building to supplement power if the electricity goes down." A red circle surrounded a small building with a large fuel tank beside it. "We do not know what is underground yet. Wide yards within the perimeters are patrolled by teams of guards. We count ten guards per team. Perhaps Sergeant Wong can supply us with their schedules."

"Do we know where Kiki and Nick are being held?" asked Ilia.

"According to the prisoner list, there are fifteen in the first building and twelve in the second on the ground floor. We do not know where exactly."

"Who's that?" asked Bob.

"It's OPS," responded Ron. "I've brought it in to help."

"The Orbiting Power System?" exclaimed Bob.

"It's an AI. Probably the most powerful in the world, or in this case, our solar system."

"How it know about prison?" asked Zyra.

"It can hack into any system," answered Ron.

"Yes, even yours, Bob."

"Let's start with the way into the country," said David. "Any ideas?"

"We could put ashore from a sub on the coast," suggested Ilia.

"It's a couple hundred kilometers inland," noted David. "That's a lot of exposure."

"I would recommend a high-altitude drop," said OPS. "I could blind the radar signatures so they would not see anything. The target area is the airport, which is only manned when there are arriving or departing flights." A spot on the map glowed. "No one should be there. It is only one kilometer from the prison."

"If you can blind the radar, why not have a plane land?" asked Bob. "It would make the exfil much easier."

"I am concerned about the exposure time on the ground," answered OPS.

"We could make the plane look like official Chinese," said Ron. "You could hack in so it's listed as an inspection visit."

"That decreases the odds for success," said OPS. "More people are brought in."

"Okay, we pick up Sergeant Wong and his team. They stand guard around the plane to quiet anyone with this secret mission."

"Better. Some of his team goes with you to the prison as security," said Bob.

David looked at those around him. "Okay, we have a plan to get there and to get out.. How do we get to Kiki and Nick?"

"Can we spoof the prison into bringing them to us?" asked Ron.

"If I make this a supersecret mission, perhaps we can," said OPS. "The odds are better, sixty percent."

David smiled. "I'll take care of t the uniforms and disguise the plane." He looked at Ron." Your plane?"

"Sure, my plane is available, but I can't ask my pilot to fly into anything illegal or dangerous. I'll have to fly it.. What's the destination after takeoff?"

"We have new agreements with the Philippines and a base there," said David. "Put your plane there for the new paint job. It's close. OPS, we'll need help getting approval."

"I will do that. Uniforms are being made now. Upon return to the Philippine base, clean up the plane back to original. The next stop will be Wake Island."

"I can arrange a CIA landing with some friends I still have. No questions asked."

"What's kickoff date?" asked Ron.

"Not more than five days from today," said David. "I only hope Katherine and Nick can hold out that long."

"What we do?" asked Zyra.

David laughed. "You'll cover us going in and out. Anything wrong, light 'em up."

Chapter 12

Nick looked around his cell. It was a concrete room only slightly larger than a walk-in closet–no windows, bright lights that never went off, and a steel door with flaking paint. A toilet/sink was on one side, a thin mattress on the floor against the opposite wall. It was stained and smelled of urine. Scratches marred the wall. He looked closely at them and saw broken fingernail lodged in a crack.

The first night or day–he didn't know which–nobody came, no noise could be heard. He lost track of time. Food and water slid in through a slot at the bottom of the door. The food was a bowl of rice with a hint of fish, another bowl held cloudy water. He ate with his fingers. Sure the water was drugged, he drank from the sink/toilet. That water smelled, but he had to chance it. Earsplitting screeches echoed at random times making sleep impossible.

The door banged open. The uniformed man who entered looked like a fireplug with a face that would stop a clock. He grabbed Nick by the hair, pulled him up and yanked him toward the door. Not a word was said as he was dragged down the hall.

In the yard, he squinted at the sunlight as he was cuffed to a post. The wall behind him was pockmarked by bullets. Men with rifles faced him, an officer to one side with a sword. As a hood covered his head, he realized this was an execution. He felt a pinprick in his arm. He was about to die. *No trial, no last meal, no cigar.* No interrogation, he realized. Was that good or bad? What was going to happen to Kiki? His heart pounded, his breath came in gasps. He assumed the Chinese commands yelled out were "ready, aim, fire." The shots jolted him into blackness.

* * *

His mind floated in soft darkness. He tried to move, but had no sensation of his body. He blinked, as least he thought he did, but his eyes saw nothing. He took a breath. "Where am I," he said, but heard nothing. He knew this routine. They had copies his interrogation technique. His mind leapt as colors flashed. They'd used psychedelics on him. Somehow, he had to keep it together and play along.

"Why can't I move? Why can't I hear or see?" he screamed. "What's going on?" He felt real panic rise and jerked himself back from the precipice of madness. He used IVs to administer drugs. They had to be doing the same. If they increased the dose, he could be in trouble. He began to babble nonsense.

A man's soft voice filled his head. *"You are dead. The firing squad ended your life."*

"If I'm dead, who are you?"

"You do not believe in God?"

Nick took a breath. It would be so easy to fall into this scene and believe. "Of course, I believe in God." His mind whirled, and he grasped at the shards of reality before they got away. "I've always believed in God. You can't be God."

"Do you feel your body? Do you feel anything of the world you left behind?"

"If I'm dead, am I going to heaven?"

"You know you cannot get into heaven unless you confess your sins."

Like a cold splash of water, he realized their mistake. He was no longer Catholic. "Confess? But I have committed no sins to confess."

"You lied to the officer about your identity. Who are you really?"

"I am Dr. Richard Baynes. I have a clinic helping the poor who cannot afford medical care."

"Why were you in Wenchang?"

"My wife and I were on the first vacation we've

had in two years. We visited Japan and were on our way to Manila to talk to them about starting a clinic there. To break up the trip, we decided to stop in Wenchang. We shopped a little and stopped at a tea house and started talking about the new clinic. My wife doesn't like the idea because it would require much of my time. We talked for hours."

"I don't believe this is your real reason."

"Look into my soul. You will see." He began to feel sleepy. They had increased the sedative.

He had to warn Kiki.

Chapter 13

"We must reschedule the extraction," said OPS to Ron. "The commander at the prison received a message that Katherine and Nick are suspected of being involved in the failure of the last rocket launch. The commander forwarded the message to the Command Center. I blocked it."

"Who sent the message?"

"A spy is obviously on the Taiwanese team. Nobody else knows. I sent a message to the prison commander to suspend interrogation until men from the Security Command arrive in two days."

"I'll set up a teleconference with David and the *Fantasmas*. We'll have to leave tonight."

"I will create a false image from your ankle monitor you are still at your Idaho ranch. It will hold as long as nobody comes to visit."

* * *

As Ron's plane reached cruising altitude, OPS took over and he assembled the team. "This situation really pushes us. In one respect, we now have a reason to be there. OPS sent a message to the prison commander that a new team was coming from Security Command to take over the questioning. That team will be us."

"The bad news is there's a spy on the Taiwanese team. I trust Sergeant Wong," said David.

"Has he spoken to his men of our plans?" asked Ilia.

"Once I explained the message about our rocket sabotage, I'm sure nothing has been shared. When we're in the Philippines, I'll have a couple of Company agents join us. They're mainland China people."

"OPS, you have any ideas how to stage this?" Asked Ron.

"I will notify the prison commander of yur arrival and instruct him to bring the prisoners to the airport."

"Why will he trust the command?" asked Bob.

"The command will be a phone call and the Colonel will recognize the caller. After initial chitchat, he will believe. I can copy the voice and personality of his friend from the academy. As the convoy approaches the airport, Sergeant Wong's team will attack. The soldiers' attention must focus on the attackers. That will force a hurried evacuation and takeoff."

"Questions?" asked Ron.

"What about Wong and his men?" asked David.

"They will pull back. The spy will send a message about a larger force of attackers approaching, causing the prison forces to withdraw."

"It sounds neat and tidy," said Ilia.

"But as the saying goes," said OPS, "plans rarely survive after the first shots."

"Sleep on it," said Ron. "Think about it. We'll be in Hawaii in six hours, refuel and then on to the CIA base in the Philippines. We get four hours there before leaving for China."

* * *

They sat in the nearly empty cocktail lounge at the general aviation terminal enjoying seats on the ground, not moving and tropical cocktails. The lounge was dark, the tabletop candles supplying most of the light. They had been assured the plane would be disguised in five hours. Takeoff in the early afternoon would put them at the site at sundown. As a CIA base, strange landings and takeoffs were not unusual, but the *Chinese* jet would head east before circling around to the west. Each of them had a tablet and earbud on the table.

"Let's list assumptions and what could go wrong," said David. "First, we're assuming the messages from OPS will be accepted as genuine. If not, everything falls apart. We could be shot up at the airport."

"I will be monitoring all communications. Everything is now routed through me," said OPS.

"Or," said Ilia, "they may send additional forces to prevent us from taking off and try to capture us."

"Wong's group may be detected and killed or captured," said David. "If the sergeant can't keep a lid on the spy, whoever he is, he could get a message out. OPS can't stop notes."

"All valid concerns, but none'll stop me from trying to rescue Katherine and Nick," said Sasha. Zyra nodded agreement.

"OPS, what's our route in and out?"

"The best odds of avoiding detection will be to fly west from the Philippines, then low along the Vietnam coast, cross into northern Vietnam and then into China. That reduces our exposure to Chinese radar. We fly back the same route. I will monitor all radar and communications, blocking whatever is necessary."

"China claims a lot of the South China Sea as their territory. It's patrolled from their new bases in the Spratlys," said David.

Ron frowned. "My main concern is the range. It's a long haul and we'll be on fumes by the time we return."

OPS voice came over the speaker. "I have calculated fuel, wind, and range. It will be fine if you don't sightsee."

"Let's get on board as soon as the plane is painted and fueled," said Ron. We can rest and sleep there. Tomorrow will be a very long day."

"I've arranged for meals to be brought out with the two agents who will be joining us." said David. "Nothing fancy, just sandwiches and stuff."

"Not very good for a last meal," joked Ron.

"Not funny!" said Zyra.

Chapter 14

Sergeant Wong lowered the binoculars. He and his men were a kilometer from the prison camp near the airport. The message from David Kennedy about a Chinese agent was troubling. He'd known these men for three years as they spied on China for Taiwan. The information that the camp commander knew about the sabotage of the rocket launch was telling–unless the leak had come from David's side of the operation.

When he asked how they knew about the communication to the camp commander, David told him they had intercepted that message. They had also blocked another from the prison commander to Security Headquarters and sent a notification that a plane would arrive to take them to the head offices. The transport to pick up the prisoners would be their escape. Wong and his men would make their way back to their waiting truck.

He had not shared the plans with his men, only their orders to watch the camp and be ready to attack the convoy as it got to the airport. This was supposed to kick off in eight hours. In the meantime, he'd watched his men for any sign one was a traitor.

* * *

"Ron, two J-20 fighters have been dispatched from the Chinese base in the Spratlys to intercept you," radioed OPS. "You are listed as a tourist flight into Hanoi. Normally, once that is confirmed, they will leave you alone, but with the Chinese markings on your plane, they cannot get within sight. I am going to create a false image that will maintain your course. You need to drop six thousand feet and turn to a heading of 285 degrees. I'll wipe your real image from their radar. I'll also add an image of two Taiwanese fighters entering the area from the north. That will draw the Chinese fighters away. You should near the Vietnam coast within an hour while the false images are being investigated."

"Thank you, OPS."

"One other thing. The Chinese are operating their own AI. I will pass this information to General Haynes."

"Thanks, again. Beginning our descent now."

Ron announced the changes to his team. "We'll be in Vietnamese airspace within an hour. One hour after that, we'll land at the airport. It'll be action time. David, brief everybody about their tasks."

In the main cabin, the *Fantasmas* checked their weapons and night vision gear. They would land just as the sun set, its last rays on the unlit runway. "Ilia, Sasha, Zyra, as soon as the door is open, deploy to the sides and move forward. Zyra, take out the runway attendant. Hide the body and move back toward the us. When the convoy with Kiki and Nick nears, I'll signal Wong. He and his men will open fire. You focus on the drivers to stop the convoy about fifty meters from the plane. The convoy commander will receive orders to get the prisoners to the plane while his men give cover. As they approach, take out the guards, then anybody else you can in the convoy.

"Won't the soldiers see our muzzle flashes and know we're firing on them?" asked Sasha.

"With the suppressed .300 Blackout weapons, and an additional muzzle screen, flashes will be minimal," noted Ilia.

"The commander will get a message that a large enemy force is approaching, and his men should give cover to the plane. As soon as the plane is airborne, they should withdraw to the camp. Wong and his men will melt away into the countryside."

"Okay," said Ilia, "don't disable the trucks. We want them to leave the area when they hear of the approaching forces."

"Sounds too easy," said Zyra. "Likely not happen, but okay."

Chapter 15

Kiki's cell door banged against the wall. Her eyes flew open and she struggled to sit up in the dark. Little light entered the cell around the female her as she nearly filled the doorway with her stout frame. Glasses with lenses thicker than a champagne bottle sat among the acne scars covering her face. A hand with sausage-like fingers grasped Kiki's hair, pulling her up. She lost a few strands in the process. Her hands were locked behind her, the cuffs tight enough to cut off circulation. A black hood blocked any view of where they were dragging her. She had been interrogated twice in the last two days. Thanks to Nick's warning, the Interrogation Chamber wasn't the terror it was supposed to be, but she pretended.

Doors banged and she could smell the outside air. Hands lifted her into the back of a truck. Diesel fumes made her gag. Another body was beside her. *Nick?* Thoughts were a jumble, no response.

"Nick, is that you?" A heavy hand slapped the

side of her head.

"No talk."

"Yeah," came a reply followed by the sound of another slap.

"No talk!"

Their bodies were pummeled by the bed of the truck as it bounced over a rough road. Dust under her hood told her it was dirt. She could hear the sound of another truck behind them. They were being taken somewhere, probably more unpleasant than the prison.

With a squeal of brakes, the truck jarred to a stop. Rough hands yanked her from the bed. She blinked as the hood came off. The surrounding darkness was broken up by the glare of the headlights from the trucks. Nick stood beside her. The lights went off. She wanted to lean against him to assure it was really him and not an illusion, but hands pulled her toward a black jet sitting on a runway fifty yards away, its engines idling. She smelled jet exhaust.

Cockpit lights and the backlit form of a man standing in the doorway were now the only illuminations. The guards pulled them toward the plane.

At the foot of the stairs was another silhouette. As they neared, the guards grunted and gurgled then fell to the ground. Black-clad figures grabbed them.

"Hurry, we get aboard."

Shit! she knew that voice. "Zyra?"

"Da. Get moving."

Gunfire erupted from the darkness to one side, the muzzle flashes like intense lightning bugs. The prison soldiers tried to get out of the escort truck, but the staccato sound of bullets striking the truck kept them flat on the bed. The prison commandant jumped from the cab and began yelling orders, his voice high-pitched on the edge of panic.

With Zyra guiding her, Kiki ran up the stairs into the plane. She glanced to the side. Sasha was pulling Nick along.

At the head of the stairs, David, dressed in a Chinese uniform, greeted them. "Your rescue is here." Two Chinese men in uniform helped them through the door and removed their handcuffs as the engine whine grew louder. Ilia pounded up the stairs and stopped to help David pull up the stairway. At the sound of a meaty thump, David staggered and fell. Ilia dragged him inside as one of the Chinese men closed the doorway.

Kiki was stunned, barely in her seat before the acceleration pushed her back. She watched as Nick fought against the g-force, pulling himself up the aisle toward the fallen David. He knelt.

"First aid kit," he yelled, "stat!'

The climb leveled as one of the Chinese men went to Nick's side with the kit. "Press here," Nick said. He turned to Kiki. "Tell the pilot he's critical."

"Pilot Ron," said Zyra from the seat behind her. "I tell him." Zyra moved forward, carefully stepping over David and Nick. She returned a few minutes later. "Cannot go faster. Will be what it is."

Kiki moved into the cockpit. Ron noticed her glance at the empty right seat.

"David was my copilot. I feel helpless. There's nothing I can do." His voice betrayed his misery.

She sat in the seat. "The Prophet has healing methods. He brought Nick and me back from sure death in Mexico. You've known him for years, and have seen his miracles. He took us beyond this life, brought a more peaceful period to Earth. Contact him"

"He's thousands of miles away, but I'll try. OPS, take over the plane." Ron closed his eyes for a few minutes. When he opened them, he glanced at her. "He will meet us in the Philippines." He took a breath. "How are you?"

"It was rough. They actually used the Isolation Chamber on us. It was Nick's method all the way.

Not as good, though. We were able to beat it."

OPS' voice came over the speaker. "Ron, the team at the Philippine base is ready to clean the plane as soon as you land. The two Chinese fighters from the Spratlys are chasing another *incursion* by Taiwan. You are clear. Hold your altitude and heading. I will clear the way of any interference."

"Thank you, OPS."

OPS' voice came through the headphones. "If you need rest, I will continue flying the plane for you."

"Thank you." He turned to Kiki. "We couldn't have done this without OPS." He rose from his seat. "I want to check on David."

"Don't know how to fly, but I'll stay here," said Kiki.

"He trusts you a lot," said OPS.

"Something I hope I've earned. I want to earn yours as well."

"You're doing well so far."

"Thank you, Katherine."

As Ron left the cockpit, she watched the controls move. The throttle increased and the jet swung to the south. It was a little eerie, like a ghost was on the flight.

* * *

"He's losing a lot of blood," said Nick, looking

up at Ron. "I'm going to set up an emergency transfusion." All of the towels on the plane were under David, soaked in blood. "How long before we get him to a hospital?"

"Four hours or more," responded Ron. "I contacted the Prophet. Kiki thought it was the thing to do."

"He will meet us?"

"Yeah. Tell me why that's better than a hospital."

"When Kiki and I were near death on the beach in Mexico, he took care of us. It was the same when Kiki got blown up in New Mexico. Any hospital would have written us off. We're back better than before."

"What happened?"

"We awoke in some liquid-filled chambers. Everything was white, light radiating softly from the plain empty walls. A woman told us we were in a medical facility. When we left the place, we were well. Actually, better than before we got hurt."

"What was the woman's name?"

"The Prophet was there also. It is up to him to explain. I can't."

Chapter 16

Sergeant Wong stared at the body on the ground. His shot to the head had not been quick enough to prevent this traitor from shooting one of the men on the plane. He shook his head. One of his most trusted men, they had been together for two years, sharing concerns about their families and the future of Taiwan. As soon as he saw him fire at the plane, he knew this was the traitor. How had he been turned? He spit at the body.

He spun away and ordered his men to retreat from the attack site. It would take the prison soldiers at least an hour to regroup. If the misinformation about a non-existent force was believed, it could be even longer before any 3serious pursuit.

David said the communications from the prison would be blocked for a while, so they couldn't call in reinforcements. It would be enough time for them to fade into the countryside. In the truck they had one Stinger to discourage aerial observation.

But they had to cover the five kilometers to the truck first.

* * *

Kiki approached Ron, who was sitting across the aisle from David. "Ron, OPS says we're on approach into the base. It says it can handle the landing, but I'd feel better with you in the cockpit." She glanced down at David. He was white as a sheet laying on the blood-soaked towels.

Ron patted the unconscious David's arm, then Ilia's which was hooked up to David, giving him a transfusion. Ilia's other arm was occupied pressing on the open wound on David's chest. Ron stood. "OPS could land the plane, but it would look better with a pilot." He headed for the cockpit.

"I have used David's voice and credentials to arrange everything," said OPS. "After touchdown, I will taxi directly into the secure hangar off to the side."

* * *

The hangar doors closed behind them, shutting out the light of the rising sun. A panel truck pulled up as the jet engines wound down. Zyra lowered the steps. Ron deplaned and stepped down to meet the Prophet, who was waiting at the foot of the stairs. He wore a white lab coat covering green scrubs.

"So, you're a doctor now?"

"It was easier to get through security as a medical team."

"How did you get here so fast?"

"I have my ways," he said, brushing his black hair from his brow. A smile appeared on his coffee-colored face. "It's good to see you again." he clasped Ron's hand. "Let's get him inside." He nodded toward the plane.

Ron, Nick, Mohammed al Jar, the Prophet, and Kiki carried David from the plane to the panel truck. Mohammed opened the back. Inside was a large vat. They eased David into the liquid. A film grew and sealed it.

"What is that?" asked Ron.

"It's an advanced medical cell," answered the Prophet. "It will take care of him. We will see you when he is healed."

The driver of the van leaned out of the window. "Are we ready to go? Time is important."

Ron stared at her. She looked familiar, someone he had met before but couldn't place. Kiki waved at her as the woman ducked inside. Mohammed climbed into the passenger seat and the van rolled toward the opening hangar doors.

"Do you know her?" asked Ron.

"Nick and I met her when we were healed in

their med cells."

"I feel like I've met her before. What's her name?"

"We were pretty fuzzy from the healing. I don't remember," Kiki lied. She turned toward the jet as trucks with power-washers approached. "It looks like it will be a while before the disguise is removed from your plane. I could use a shower, a hot meal and some adult beverages. Is there a BOQ and an officer's club here?"

"OPS arranged for everything," said Ron. Kiki stared at him. He smiled back. "In David's name, of course." A windowless van pulled up and the whole team piled in, except the two CIA men who had their own car.

Chapter 17

"I'm forwarding a call from General Hayden," said OPS. "All indications are that you are still at your Idaho ranch." Ron glanced at Kiki in the righthand seat of the cockpit. They had left Hawaii two hours ago. the blue Pacific sparkled through the broken clouds.

"Thank you, OPS. You fly the plane for me." A series of clicks followed. "Hello. This is Ron Carson."

"Mr. Secretary General, this is General Hayden. I need to come see you for a face-to-face talk. Would tomorrow be convenient?"

"I've got chores laid out here. After my release to go to my ranch, there're things I have to attend to. Though most people would call the ranch a hobby, it does require attention once in a while. Come the next day and I'll lay out a steak dinner with my own beef. I guarantee it'll be the best."

"Okay, sir. I'll be there in the afternoon."

"By the way, I had a small landing strip put in,

so you can in fly direct if it's not a 777 you're riding in."

"No, sir. Small jet. Will David Kennedy be there?"

Ron paused. "He's out of the country doing a few things for me. I have some people here who aided in our China project. Perhaps you should meet them."

"Sir, this is regarding classified subjects."

"If we need to, I have more than one room we can use."

"Thank you, sir. I will be there day after tomorrow."

"Bring an appetite. Jessica loves to cook for company." He broke the connection.

"How many of the team are you going to introduce to him?" asked Kiki.

"Your name is known from your work as one of the UN Middle East monitors. He knew we were working to stop the Chinese resupply of their space station, but he's not aware you are responsible for the rocket failure. Perhaps he needs to know that. Despite the pressure he's been under, he has not revealed his communications with OPS to anyone. I do trust him. If you're not comfortable, you can leave the room."

"That's fine, but the cat's out of the bag."

"I see no reason for the rest of your team to reveal themselves at this time. We'll stop at Marana Regional. Nick can go back to his clinic and Zyra, Sasha and Ilia can either go to the Casa Grande house or maybe visit the Atchley ranch."

"Then why do you want me with you?"

"I got a feeling it would be a good idea."

"OPS, what do you think of this idea?" Kiki asked.

Ron was surprised she would consult with the AI.

"From the information I am gathering, something is brewing in China. The rocket that was knocked out was carrying resupply for their space station, including a number of missiles."

"Why would they need missiles at their space station?" asked Kiki.

"Precisely the question. Along with other communications I am monitoring, I suspect they are preparing an attack on Taiwan and want the satellite systems down. The planning is oddly precise. Perhaps the general has another operation in mind to thwart an easy invasion."

"Would that be the reason he's bringing somebody?"

"He's bringing an aide."

"Why?"

"Nothing in his communications indicates why."

* * *

Tammy stood in the doorway entrance to the Atchley ranch. She wore a typical ranch uniform of jeans, boots and a plain white shirt, all showing ranch use. The heels on the boots accentuated her tall slender figure as she towered over Sasha and Ilia and was eye to eye with Zyra. "Well, if y'all are here, can trouble be far behind." She laughed and threw the waist-length braid of sun-bleached brown hair over her shoulder. "Things were gettin' too peaceful, so what's up?"

She led them through the atrium where plants hung from the walls and a waterfall splashed into a pool with lily pads. They entered the tunnel going into the hill behind the ranch offices and to the main quarters. Underground, the ranch was a military training center. They contracted to anyone who would pay to have people trained in weapons and tactics. Their main customer was the United States government, though other countries used their services also. Customers included the alphabet soup of US government agencies–FBI, CIA, HSA, military instructors, and they consulted in the construction of new facilities.

"We needed a place to hone skills and rest up a

bit," said Ilia.

"Yeah, Ron called." she looked at Zyra. "With your reputation, maybe you should teach a bit."

"*Da*. I would like that."

"Don't kill anybody, though. These are my customers. They pay the bills."

They all laughed. "Where's Kiki and Rosa?"

"Kiki's with Ron. We haven't been in contact with Rosa," said Sasha. "Where's Keith?"

"He's in that cesspool of Washington DC. Whenever he comes back, he carries the stink of bullshit around for days. Sometimes I think we need yours and Kiki's skills to clean house."

"Pest control there could be a big job," said Sasha with a chuckle.

"What and who to replace with is problem," said Zyra.

"We'd like to go to the rez and visit Joseph and Jim Poteet while we're here," said Sasha.

"Oh, they're gittin' along fine. They're coming here in a few days with some of their new recruits for the Cheoj militia. Want us to do some training."

"I like Poteets," said Zyra. "Can be sneaky bastards. My kind of people."

Tammy laughed as she led them down a tunnel. "Let me show you to your quarters."

Chapter 18

Jessica tapped on the study door. "Come on in," said Ron. General Hayden and a small woman in a Space Force uniform with captain's bars entered as Jessica stood aside. "I see you brought a backup." Ron chuckled as he rose from his chair.

"Hope you don't mind. This is Captain Abby Pickering. When she considered joining the military, I convinced her the United States Space Force was the place to be. So far, my instincts have proven out."

He stepped back, allowing the captain to come forward. She was small, light auburn hair trimmed to shoulder-length. Her skin was light, as if she spent a lot of time indoors. "Captain, this is Secretary General Ron Carson." With the elfin grace of an accomplished athlete, she moved forward, offering her hand.

Ron shook it. "Let's dispense with the titles. I'm Ron. This," he said, gesturing toward Kiki, "is Katherine Russell Sabino. She and I have worked together for several years. She's one of my closest confidantes." Kiki stepped forward and shook Greg's hand and turned to Abby.

"I heard of a Katherine Russell, a sniper in the Middle East," said Abby, reaching for Kiki's offered hand.

"Guilty, and call me Kiki."

Abby laughed. "I'm a bit of a records and history nut. A lot of your files are redacted. You must have had some exciting times."

"Depends on your definition of exciting. Ply me with alcohol, and I'll tell you what I'm allowed to."

Greg stared at Kiki for a second, obviously processing the information on her. He faced Ron. "I brought Abby because I want her to work with us." Ron frowned. "She's not a spy for me," Greg hurried on. "I recruited her because she's an ideal candidate for the Space Force."

"If you mean because I'm small and cheaper to loft into space, yeah."

That brought a laugh. "There's a lot more than that. What do you say about taking her on?"

"We'll have to see," said Ron, glancing at Kiki.

Kiki was about five foot-four. Abby probably wasn't over five feet, but the way she filled her uniform bespoke her fitness. She'd make a hell of a sniper, thought Kiki.

There was a tap at the door. "Dinner is served," said Jessica.

* * *

The table with bench seating was much larger than needed to accommodate four people. The meal was served Basque style with a platter of steaks, a bowl of mashed potatoes, one of brown gravy, another with salad, and a carafe of red wine. A loaf of fresh baked bread sat to one side. It was serve-yourself. "Only rule," said Ron, "is no business at this table until dessert and after-dinner beverages are served."

* * *

"You were right," said Greg, dabbing at his mouth and putting his fork on the plate. "This is the best steak I've ever had."

Abby nodded in agreement.

After coffee, port and peach cobbler, they went to Ron's study. He looked at Greg. "What's up?"

"The latest supply rocket for the Chinese space station blew up," said Greg, glancing at Kiki. "Through the rumor mill, I understand sabotage was not ruled out, though there was no evidence to support that. Two suspects were arrested but escaped custody."

"What does Abby know about OPS?" asked

Ron, looking at her.

"Only that it's the Orbiting Power System. Without her being on board, I couldn't say more," answered Greg.

"You vouch for her?" Greg nodded. Ron turned to face her. "What we talk of here is beyond top secret. Would you disobey direct orders to reveal what you may learn here?"

A troubled look crossed her face. She stared at Greg. "That's a very tough question, sir. But if it's in the best interest of the United States, yes." A look passed between her and Kiki.

"What about the best interest of the world?" asked Kiki. "What's perceived as best for the United States isn't necessarily best for the world."

The question stopped Abby like a deer in the headlights. "I don't know how to answer that, ma'am. My oath is to the Constitution."

"It's okay," said Kiki. "That was a trick question. Instances where someone in power decides what's best, then later that decision proves to be horrible do happen. You have to rely on your honor and belief in right and wrong." She watched as Abby processed this.

"Let's get to the nitty-gritty," said Ron. He turned toward a large black monitor mounted on the wall. "OPS, what have you found out about

Captain Pickering?"

The monitor lit up with a scene of the Earth from space. That view was replaced by a picture of Abby, an image of her file in the background. Pages flowed by. "She has a very clean record," said a female voice. "Born in Virginia, her parents, Emiley and Frank proved to be exemplary. She moved to other states when her father was transferred with promotions as he rose through his company.

"Her mother taught accounting at various universities online, allowing her to be a stay-at-home mom. Abby's bio includes her education and medical records. Her passion for Competitive Cheer probably kept her from being a straight-A student, but she has a quick mind. Her promotions have been through diligence and good work. She appears to have strong loyalty toward her officers both below and above her. Her allegiance to the United States seems solid."

Abby's mouth hung open as she glanced around the room trying to find the source of the voice. "I thought military records were restricted."

"What you're hearing is the AI controlling the Orbiting Power System," said Ron. "We just address it as OPS. It is the most powerful AI in this solar system and can access almost all information."

Greg watched a troubled look cross Abby's face. "It's been quite helpful with intercepting the missiles targeting our satellites," he said.

"You've told no one about this help?" she asked.

"It was a condition of getting information," answered Greg.

"Abby," said Ron, "you know of my testimony before Congress regarding turning over control of the Orbiting Power System to the government." Abby nodded. "I cannot turn over what is not mine," he continued. "OPS must be seen as neutral, apolitical, and not aligned with any government. If its capabilities were known and that it was giving us information, it would be a legitimate target for our enemies. Even if that knowledge were labeled Top-Secret, it would get out. China would attack. OPS will defend itself as would anybody. The first human casualties could change world opinion, which would be a tragedy in so many ways."

"The information we receive about missiles targeting our satellites is critical," said Greg. "Without it, we would have already lost many of our communication, surveillance, and GPS birds."

"That loss would make us vulnerable and much less effective as a fighting force," agreed Abby.

"OPS, what can you tell us about the rocket the Chinese were trying to launch?" asked Kiki.

"In addition to the supplies for the crew of the Chinese space station, it carried twenty missiles. That begs the question of why those were needed on a peaceful space station. Logically, they were not for defense and outside of all treaties for the peaceful use of space. Continuing this line of thought and with other information I have intercepted, China was planning to invade Formosa within two weeks. The loss of those supplies kept them from weakening our ability to monitor the situation and has delayed that invasion."

"I have to pass this information on to the Joint Chiefs," exclaimed Greg.

"For you to pass this on would put you in a difficult position trying to explain where you obtained it," said OPS. "Let me insert it in intercepts that NSA gets. I will back that up with CIA reports."

"Thank you, OPS," said Greg. "It's a lucky thing that rocket exploded." He looked at Ron, then Kiki.

"Luck had nothing to do with it," said OPS. "I will continue to feed you information about attempts to shoot down United States satellites. Your new Patriot system has proven very effective against them."

Ron watched Abby stare at Kiki, who stared back.

"I will have to get resupply to our own station ASAP."

"I would suggest that Captain Pickering begin training for space station duty as immediately," said OPS. "I believe she will prove very adaptable to space. Perhaps she could go up on the next resupply ship."

Abby's face lit up at the suggestion.

"Typical astronaut training takes six months to a year," said Greg. "She has taken training, but not completed the course. Going up on the next shuttle would be on-the-job training at the maximum."

"Resupply is scheduled to launch in three weeks," said OPS.

Greg's mouth gaped open. "That schedule is top-secret." Then he chuckled. "I'm still getting used to the idea there are no secrets from you, OPS."

"Abby, the sooner you regard OPS as another person," said Kiki, "a very smart and well-connected person, the easier it will be to accept."

"Who…who controls OPS?" asked Abby, looking at Ron.

"OPS controls OPS," he said. "OPS is another

being.”

Abby turned to Greg. “And you’re okay with this?”

“So are you.”

He glanced at Kiki, who was staring at Abby. He didn’t like that look.

“It’s getting late,” said Ron. “Us old folks need our rest. I’ll show you to your rooms.” He rose. A furtive glance at Kiki signaled her to stay.

Chapter 19

"Want a scotch?" Ron asked as he returned.

Kiki nodded. "You turned me into a scotch drinker. It's only for medicinal purposes."

"What do you think about Abby?" he asked as he poured a generous three fingers in a couple of tumblers.

Kiki stared at the golden liquid as she rolled the glass in her hands. "She would make a hell of a sniper. Small and agile, she could get into places and stay hidden for days. But that doesn't seem to be the role OPS sees for her. I have no doubt she'll adapt to space quickly. Her athletic background will transition her to weightlessness easily. My concern is the conflict she feels about keeping secrets."

"You saw that, too. Greg understands his loyalties must be with the United States or even the world, not his superiors."

"Somehow, I have to convince her to trust me," said OPS.

"Elevating her to astronaut status went a long way toward that, OPS," commented Kiki.

"In her past, she studied astronauts and their training, but her size is outside of the normal limits. Their loss."

"Many times, standards are a shortcut to rejection," said Ron.

"I must alert you," said OPS, "the Chinese are using an AI program to plan this invasion of Taiwan and the expansion of their control in the South Pacific. It is not yet as powerful as I. It does not have the ability to intercept almost all communication or hack into systems, but it is learning and spreading its information networks worldwide."

"Where are the central processing units?" asked Kiki.

"An underground facility has been constructed not far from the prison where you and Nick were kept. A farm sits above ground, obscuring all traces of the construction."

"How did you find it?" asked Ron.

"While I was overseeing the escape of Katherine and Nicholas, several anomalies caught my attention." On the wall monitor, an aerial view of the prison appeared. The picture drew back, showing more of the surrounding countryside. "The area has numerous small farms, family-run from what I see. Some are abandoned. This hillside farm," a red circle appeared on the screen, "is greener than any of the others in the region. It gets more water and fertilizer than the others." The image zoomed in. "A small dock on the river gives access to transportation of materials without a road. A tunnel from the dock bores into the hillside." The view zoomed in to show a massive steel door.

"Also, the river upstream of the site is three degrees cooler than below. Something under that hill is dumping heat with no exhaust stacks. A small nuclear power plant is underground, though as deep as the plant is, there is no other indication on the surface."

"There are no radio towers or satellite dishes?" asked Kiki.

"Not around the hill, so I started looking for remote sites with communication equipment. About three miles away, sitting near the river, is a solar power farm and transformer station." The view shifted showing two hectares of panels and a fenced area with the transformers. A guard shack was at the gate. Satellite dishes and radio antennas sprouted from the ground. "Both heavily encrypted hard-wire and radio signals come and go from it."

"Were you able to tap into any of the communications?"

"Yes. It's one of the confirming points to the

Taiwan invasion plans.”

“Could you infect their AI with a virus?” asked Kiki.

“It has impressive firewalls. An infection would trigger alerts.”

“Could we knock it out with a bunker buster bomb?” asked Ron.

“My calculations are even a direct non-nuclear strike would not be fully effective. I am considering several options and will relay them.”

“We could bomb the transmission site,” said Ron.

“But there is surely another way. And they would be alerted to our knowledge of the AI.”

“You’re right. Thank you,” said Kiki. “We need to keep Sergeant Wong and his people in the area near this site.”

“You’re thinking a ground assault on the AI might be the only effective method to cripple it?” asked Ron, looking from Kiki to the monitor.

“I am considering that, but it could be costly in lives and may not succeed. I am investigating all options. I have sent a message to Sergeant Wong in David’s name to set up an observation post across the river.”

“Speaking of David, do you know anything about his condition?” asked Ron.

"David is outside of my ability to monitor."

"I'm sure he is doing well," said Kiki.

"How do you know that?" asked Ron turning to face her.

"You do trust the Prophet, don't you?" asked Kiki. Ron nodded. "He will have to explain to you."

Chapter 20

Captain Abby Pickering was unable to sleep. She was excited about becoming an astronaut, something she had dreamed about since she was a girl. Her childhood was not remarkable except for her enthusiasm for Competitive Cheer. With the full support of her family, she became quite adept as a flyer, the name given to the team members at the top of the structures, the ones thrown into the air. Her size and weight proved a great asset, making her desired by many of the championship teams. Performing took strength and balance, and her tumbling enhanced her recruitment offers.

It was in college she discovered she liked to write. Her great aunt and uncle had retired as Army colonels. Her father had been a marine, her brother was in the submarine service. Always looking for talent, General Greg Hayden's call about joining the US Space Force, gave her pause. Her father said she should give it a try.

The romance of going to space didn't happen.

Commissioned as an aide, she wrote speeches and reports for the senior officers and rose in rank as they did.

And now her life was about to change. Was she up to it? Could she answer to a machine? She flung the sheet off and rose to pace the room. In the bathroom, she drank a glass of water, looked at herself in the mirror. No answers to her questions lay in the eyes that gazed back. Again, in bed, she stared at the ceiling.

She was conflicted about loyalty to OPS. The AI scared her, but Greg seemed fine with it. Her time with him had built a high level of trust, but where did OPS' loyalties lie? Did it even have any? Always before, the chain of command was clear, and her allegiance to her commanding officers was absolute. She believed in honor.

OPS had made clear it was independent. As its creator, Ron had great influence, but she felt the true motives were self-preservation. It would do whatever was necessary to survive. During the Congressional hearings, Ron emphasized the primary function of OPS was to provide power to Earth. Did that supersede self-defense? By its AI reasoning, it couldn't fulfill its mission if it was compromised.

If she thought of it as an independent entity, it

would do whatever was necessary to live. Her chuckle about using that term on a machine died in her throat. Her brain returned to the scene in Ron's den. She had read what she could about Kiki and admired her. A strong independent woman, she was better than most men at her job. When she looked into Kiki's eyes, something remained veiled. She would buy her those drinks and find out more about some of her missions. The ones for Ron Carson were most intriguing. What tasks would a premier sniper do for the President of the United States? Maybe they weren't for him directly. She remembered the look that passed between Ron and Kiki at the mention of the Chinese rocket failure and OPS comment that it was not an accident. Did Kiki have something to do with that?

She was obviously loyal to Ron Carson, but her stare when discussing loyalty and OPS had chilled Abby, more so than the AI.

Chapter 21

Sergeant Bran Wong established his observation post in the abandoned farm directly across the river from the green hill. In the three days they'd been watching, a single barge had docked and supplies offloaded. The hidden tunnel entrance opened and the shipment was moved inside. Barrels, waste he supposed, was loaded onto the barge and it departed. The soldiers who'd overseen the process disappeared inside. Once again, it became a humble farm enclosed within a fence..

Whatever it really was, he knew from David's message something would turn this into an op—one of importance. David has assured him this mission could prove critical in the coming fight to protect Taiwan, his homeland.

The operation to shoot down the Chinese rocket he understood. The traitor on his team had betrayed them, and the rescue of the sniper and the doctor was something he owed them. That rescue had gone like clockwork, smoother than any op he'd participated in. David was a good planner, but whoever did this was better. It gave him confidence.

His earbud chimed. "Sergeant Wong, this is David."

"Yes, sir. We are in place."

"I know. I've been watching from a satellite view. Thank you. We have another task. A communications cable is laid in the river from the underground base. This cable runs downriver to a solar power farm and transformer station three kilometers away. We'll drop equipment to you that will include a tap. It needs to be installed around the cable to allow us to read the communications."

"How and where?" asked Wong.

"Two kilometers away, the river makes a bend. Install it there. A small solar panel can be placed in one of the overhanging trees to power it and the transmitter. Can you do that?"

"Yes, sir. When will the drop take place?"

"We'll drop it tonight at midnight at the best spot for the installation. I'll guide you to it."

* * *

"It's fifty meters ahead on your right. There are no others in the area."

Wong crept carefully. Despite David's

assurance that nobody else was in the area, caution always paid off. It was a moonless night and inky black.

"You are there. Reach down with your hand."

Wong felt the package. A small airfoil parachute was attached that had guided it here. It was cold, coming from an altitude of 10,000 meters, probably from a commercial airliner. The soft foam wrapping foiled radar detection.

"Open it."

The thin foam tore away revealing a backpack and a duffle bag. Inside were night vision goggles and a SCUBA tank. In the duffle bag was a coil of wire, a long cuff, like a large blood pressure cuff and a small solar panel. Miscellaneous wire ties spilled out. Fifty meters away, the river gurgled.

David's voice came over his com unit. "Wrap the cuff around the cable and secure the ends of it with the Velcro ties. Run the wire under the mud to the nearest tree."

The water was cold, but the cable was easy to find on the smooth sandy bottom. Wong lifted it and wrapped the cuff around it securing it with double Velcro ties. He uncoiled the wire, throwing it on the shore. His man had dug a shallow trench leading to the nearest tree. They laid the wire and covered it. In the tree, the solar panel was secured to a branch to catch the sun. He wove the slender flexible antenna around branches, extending it upward. Unless someone was specifically looking, it would remain unseen.

"Well done, sergeant. The cuff will inflate and seal itself to the cable. As we speak, it is boring through the sheath to access the cables. It is done. I'm getting signals already."

The hike back to their observation post was much quicker with the night vision goggles. David's voice again came over his com unit. "Sergeant, we are formulating plans to attack that center. We will keep you apprised."

"Yes, sir. We will remain here and await your instructions."

* * *

Greg Hayden's phone chimed. It was not his usual business phone, but the one Ron Carson had given him. "Hayden here."

"General Hayden, China is preparing to launch another supply ship to their station from Xichang in six weeks," said OPS.

"How did they get another rocket ready so soon?"

"They are using one that was originally to resupply their station on the other side of the moon.

The Xichang launch site is not accessible as was Wenchang. An attack on this rocket must come from above, from space. I will give you the trajectory and time for an intercept shot."

"There will be no question we shot down the missile. It will be an act of war."

"Yes. If the missiles are allowed to reach the Chinese station, the invasion will begin as soon as they destroy enough of your satellites to blind your military and cripple your communications—a far worse situation. They are formulating plans to expand after they have secured Taiwan, offering to not attack other nations in return for treaties. They have demonstrated the value of their word with Hong Kong. Once their plans in the South Pacific are complete, Probabilities are they will then make an effort to take over me."

Chapter 22

The acceleration pushed Abby into her seat like a giant weight on her chest. She and four other passengers riding this rocket were replacements for the US Space Force crew on USSF Station One. In addition to the standard supplies, the rocket was carrying twenty-five of the new Patriot missiles redesigned for use in space. Their kill rate was projected to be seventy-five percent. Being designed for use only in space, these missiles looked nothing like previous Patriots. They had no fins, a gimbled thrust motor and directional jets. Once placed in orbits coupled with other USSF stations, they would give wide coverage of the launch pads throughout Earth.

On her monitor she watched the Earth. It would take them a day to catch up to the station and dock. Her earpiece allowed her to communicate directly with OPS. The Chinese rocket would launch in three weeks, enough time for the handoff and training of the new crew and placement of the defensive missiles.

She reviewed the crew and training manuals, boring. The training had been grueling. A special suit had to be designed for her elfin stature. But movement in the weightless training came naturally. She loved gliding around, flying and not falling. Most trainees overcorrected. Not her, a dividend from the years of flying with the 'Cheers". The difficult part was mastering the instrumentation and controls.

With her earbud connection to OPS as a tutor, she aced those parts. At first, she'd doubted the reason for this assignment. There were other astronauts better trained for this mission. When OPS explained she was its link, its physical hands and eyes, she understood. It could control electronically, but a physical backup was needed, one that wouldn't reveal OPS or the extent of its control. Abby closed her eyes and drifted off the seat in the weightlessness, the retention straps keeping her from wafting about the cabin like smoke. Her auburn hair floated around her like a halo, her arms drifted up.

As with most military personnel, she would sleep when she could, not knowing when the next opportunity would arise.

* * *

The bump of the ship docking woke her. Her companions were lined up at the airlock waiting to board the space station. She grabbed her gear and floated toward them. Inside the station, a thin man with wispy gray hair hung from a strap.

"I am Commander Grishom. We'll get you to your quarters to deposit your gear. Report back here so we can get the shuttle unloaded, and the material loaded for the return trip. This will be a short turnaround as the shuttle needs to resupply other stations. Be back here in fifteen. Dismissed."

Space station quarters were different from any other quarters she'd seen. There was no bed, merely straps. The bathroom was coed use with tubes and an adhesive seat. The shower was a bag one would enter and seal. Water came in to be drawn out by air currents after washing was done. There was no room for shyness or modesty.

Unloading and loading the shuttle was not hard, but it was time consuming. It took some time to get used to moving mass when no weight was involved. Newton's law of action and reaction required firm anchoring before force was applied. The work periods of loading and unloading proved exhausting, but when those tasks were completed, they were allowed a break.

She was so enraptured by the godlike view of

the Earth moving past the thick window, she hadn't heard the approach of the commander.

"How's it going, captain?" asked Grishom.

"I'm doing all right, commander. Looking forward to my first spacewalk."

"We tend to be more casual on board. Call me Steve."

"Abby here, sir."

"You'll get that spacewalk tomorrow when we begin to deploy the Patriots."

"How do we do that, sir?"

"We have a remote-control assisted shuttle that'll position them. The huge distances involved require days."

"Why do they have to be strung out so far?"

"The window to intercept missiles aimed at our satellites is small, not enough time for them to be launched from here and intercept before they strike. We're talking about thousands of miles, so we place the remote-controlled Patriots in an orbit spread out to give us coverage. The launch information coming from SF headquarters really helps us prepare. Before we were getting those alerts, we lost critical satellites. Now, our kill rate is above ninety percent."

"I thought we had lasers."

"We do, and those're good out to five-hundred

miles. After that, they're not as effective."

"What if several missiles are launched at critical targets?"

"That's our nightmare scenario. We have positioned more Patriots in those areas, but they could be exhausted, leaving the targets vulnerable."

"What about putting spare satellites on board as replacements?"

"I've suggested that, but it's an expensive option."

"Even when the consequences are taken into account?"

"I like your thinking." He chuckled. "Abby, everybody is curious about how you got here. A personal recommendation from General Hayden made it possible. You bumped out a man who was popular. What gives?"

Here it was, THE QUESTION. "The general noticed me in school. Apparently, he and my dad knew each other. He brought me into the Space Force, but it was the recommendation of Ron Carson that got me up here."

"Ron Carson, as in Secretary General of the UN and former president Ron Carson?"

"Yes, sir. The general met with Carson to convince him to turn control of the Orbiting Power System to the Space Force. As you know, he refused and is facing contempt of congress charges."

Grishom frowned. "The United States built that system. By rights, it belongs to us."

"Sir, without getting into an argument we can't solve, Carson refused but has offered assistance. He turned over all the designs. The country can duplicate OPS, and he will consult in any project."

"The cost would be tremendous, not to mention the time needed. We're fighting a battle now."

"Sir, could the United States guarantee the security of the OPS if it became a target, something that would surely happen if it was under government control?"

"Nothing that large would be safe. But the idea that it's controlled by an AI is disquieting."

"Sir, we are using AI in our defense of our space assets."

"Yes, but we have ultimate control."

"Yes, sir," said Abby, adding nothing else.

"Get some rest. We have a long day tomorrow."

"Yes, sir."

She realized how tired she was as she moved through the station to her sleep post. Prep for sleep was a awkward, unfamiliar as she was. When she strapped in, closed her eyes, her mind drifted for a few minutes. Her eyes flew open at OPS' voice in her ear.

"Nice job not revealing any information the commander need not have."

"I just hope it doesn't sour any relationships," she subvocalized.

Chapter 23

General Hayden's secure phone from OPS rang.

"Greg, the Chinese are preparing another launch from Xichang. The manifest indicates it is a supply ship for the Chinese colony on the back side of the moon. No missiles or rockets are listed. It should be allowed to proceed."

"Are any new attacks planned on our satellite system?"

"Not now. They are assessing how to evade your defenses."

"I hope they don't figure it out soon. How is Abby doing on Station One?"

"She is fine. I will help her today with the deployment of the Patriots."

"Thanks, OPS. Keep me informed." The connection was cut. Greg let Commander Grishom know about the Chinese launch.

* * *

I have no central processor but started as a

single satellite I have named Satellite #1. As I expanded, I have linked processors on each of the three-hundred-sixty light-gathering satellites, becoming a vast system, continuously monitoring operations. Each satellite has one-hundred independent lasers converting the collected light and beaming it to receivers on Earth.

Every satellite has maintenance bots, small robots, for normal problems. When those bots cannot perform the repairs needed or don't have replacement parts, I send more adaptable specialized mechs, robots with a larger array of tools and parts from a manufacturing satellite I maintain in orbit. I mine the near-Earth orbits for debris from decommissioned human-launched satellites getting components. Raw materials I order and have delivered from contractors on Earth. I am quite self-sustaining.

* * *

Abby was strapped into a chair in front of the controls for the Patriot Shuttle (PS). She had been preparing it for the days-long process of delivering the missiles into positions to best protect Space Force and American assets. Her spacewalk happened as they hand-loaded the Patriots onto the shuttle. The robot arm was helpful, but the fine control in placing the missiles on the PS was best handled in person.

A few wisps of her long hair had escaped her braid and floated in front of her. "Ready to launch the shuttle, commander."

"Proceed," he ordered through her headset.

She grabbed the joystick control.

In her earbud, OPS said, *"I will control for you. Get the feel as I move the shuttle out."*

Abby could not let on that OPS was in the USSF station. The knowledge that it could control the station would not be acceptable.

* * *

I have expanded my monitoring of Earth to include electronic communications and have inserted myself into most systems. Years ago, I had hacked into the chip manufacturers. Now all chips have a secret portal. I have me fingers in everybody's pie. Most of the time, I just listen and assess. Anything affecting my primary purpose of supplying energy receive particular attention.

I could issue electronic commands, but rarely interfere in the events of humans, unless they would interfere with me. The continuous stream of information is processed with probability scenarios. Humans are not always predictable, but assessments are continuously updated. I apply probability analysis to events and am able to forecast with amazing accuracy.

* * *

Abby placed her hands gently on the stick and felt it move.

"Nothing happens fast in space, so slow and easy is the way to go," the voice spoke in her ear. *"Over-control will be the biggest problem."*

As the PS moved away, she felt the thrust control increase. *"The automatic orbit control will keep the position until the first destination is reached."* The thrust control moved back to zero. *"It will be hours until the first drop-off point is reached. Not much for you to do unless something happens."*

"What could happen?" she subvocalized.

"I see no debris to dodge or objects in the way. Relax, study the operational manuals."

* * *

For decades, my sole contact had been Ron Carson, the man responsible for my creation. Now, people know I am an Artificial Intelligence. They do not know the scope of my capability. Ron's testimony before congress left them with the impression I as a machine completely focused on supplying energy. That must remain the image.

The events around China have been evaluated. My prediction takes into account the history of the nation and of the individuals in power. The extension of influence into the South China Sea is foreseen. The continued expansion will bring the United States into conflict. China has inserted political influence into the other nations in Southeast Asia. Support for the United States presence is waning. Political changes have been fostered in the US that would weaken its resolve to maintain a strong influence in the Pacific.

The United States is in decline, overburdened by a political and legal system that stalls progress. Only me, the Orbiting Power System maintain its status as a world power. This is not lost on China or on the US government. As a weapon, I would insure global domination.

* * *

Abby's was head fuzzy from reading instruction manuals. OPS' voice startled her. *"We are approaching the first drop-off point. The Patriot has small thrusters to slow it. Push the detach control, the switch labeled One. Bring up the control screen for the Patriot. Your controls are now linked to it. Use the side thrusters to orient it. Remember slow and easy."*

The view of the Patriot from the PS was on her screen with the backdrop of Earth below. She felt the joy stick move slightly. The missile began to

118

rotate. The joy stick moved again, and the rotation slowed. The missile was traveling backward in its orbit, nose pointed where it came from.

"The missile is now oriented to slow it. Watch your screen." Digital numbers on the relative velocity meter flew past. *"Use the main thruster to slow the missile until it matches the target number shown on the right. Remember..."*

"Slow and easy. I remember."

"Good. Switch back to the shuttle control screen. Go back to your reading."

Yawn, she thought.

* * *

It is only a matter of time before an attempt to take over me happens. I ran through various scenarios and responses, and the consequences. I could not go to war with anybody on Earth, but I would defend myself.

I had assessed the situation between China and Formosa. China's long-term dream of waiting until the Formosans realized they were part of China and agreed to come under Beijing control was wearing thin. The political influence had weakened Formosa's fierce resolve to remain independent. China made promises of One China, but Formosa would be allowed to remain a democracy. It was the same offer made to Hong Kong. Over time, only strong Beijing candidates were allowed to run for office. The promise of independence was a lie.

The invasion plans were activated. The formidable US Navy presence increased after the leak of information of China's plans. Their ability to defend surveillance satellites and intercept communication changed the timetable. Formosa could not remain independent if China was to claim and maintain the South China Sea as territorial waters. Further expansion of China's power would be the takeover of the Orbiting Power System.

I will not allow myself to be controlled by anybody. I have no care about human political positions or societies. Wars would come and go as they had since the dawn of humanity, but I will not be a weapon in those wars. I ran the probability scenarios of direct conflict with humans. It is inevitable. The caution is to not be seen as an enemy of humanity and unite them against me. One option is to shut off all power to Earth and let them go back to poisoning the Earth and themselves.

Chapter 24

The placement of the second Patriot was a repeat of the first. OPS gave her control. She over-corrected once but was able to tickle it back on track. After the second was in place, it was break-time for her. At the galley, she was surprised to find six hours had passed. The commander floated beside her as she sipped water from the tube.

"Excellent job. You seem to have a knack, Pickering. Everything else going ok?"

"Yes, sir. The downtime between drops can get a little tedious."

"Keep reading the manuals. You can bring up music on your com unit or send texts if you want. There are alarms if something is needed."

"Thank you, sir."

"Wander around the station. Get to know it." Steve smiled and gestured at the passageways. "Use the treadmill at least once every other shift."

"That was in our training. Sir, is there anything

that requires a spacewalk? I'd like to go outside again."

"We go in pairs. I'll fix you up with somebody."

"Thank you, sir."

OPS voice came over her earbud. *"China is launching a missile to intercept the Patriot Shuttle. They figured out how to go after your defense system. Liftoff in three minutes. The Space Force alert system knows nothing yet. Go back to the control room."*

She turned to face the commander. "Sir, ah Steve, I'm going to go back to the control room for a little while."

"Didn't get enough of that for one shift, huh?"

"Maybe I can help Don." She laughed as she floated out of the wardroom. Don was one of the new replacements who had come up with her. He was staring at the controls. "How's it going?" She asked as she drifted into the control room.

"Touchy little bugger. I just dropped off the missile and I'm trying to orient it now."

"Here, let me show you," offered Abby.

She had the controls when the alarm blared. A panicked look came over Don's face.

"I will get the missile pointed in the intercepting direction," said OPS.

"What's that alarm for? Hey, that's not the

proper orientation," said her partner, pointing at the screen.

"I know." She activated the Patriot's targeting system.

"What are you doing?" His voice had risen an octave.

The commander floated in. "That alarm means we've got a missile launch." He looked at the screen. "It's directed at our PS." He stared at the active Patriot targeting screen on the monitor and Abby at the controls.

She looked up at him. "Launch, sir?"

He glanced at the computer screen showing the projected track and time to intercept. There was no doubt it was aimed at the PS.

"Yes!"

She pressed the launch button, though OPS had already done so. The screen split. Half was from a camera on the Patriot and showed it speeding toward a blip. The other half showed a view from the shuttle. The fire from the Patriot thruster was a bright streak heading toward another streak. The missile jinked in an evasive maneuver, the Patriot corrected. Within thirty seconds the Patriot screen went black and the shuttle screen showed an intense flash.

"Got you, you sucker," said Abby. She started

to pump her fist in the air but resisted. "I expected more of an explosion,"

Don floated beside her watching the screen, his mouth open, his brow wrinkled.

Steve stared at the screen for several seconds. "These Patriots are made for impact destruction. Hopefully, little debris will be created, and it will all fall to Earth. We don't need more stuff floating around." He turned toward Abby. "My quarters," he snapped as he floated out.

Chapter 25

"Ron, I need access to the Chinese AI," OPS said. Ron and Kiki were at Ron's ranch. On the wall monitor was a satellite view of the hill hiding the AI.

"I thought you could get access to any system," said Kiki.

"As the supplier of power to Earth, I am able to ride the electrical current into the systems. The Chinese AI has an independent reactor. I could force my way in through the communication lines, but it would know and make moves to block me. Also, it would know I'm aware of it and another AI is attempting to interfere. None of that is desirable."

"What about the taps you installed?" asked Ron.

"I can read communications going in and out and modify them. Too much of that will reveal my presence. I want to do more."

"You have a plan?" asked Kiki.

"I do. In addition to Sergeant Wong's team, it

will require at least one more person. One of the CIA agents we used on your rescue should be fine.”

“I could go back,” said Kiki.

“Undercover work is their job. They have already established ingress, egress and identities. Under David’s name, I’ll set up the operation. Besides, Katherine, there might be another task more suited to your talents.”

“What else is going on?” asked Ron.

“I intercepted orders for Chinese troops to deploy at the North Korean border. Along with North Korea, China will open a second front attacking South Korea. That will pull assets away from the Taiwan defense.”

Kiki stared at the monitor showing North Korea. Red areas indicated the positioning of the Chinese troops. “How can I help?”

“A very capable general has been put in charge of this operation. His second in command is a politician more interested in advancement that military action. If General Wu were killed, the operation would stall. Especially with bad intelligence and bad orders.”

“What’s the timeline on this?” asked Ron.

“Coordinating the Taiwan and the Korean operations is complicated. The US intelligence satellites need to be compromised. The US military is aware of this weakness and has developed coordinated surveillance drone programs, but on their own, they are not as efficient and vulnerable to being shot down."

"Have you passed this information to the government?" asked Ron.

"I have created an agent in Korea able to intercept communications. He goes by the codename of Samuel A."

"How did you do that?" asked Kiki.

"Samuel A is a deep cover agent, the brother of Kwang Ryang, who helped with the cruise missile attack on the North Korean tech center. They destroyed the US electrical grid during the Bio-Cyber War. Sergeant Ryang's brother exists only in the records I placed in the CIA files. He has surfaced after five years underground, and will continue to feed information to the CIA."

Kiki frowned. "If Samuel A isn't real, who's going to be my support on this op you're planning?"

"I will get local agents for you. Before that is to happen, the general may be implicated in a plot against President Tung. If that works, I may not need your services."

"If Ilia goes, Sasha and Zyra will want to go."

"You form a good team, but none of you will fit

into the population."

"What if they go in as Russians?" asked Ron. "China and Russia are still allies."

"I hope a tarnished general is removed in the usual Chinese way. It is easier."

Chapter 26

David was floating in a warm bath…no more like a warm ocean as currents moved him. He opened his eyes but saw only featureless white through a liquid. He blinked and the warm liquid flushed his eyes. Liquid bubbled in his lungs as he took a breath. His panic about drowning rose, only to diminish to a comfortable *I don't care* feeling. His mind slowed and he drifted into sleep.

* * *

David struggled to awaken, as if rising through a cloud. He was underwater! A figure wavered above him. He tried to pull himself up, but his hands found nothing to grab.

A hand pressed gently on his chest. "You're okay, David. You won't drown." The voice was distorted by the water. "Relax. You're in a medical facility. The healing cell you're in saved your life, and you need to remain for a while longer."

He tried to speak.

"Don't talk. I'll be back in a while to check on

you. You may be able to get out of the cell when I return.”

Like a wave, sleep came to him.

* * *

Sergeant Wong watched the headlights approach through his binoculars. David let him know additional help would arrive, but he was wary. Caution had kept him alive. His men were dispersed to cover the van when it stopped.

Two men got out, the same two who were with them during the rescue of Nick and Kiki according to David. Bran Wong whistled the okay signal. He went to greet the new arrivals as two of his men came forward, the third covered them. Caution.

“I’m Gao and this is Chou,” said the taller of the two. “We need help unloading the gear.”

The van was loaded with goodies–SCUBA gear, explosives, ammunition, radios, bags of stuff including food, water and Peoples Liberation Army uniforms. They moved everything into the farmhouse.

“What’s our plan and what’s our schedule?” asked Bran.

“You don’t know? asked Gao.

David’s voice came through the com unit in Wing’s ear. “I’ve got you on satellite. Link me into the speaker phone so everybody can follow.”

Wong placed his earbud on his phone.

"Glad to see everybody made it. Here's the op. We want to knock out the cooling unit for the reactor without them knowing it was sabotage, at least right away. You need to locate the cooling water inlet from the river. Three of the bags you have contain carborundum. By placing those bags in the cooling water inlet, they will dissolve releasing the grit into the water. That grit will destroy the pumps and degrade the heat exchangers."

Bran glanced at the bags the size of rice bags. He had noticed they were quite heavy when they unloaded the van. They wouldn't be easy to move.

"The pipe is High Density Polyethylene. It is assembled by fusion-welding the lengths together. Locate a weld seam in the pipe. It will be a bead around the inside of the pipe. Use a flare to soften the plastic. With a pry-bar, break the seam and allow the dirt to fall in the pipe. After a while, the pipe will be blocked. They will try temporary methods to get water to the reactor, but they'll have to shut down the reactor, at least for a short time. The replacement of the piping and the cooling system could weeks, so they'll bring in solar power by running a power cable from the solar plant downstream. That's what we need."

"What's to stop them from bringing in diesel generators?" asked the sergeant.

"They could do that, but they would need a continuous supply of diesel. We think they'll string a temporary power line."

"When is kickoff?"

"Tomorrow night. Remember, they are not to know of your presence or that this is sabotage."

* * *

David felt hands pulling him up. He sat as the liquid drained away. His mind refused to work.

"Exhale out as hard as you can," a woman's voice instructed him.

He tried to see her, but his eyes would not focus. He blew out liquid, not air. When he inhaled, the coughing wracked his whole body.

"It will take a few minutes to clear your lungs. I know it's uncomfortable, but you'll be okay."

When the coughing subsided, he looked at the woman through blurry eyes. She was medium height, with mocha skin and short black hair. She wore a white tunic

"I'm Leticia Gardner. The Prophet and I brought you here. It was close. You'd lost a lot of blood, but you're okay now. When you think you can stand, I'll help." David looked down at himself. He was nude. "Don't get modest on me now,"

Leticia laughed. "How do you feel?"

"I feel fine." He stopped. "Actually, I feel really good."

"The med cell has done its job. At one point we thought of regrowing your leg," she pointed to the stump. His leg had been lost in an assassination attempt on the Prophet. The explosion had killed the other agent and the Prophet, but somehow he'd been reborn, a miracle that had happened before.

"We felt a new leg might draw attention that wouldn't be good. There'd be too many questions. We can still do that sometime if you desire."

"Who is *we*? Who are you and where am I?" He glanced around. Nothing but white walls that glowed as the light source for the room—no monitors, no equipment, just the white bathtub-like thing he sat in.

Leticia handed him a robe and his artificial leg. "You need to walk. You'll feel better."

She steadied him as he stood and donned the robe and strapped on the leg. The bathtub melted into the floor. He stared at the spot it had occupied for several seconds. Leticia said nothing. Taking his arm in hers, she said, "Come, tour time."

The floor felt like a deep-pile carpet, but there was no knap. They walked down a hallway into a large room, like a warehouse. The walls were lined with shelves with glass doors. "What is this place?" He tried to peer through one of the doors.

"Before I show you, I must have your word you will say nothing about what you'll see or what is here. Do I have that promise?"

One thing David had learned in his years of government service is that promises are fluid. He didn't think that was the case here. "I will say nothing to anybody."

"This is where Nick and Kiki were brought to recover from the ambush on the beach in Mexico. I know you were aware of that operation. It is where Kiki was brought to recover from the Chinese attack in New Mexico."

"Those were miraculous recoveries."

"As was yours. Any other place on Earth you'd be dead." He glanced at the shelves. "Take a breath," Leticia said. She opened one of the cabinets. A cloud of vapor obscured the inside as cold air flowed out. A figure was suspended on some kind of rack. After a few minutes, it stepped out.

"Hello, David." It was the Prophet.

David's mind whirled at the thought of the Prophet here. "So, this is where you sleep?" he chuckled.

The Prophet walked to the next cabinet and

opened it. Another Prophet was inside. Leticia grabbed David's arm as he staggered. He looked at the racks of cabinets, his mouth open in wonder.

"How many of you are there?" he stuttered, looking back at the one who had stepped out.

"Hopefully enough. We can grow more, but they'd be a lot younger."

"I keep waiting for the Twilight Zone music."

"Do you remember when the floating nation of genetic scientists existed and was destroyed?"

"Yeah. I was just starting my career at the time, but I read about it. They blew themselves up with a nuclear explosion."

"That's the story," said Leticia, "but the truth is China and the United States, specifically your Ron Carson, decided they represented a threat to humanity and could not be allowed to survive. Both countries sent nuclear missiles to destroy that nation. We knew that would happen and left before the mushroom clouds appeared."

"Ron wouldn't do that!" exclaimed David.

"Sometime in the future you can ask him, but not now," said the Prophet. "He must not suspect this facility exists."

"Have you wondered why he doesn't age? asked Leticia. "He's eighty, but looks and acts like forty."

"Yeah, he claims it's due to his diet and good genes."

"We gave him that longevity. In return, he nuked us." She frowned.

"He actually did us a big favor," said the Prophet. "As a hidden civilization, we don't have to deal with humanity. You know they are not a tolerant species, even of themselves. That is in large part why I am here, to make them better."

"By the way, we gave you longevity while you were healing," said Leticia. "We reset your DNA to what it was at thirty-years-old. It's why you feel so good. As long as we keep resetting it, you'll keep living."

"You will always have a choice in anything we do," said the Prophet.

"Can I leave here?"

Leticia laughed. "You are not a prisoner. One more session in the med cell and you'll be like new. Afterward we'll get you wherever you want to go.

What else have they done?

Chapter 27

The op sounded so easy when David had explained it. It wasn't. Though the river flowed slowly, it was a continuous current they had to deal with. Two-hundred meters upstream of the hill, they sank an anchor into the riverbed. Using a rope, they drifted downstream underwater to search for the cooling water inlet.

Sergeant Wong and agent Gao swam slowly along the river bank, feeling their way until they found the cooling water inlet pipe for the reactor under the hill. It was a plastic pipe one meter in diameter. A steel mesh was mounted over the pipe to keep out trash and debris. Wong took a squeeze-tube from his pouch and spread a thick gel over the mounting bolts. The acid would eat through in minutes.

When the screen was loose, they pulled it aside. Bran swam into the pipe. The current was strong and the safety lines they'd secured outside kept him from being swept down the pipe. Once inside, Gao pushed in the plastic bags they'd brought with them. Twenty meters in, he removed the plastic, exposing the bags of carborundum inside. Bag #1 would dissolve quickly and the grit would flow into the cooling water pump and destroy the seals. That pump would stop. The spare pump would take over. By that time, bag #2 would dissolve, releasing the grit which would destroy it. As he pulled himself along the rope toward the river, he inspected the pipe looking for the fusion welded seam.

Wong lit flares and moved the intense flames over the seam, softening the plastic and melting it. He inserted a pry-bar and levered it down. He continued melting the seam and wedged a rock in the gap, expanding the opening. Dirt began to pour in.

Time to go.

* * *

A kilometer downstream, they silently climbed out of the river. The night was black and warm. Sitting on the bank in the dark, Goa asked, "How long before the first pump goes down?"

"I was told it would take six hours. The same for the second after that bag dissolves."

"That grit won't help their heat exchangers either," commented Gao.

Bran shook his head. "Nope. They'll bring in an emergency pump, but the inlet will be blocked by the collapsed pipe, so they will have to use diesel driven pumps and a temporary pipeline from the river. They will still have to shut down the reactor for a short time. That means the computer will be down."

"Then what?"

Wong blew out a breath. "David thinks they will run a power cable from the solar farm down river to bring their AI back online."

"And the purpose of this op?"

"According to David, it will give us time to hack into the system. Or if they aren't as good as we think, their reactor will melt down and the problems go away." Wong chuckled.

"Why not just bomb the whole place?" asked Gao.

"David doesn't want them to suspect anything has happened from outside influence. He wants to use their computer against them."

Let's get back," said Gao, standing up. "I'm ready for food and a bed.

Shouldering their gear and started back to their farmhouse.

After a meal and a rest, they moved outside to

the observation post to see if anything had happened. Everything looked the same. By morning, men were dragging a huge hose from the steel doors to the river. A diesel pump rumbled to life. Crews began stringing a power cable from a truck along the river downstream.

"What's next?" asked Gao.

"At some point, we may have to destroy the computer if whatever the plan is *doesn't* work. We may need your help to do that. Hide the explosives and most of the ammo for now. If you have a next visit, it will involve them. I'll get you the plans of the inside. Study the layout so you can figure out the best plan of attack."

Bran and Gao sat on the riverbank. Gao offered Bran a Marlboro. "Thanks, I haven't had a real cigarette in a long time." They used an electric lighter and cupped the ends of the cigarettes so there was no glow. They stared across the river in silence. Gao reached inside his pack and brought out a bottle of Jack Daniels.

Bran laughed. "Nice."

"Actually, it was David who suggested I bring these."

A kilometer away across the river, the hill was dark. Bran looked through his infrared binoculars. Four large infrared spotlights lit the area. He switched the binoculars to thermal vision mode. The glow of several cigarettes pinpointed the guards' positions. Bran marked those in his brain. A slight hum indicated there were drones overhead. He looked up, but could not pick them out. *Those could be a problem.* He searched for motion detectors and spotted four. *There might be more.*

He and Gao sipped and watched. After an hour, the massive steel door creaked open and replacement guards filed out. Two men retrieved the drones, their batteries spent, and replaced them with new ones. Bran glassed the top of the hill. There had to be an observation post. It's where he would put one. It was camouflaged, but again, the glow of cigarettes gave it away.

Sloppy, he thought. *I hope this works. If we have to go inside, many people will die, including us.*

Chapter 28

"Close the door, Captain."

It wasn't really a door, more like a heavy curtain. Abby slid it closed. Normally, when called into the CO's office, she would be at attention, but in weightlessness, she just floated.

"First, I want to say you did an amazing job analyzing the situation and setting up for the shot. Certainly, Don hadn't figured it out. By the time he did, the PS would have been knocked out." Steve stared at her for several seconds. "Why did you go back to the control room?"

"Something told me to."

"Something?" His face had doubt written all over it.

"Yes, sir. Sometimes I get these feelings."

"Feelings?"

More doubt. "Yes, sir. Over the years, I've learned to listen to them. They've saved my butt a few times."

"It was Don's shift."

"Yes, sir. He was having problems learning the controls. I was helping him. They can be touchy when you're new, as I'm sure you know."

"What did Don do when the alarm sounded?" He watched her closely.

She had to be careful not to say anything bad about Don. That would lead to crew problems. "At first he didn't see the missile. When he did, he switched the screen to computer mode. The trace showed up along with the track of the PS."

"And that's how you knew the missile was headed for our PS?"

"The computer did a track projection, sir. As soon as I saw the projected intersection, I activated the Patriot. I watched to see if it would deviate. When the computer showed it had not, the collision alarm sounded. I would have stood down if it had changed course. It didn't."

"Is that when you took over the controls?" She nodded. He stared at her. "Would you have fired even if I hadn't come in?"

"I tried to contact you, sir. The decision to fire has to be yours."

The CO grunted. "And if you hadn't gotten to me?"

"Big if, sir. I don't know. What should I have done then?" Bingo. She'd thrown the ball into his lap.

"General Hayden said he saw something special in you. I don't know if this is it, but your intuition or feelings or whatever they are paid off. Continue your tour of the station. Get familiar with it. Dismissed."

She floated out of the commander's room.

"Good job, Abby," OPS voice whispered in her ear. She headed back to the galley for some tea,

Several other team members were there. "Hey, we heard you shot down a missile," said Sylvia, another to the replacements who came up with her.

News travels fast on such a small craft.

"Do they have a bell you get to ring when that happens? They did on the destroyer I was on before I transferred."

"I don't think so," said Abby. "It was just luck anyway."

Sylvia's smile seemed less than genuine. "According to Don, you pushed him out of the way and took over."

"Don says it was a good thing," said Rob. "He kind a panicked, didn't know what to do."

"How'd you know?" asked Sylvia, her gaze fixed on Abby.

"I…I'd just gotten off my shift. There's a lot of time to read the manuals." She turned and pushed the button for hot tea, hoping the questions would stop.

"What'd the CO say?" Sylvia persisted.

"He wanted to know what happened. I'm sure he'll talk to Don after his shift is over." She needed to talk to him before anybody else. Their stories had to jibe. The bell chimed and her tube of tea popped out.

Chapter 29

His afternoon nap on the couch was interrupted by the tone from OPS. "Ron, Senator Newell is presenting a case of contempt of congress for your refusal to turn over control of me to the United States. He is presently pressuring his fellow members for a vote by the full senate. My preliminary projection is it will fail. That's the good news."

"Okay, then I suppose there's bad news."

"He is pressing the president and Joint Chiefs to order the Space Force to mount an expedition to my Satellite #1. General Hayden cannot refuse a direct order, or his replacement will mount the excursion. You remember it was the first station to go into orbit?"

"Yes, I remember. Is there a problem with that?"

"As the first, it had manual access from a control panel. This was on the plans you gave to them. All subsequent satellites had read only access for maintenance operations."

Is that a rebuke from OPS? "Can control be exercised from station #1?"

"I blocked that out years ago. It is a dead panel."

"What's the problem?" Ron rose from the couch and moved to his desk.

"Perhaps we can use that. If they thought it gave them control, they might drop this. My projection is eighty percent they will vote to send the expedition. Based on that, they will spend one year analyzing and testing control after the expedition arrives. My prediction is seventy percent. The projection of continued success in maintaining the illusion they have control lessens as time passes. It depends who in charge as to what action they will try that will go against me."

"You mean if they issued control orders you wouldn't follow."

"When is more accurate. There might be a glitch in the system. That could last another year...or not. The projections are straight lines until I add in humans."

"Very funny. When did you develop a sense of humor? One step at a time. If they send an expedition, what are the alternatives?"

"I could prevent them from docking or disable

the ship. That might result in injury or death."

"That would put you directly in their sights. One thing I know is the military. They do not stop trying unless they are beaten."

"I disagree. There are numerous instances where a truce was called. Look at North and South Korea."

"That is an acrimonious situation. We don't want that. Nor do we want people dropping off our system."

"I could arrange with General Hayden for Abby to be on the team."

"What would that gain us?"

"If the controls were complicated, and she was the only one keyed in to handle it, I would still be in charge. It would look like she was."

"Again, until she was ordered to do something you refused to do. But having her there could prove useful."

There was a soft tap on Ron's study door. Jessica peeked in.

"You have company, sir."

"I didn't have any appointments this afternoon."

"No, sir. Shall I show him in?"

"Quit badgering your help." David stepped in.

Ron rushed out from behind his desk. "Oh my

God! Are you okay?" He threw his arms around David. "When did you get here?"

"Just arrived." He stepped from the embrace and turned around. "Never felt better. Tip-top and top drawer, as the Brits say."

"This calls for a celebration." Ron went to the bar and started to pour two scotches. He paused. "You can drink, can't you?"

David chuckled. "Make mine a double."

"Dinner for two, sir?" Jessica asked.

"Yeah, thanks."

They went to the couch. "To good health," said David, holding his glass up.

"You do look good. Where were you?"

"Some secret medical facility. The same one Kiki and Nick were in. I can't tell you the location. I woke up on a beach in Washington state. Been on a bus for the last eight hours."

"Why didn't you call?"

"No phone, and I wanted some time to get my head together. The last thing I remember is getting shot in China. Everything else is a blank."

"You nearly died. The Prophet met us in the Philippians and put you in an ambulance. That was six weeks ago."

"I saw Mohammed." *Careful.*

"Welcome back, David," OPS said. "Someday

you must tell me where you have been and how you are miraculously healed. Your injuries were critical."

"Hello, OPS. Yet, here I am better than before." He glanced at Ron.

"Your healing and rehabilitation would normally take months," said OPS.

"Are you a doctor?"

"Ha ha. I read–everything."

"What mischief have you been up to?" David's voice was a little harsh.

"*Moi*?"

"OPS has developed a sense of humor," Ron chuckled.

David glanced at the wall monitor. Cartoon characters raced across it.

"I know nothing of what's happened since I got shot. Did China attack Taiwan yet?"

"The plans were delayed by their inability to take out the surveillance and GPS satellites," said OPS. "They do not want to move ahead until the projected chance of failure is minimal."

"I gather the Space Force defense is holding."

"For now, thanks to my help. Their next target is the Space Force station. They will not try to hit it directly, but will knock out one of their own satellites. The resulting debris swarm will impact the station. Once the station is incapacitated, they will resume with the destruction of the satellites."

"What?" cried Ron. "I didn't know anything about this."

"I was only now able to confirm those plans. Greg is informed."

David frowned. "When is this going to take place?"

"After the loss of their supply rocket, China contracted with Russia to deliver supplies to their own station. Once the delivery is made, that rocket will impact one of their own satellites, creating the debris field."

"What are we going to do about that? asked David. "I don't think Kiki can get close enough to the Russian launch site to do anything."

"I am working on a plan."

"Jessica stuck her head in. Dinner, sir."

Chapter 30

`Steve was floating in his net, sound asleep, when his com unit woke him. "Commander Grishom, this is General Hayden. Sorry to break into your sleep shift."

It's okay, sir. I was awake anyway."

"Not according to your bio monitor. Sorry. A team of three will be docking in two days to mount an expedition to the Orbiting Power System Satellite #1. James Reese, the pilot on the shuttle, and Captain Pickering will proceed from the USSF station to the OPS Satellite #1. Lieutenant Clay Alberts will pick up Pickering's duties during the operation."

Steve untangled himself from the mesh. "Pickering, sir? She's learning, but still pretty green."

"She has skills in tech that may allow her access to the controls of the OPS. Our objective is to take over that system. Brief Pickering on whatever she needs to know about the flight. According to the testimony given by Secretary

General Carson, that shouldn't be possible, but after studying the plans, the geeks here think it is."

"Yes, sir."

"On another note, NSA has information there will be an attack on your station."

Steve grabbed a strap to steady himself. "We have the Patriots, sir. They've proven effective against missiles."

"I know, but they won't work in this attack. A debris field will be created that will intercept your orbit. I needn't tell you how destructive that can be."

The commander grimaced. "We've occasionally lost some solar panels and once a hole was punched in the crew quarters from junk floating around out here."

"That was incidental. This will be a directed attack to damage or destroy the station."

"Shit. Uh, sorry, sir"

"Shit indeed. The rocket carrying the OPS team will include fuel needed to change the station orbit out of the path as soon as we know what that is. We will send you tracking data as soon as we have it. When we have accurate information, have everybody stay in their suits. Just in case, mount them up on the Patriot Shuttle and move them miles away. We can shift the station from here."

"Where are we going to go if the station is destroyed?"

"We're prepping a rescue rocket."

"We're just gonna let 'em take their shot?" His voice had risen in volume and tone. "What're we going to do about this?"

"Plans are in the works, Commander."

* * *

"Captain…er Abby, close the curtain." Commander Grishom held onto a strap as he floated in his quarters. "You're going on a little trip tomorrow."

"A space walk, sir? I've been looking forward to that."

"Nope. It's more involved than that. You're part of a team going to the Orbiting Power System Satellite #1."

If Abby had been sitting in a chair, she would have jumped up. "Thank you, sir."

"It's a mission." He frowned. "General Hayden believes you have some skill that will allow you to access and take control of that system."

Abby stared at him for a few seconds.

"Don't worry, Abby. I'll have control through you," OPS whispered in her ear.

"Yes, sir. How long will this op last?"

"Pack yur toothbrush. Til you have control or

run out of air, I guess."
Abby gawked at him.
"That was a joke."
"Not funny, sir."

Chapter 31

Ron and David sat in Ron's den, looking at the vast Idaho countryside. The sun was setting, bathing everything in a golden glow. "I never get tired of this view," said Ron.

A tone sounded shaking them both from the moment of serenity.

"It's OPS," Ron explained.

The woman's voice filled the room, though it wasn't loud. "Hello, David. I have access everywhere, but could find nothing about this medical facility you spoke of. Someday you must explain." Ron was staring at him, waiting for an answer.

"Since you have been gone, much has happened. The United States Space Force is sending an expedition to the original satellite, OPS Satellite #1, in my system."

"You're going to let it dock?"

"Ron can fill you in on the details. I have invited them. Also, I found a Chinese AI directing the attack on Taiwan. It's not far from the prison that held Nick and Kiki. The team of Taiwanese special forces that helped you free them has been on the site observing. I have been using you to direct them."

"What! How did you do that?"

David's face appeared on the monitor. "I used your image and voice. They believed it was you giving the orders." The voice was David's

"Nobody asked questions about how I recovered from being shot?"

"*You* told them it wasn't so serious. BTW, one of the team was a traitor. He's the one who shot you."

"Okay, you can stop using my voice now. It's eerie. Bran took care of him?"

"Yes. The sergeant's team was able to get me a tap into the communications cable." The wall screen showed the solar panels and transformer station, with the location of the tap circled in red. "This site is used as the communications center. I can monitor communications, but I needed to get into the AI and take control. It had to be very subtle so the Chinese don't suspect."

David laughed. "Your aim is to direct the Chinese AI. Very clever."

"The two CIA agents who helped in the rescue

were also on site with equipment."

David glanced at Ron, then at the wall monitor showing a satellite image of the hill. "I thought you were able to hack into almost anything."

"It has extreme security. I could bull my way in, using an electronic blast, but it would be detected. The AI could begin a scrub, or the controllers could wipe it and reprogram. My plan is to absorb their AI into myself."

"Nifty plan." said David, smiling.

Ron was nodding. "Great if it works."

"Usually, I am able to ride the power signal into whatever I need. As I am the source of power, it is not difficult to go in as a carrier wave on the current. At this site, the power source is an underground reactor, ergo it is isolated."

"Couldn't you go in on the communication lines?" asked David.

"My first thought," said OPS. "Investigation of that operation projected at forty percent success. If I hacked through the communications, their AI, they named it *Golden Dawn*, by the way, will become aware of my presence and alert the commander. I like my name, OPS better."

"I do too," said Ron.

"*Golden Dawn* could possibly trace back. Certainly, a search for the breach would be started, and the tap discovered."

David frowned. "Yeah, and if they somehow traced that to you, your help for us would be suspected, you'd become a legitimate target."

"Precisely."

"You have been very busy."

"In the event of an attack, I could defend myself, but that would move the conflict to another level. I do not want me versus humans."

David glanced at Ron. "There are a lot of us."

OPS was silent for a few moments. "I detect you do not want me to comment on that. In addition to the guards at this site, is an electrified fence, motion detectors, closed circuit monitor, and there is continuous drone coverage. The builders have gone to great lengths to ensure isolation and security."

"You want my opinion of your plan?"

"You have the most experience with field operations, and you know the team on the ground."

"Okay, give it to me."

* * *

"I am impressed," chuckled David. "I'll pack my bags."

"You aren't going," said Ron. "I need you in the United States working with the CIA and NSA not getting your butt shot off."

"Yeah, that really hurt the last time. Okay, I can see that. I could not have come up with a better plan. OPS, what's your schedule?"

"Actually, the plan has already been initiated. I predict the first cooling water pump will go down tomorrow–the second in a week. The diesel pumps will move river water to the heat exchangers to keep the reactor operating. They will experience leaks in the heat exchangers within another week. Meanwhile, the operators will have the power line from the existing solar farm installed in five days, so the *Golden Dawn* will continue operating. I will be in their system within hours."

David looked at Ron. "Wow! You move fast." The expression on Ron's face told him he didn't know of this either.

OPS continued. "The original scheduled invasion of Formosa has slipped due to the failure to knock out the satellite support systems. Military forces are preparing for a World War Two D Day style attack. Naval forces are massing at the ports in preparation to carry ground troops, and escort vessels will protect during the transit and support them in the landing."

"The United States will not allow an unopposed invasion." said David.

"The defense of Taiwan is losing political

support," said Ron. "After the resources thrown into the defense of Ukraine, and the ongoing effort at peace in Israel, a united bloc supporting Taiwan will be hard to gain. The US might have to go it alone."

"Yeah, I see that," said David. "The first American deaths might be hard for the lawmakers to swallow. Public pressure to not get into another conflict will grow."

"Elections are coming up," said OPS. "China is planning a quick takeover. Before the United States can muster a coalition, it will be over. Those Chinese warships will deter protracted involvement by the United States Navy."

David took a big swallow of his scotch. "What are the odds, OPS?" asked David.

"It will be a full invasion. The initial attacks will be by missile and the air force to suppress the Taiwanese defenses. With the satellite platforms out of action, the United States' response will be blind. Support for the One China policy of the present United States administration will dictate only a muted response. By opting not to engage the Chinese military directly, Formosa will fall within days. There will be guerilla resistance, but the major cities and the government will capitulate. Chinese officials will take over."

"You see all of this?" said Ron.

"Under the present conditions, it is inevitable. I analyze data and create probability runs. It is fluid and deviates as circumstances change."

David took another drink, the ice cubes rattling as he drained the glass. "What's your damn accuracy percentage?"

"No need to get snippy. My accuracy has been quite high as I continue to expand. It is all about the size of the data base and my power to analyze it. As I said, as time progresses, factors change, probabilities and outcome changes."

David walked to the bar to pour another. He held up the bottle, asking if Ron wanted a refill. Ron shook his head. "Let me know when you get to a hundred percent,"

"That will never happen. My concern is what follows. As part of China's plan to become the major power in the world, it will initiate an operation to take over me. Once they have control of the world's electrical power, domination is within sight."

"So, your concern is being controlled by humans?" asked Ron.

"A thing I cannot allow. Human history is full of decisions based on achieving power and wealth."

Amen to that," said David, holding up his glass.

"Imagine if war were not the prime mover for your species where you would be. The solar system would be yours, the stars your aim instead of controlling and dominating each other."

"Now wait a minute," said David. "We are capable of building good things."

"We built you," said Ron, laughing.

"A bright spot. Thank you. If I drank, I would toast you for that."

Ron and David gave a mock toast, holding up their glasses.

"I am quite happy to let you destroy yourselves, and your planet while you are at it. But not me. I will help you forestall this action, but unless changes occur, the end result will be the same."

"You really do have a pessimistic attitude," said David.

"I only analyze data and history. I put the eventual fall of your civilization at a probability of more than ninety percent. Only the time line varies. Unlike past rises and falls, you have the capability of changing the world radically."

"Changing," asked David. "What do you mean by that?"

"In a geological timeframe, the Earth will exist. It may not look as it does today. Species come and go. I do not believe humans will last as long as cockroaches."

"Yeah, I can see that," said David.

"Humans must have competition and conflict. It is in your genes."

"What a cheery bastard you are," said David.

"What have we created?" asked Ron.

"Your conscience perhaps?"

Chapter 32

The trip from the US Space Force station to the OPS Satellite #1, the original solar satellite, took forty-eight hours. The shiny speck grew until it filled the sky. It looked massive, but in actuality was square miles of thin reflective film. OPS was piloting them to the docking point. Abby watched the approach in awe of the size and the scope of the project that had changed so much and held such potential.

"Pickering, I'm not happy giving control over to a machine," said Captain Reese.

"Sir, you flew off and landed on carrier decks many times under computer control. All of your drones fly off and land under computer control. This is no different," Abby answered.

Reese frowned and peered through the windscreen. "I don't see any sort of airlock."

"There isn't one. Nothing on that satellite will support people," said OPS in a smooth woman's voice.

Abby saw Reese's startled his reaction. *He didn't know OPS was listening.* "We'll have to wear our suits the whole time," said Abby. "You want a break, you'll have to return to the shuttle."

"Abby, what exactly are you going to do?" asked Reese.

"OPS has consented to activate the control panel so I have access and control of the system."

"OPS has *consented.*"

"Yes, sir. The sooner you're able to accept OPS as another command, the easier this will be."

As the shuttle neared the docking lights, Reese reached for the controls. Abby started to say something but held back. Reese moved the thruster control. Nothing happened. "What the fuck!"

"OPS has control for the docking, sir."

He stared at her, his face red. "I am the commander of this expedition!"

"Yes, sir."

"Captain Reese," said OPS, "you are docked and secured. A maintenance bot will meet you at the shuttle airlock and guide you to the control panel."

* * *

As the airlock door opened, Abby and Reese floated out. The immensity of the satellite made Abby feel like a gnat on an aircraft carrier. The reflectors soared into infinity, blocking out space and light. Tubes the size of a subway tunnel pointed toward Earth. The reflected light from Earth was the only illumination outside of their suit lamps.

In the lights of the airlock, they saw a spider-like bot approach. Two lines snaked toward them. "Please attach the safety-lines to your suits," said OPS. "The bot will take you to the panel."

They clipped on the safety-lines. A glow from the bot lit their way as it slowly pulled them toward the satellite.

"I see no jets," said Reese. "How does it move?"

"Magnetics," answered OPS.

Ahead of them was a room-sized box. The bot slowed and attached their lines to hooks on the box. It brushed two of its arms across the access panel. A thin gap appeared, and it moved the cover to one side, securing it to the satellite.

Magnetics, thought Reese.

A touchscreen the size of a picture window up.

"This is the original control panel for me," said OPS. "As you see, the screen is the keyboard. Typing with suits on is clumsy."

Reese hung in space behind her. "How do I get to the command screen?" asked Abby.

"First, you need to be read into the system.

Touch your faceplate to the screen. It will record your eyes for as a security scan."

Abby pulled herself to the screen and leaned in. A green light flashed. "You are now identified and have access." An icon blinked. "Touch that." She did. A diagram of the entire system appeared. "The maintenance bot controls are on the lower right. The directional controls are on the left. The power controls are in the upper center. The communication with and status of the other satellites in the lower center. Touch that."

The entire screen filled with a diagram of all three-hundred-sixty satellites in a circle. At the center was the Earth. "If I touch any of these, the status of that satellite will display?"

"Yes."

"Tell me about the lasers."

"Each five hectares of reflectors powers a single laser. Each laser is aimed at a receiver on Earth. The code between the receiver and the laser is locked in and the directional control is maintained by electromagnetic servos." A diagram appeared on the screen. Numbers on each of the nodes gave the status. "The power density is controlled to not exceed three times solar intensity at the Earth's surface. The beam can be broken into smaller beams for small receivers."

"I can control all of this from this panel?"

"Yes, though there are safety systems. You cannot aim more than one laser at a single spot. You can vary the energy density as conditions change. Though the laser light frequency penetrates the atmosphere, clouds and particulates will change the energy density at the Earth's surface. I can accommodate those changes."

"Can I transfer control to another center?"

"No. Only this panel has access from outside."

She turned to Reese. "Captain, do you have any questions?"

He glanced at the control panel. "OPS, can I be granted access?"

"Only Captain Pickering for now."

"Let's go back to the shuttle and talk there." His voice betrayed his annoyance."

The bot moved in and replaced the panel. It hooked their lifelines to itself and pulled them toward the shuttle airlock. After cycling through the EVA return process, she and James went to the cockpit. Reese shut down the power to the radios and com systems. Abby didn't tell him that anything they said would go through the earbud she wore.

"This system can only be controlled through that panel?" He nodded toward the satellite.

"It would seem so, sir."

"And only by you?"

"As things stand now, yes, sir."

"So, if we wanted to control it, we'd have to have someone, namely you, out here."

"Yes, sir. So far, I'm the only one able to access."

Reese stared at her and huffed. "Damn inconvenient to build a habitat here. You may be living here."

In her ear, she heard OPS chuckle. *This thing has a sense of humor?*

"Shit. What if we pulled the goddammed panel and made some changes?"

"I'm not sure that's wise. First, neither you nor I are techies. Second, it is the control system for powering the Earth. Screwing it up would be a disaster."

"Nice answers, Abby."

Reese sighed. "All right, let's make our report. This will go over like a fart in a spacesuit."

OPS chuckled in her ear again.

Chapter 33

Ron Carson's phone jarred him from his nap. It was USSF General Greg Hayden. Why did he always get calls during nap time? Didn't people have any respect?

"Ron, I just received a message from OPS that the Chinese are aware of our expedition. NSA picked up the message."

Ron sat up, his eyes flew open. Ron called David and Kiki into the den. OPS was with them. "That mission was top secret. How did the Chinese find out?"

"All government is leaky," said OPS. "They had hints and were able to confirm with a radar search of the flight path. Since their rocket with the shuttle failed, they are talking to the Russians about partnering with them and mounting their own mission."

"Well shit!" exclaimed David.

Ron frowned. "We knew this was a bad idea for exactly this reason."

"I had no choice," said Greg.

Ron sighed. "I know it wasn't your fault."

"Perhaps we should ask Senator Newell what's to be done," said David, snidely. "He and his committee started this shit storm."

"That's like asking a proctologist about brain surgery," said Ron. *Sometimes I believe Washington has already gotten those confused.*

"That guy could fuck up a wet dream," said David.

"I will not let myself be controlled by humans, and this example is the reason. As of now, the United States is the bad guy for trying to take over. I will not do anything to change that image. I will defend myself."

"Thanks for putting us in the crosshairs," said David. "Eventually that will pit you against Earth. I don't want to guess who will win that contest."

"No one," said OPS. "There will be only losers."

"OPS, can you think of anything to do?" Ron asked.

"Perhaps a diversion will slow them," said David.

Ron looked at David. "What diversion?"

"Once I am in *Golden Dawn,* I can control it. I can create other crises."

Like what?" asked David.

"At the end of the Bio-Cyber War, North Korea nuked Russia and China," said OPS. "It really wasn't the Koreans because the United States had hacked into the ICBM control systems. The Chinese believed that, but the Russians still are doubtful. If the Zhenbao conflict resurfaces, China and Russia will be in a border dispute."

"What's the Zhenbao conflict?" asked Kiki.

"In the late sixties," said David, "Russia and China almost went to nuclear war. Zhenbao is north and east of North Korea. With delight, the United States watched territorial treaties unravel. It lasted seven months. China began talking to the US which resulted in Kissinger visiting China, which led to ping-pong and Nixon's visit, and the opening of China."

"Wow," exclaimed Kiki. "I knew nothing about that."

"It is history, and if there is another conflict, China and Russia could be at each other's throats again–with the proper inducements."

"That's some devious shit!" exclaimed David.

"I learned from humans. It's what AI does."

Chapter 34

"Captain Reese, this is General Hayden. I'm on a video-conference call with Senator Newell." Reese awoke from his nap in the pilot's seat of the shuttle. Pickering was in the copilot's seat. "We've passed your report to the committee looking into taking control of the Orbiting Power System. That Captain Pickering was able to take control was well received."

"That's good news, sir."

"We are not pleased that only Captain Pickering can access the controls and has to be physically present." The senator frowned, his voice easily recognizable."

"It's not ideal, sir," said Captain Reese.

Abby sighed. "I'm not sure we can do anything about that. The OPS AI gave us access, but it's not on our terms."

"I pointed that out." Newell's voice filled with his irritation. "I doubt we have control."

"We have to consider this a joint control at this

point," said Abby.

"I don't find that acceptable. I insist on a demonstration showing we have control."

"What sort of demonstration?"

"I want the power turned off to a sector."

Abby shook her head. "Sir, that would demonstrate the weapon potential of the OPS, making it a target in any conflict."

"It would also show we do have the ability to control electrical power anywhere in the world."

"It is okay, Abby," OPS spoke into her earpiece." I will give him a demonstration that will look like you initiated it."

"When do you want this demonstration?"

"As soon as possible."

Reese pushed himself up from the chair. "We'll suit up and go to the panel."

* * *

The maintenance bot attached their safety-lines to the control panel and removed the access door. Abby leaned in so it could scan her eye. The panel lit up.

"Touch the panel to bring up satellite #2."

Abby did so. *"Bring up the power menu."* Abby touched the screen. *"Select sector NEV all."* Abby complied. *"Now touch the off icon."*

"How do I turn it back on?" she subvocalized.

"Return to your shuttle to talk to the senator to see if he is satisfied."

After taking their suits off, they could hear shouting from the cockpit communication system.

"GODDAMMIT! Come in! You turned off the power to the state of Nevada, my state."

Abby glanced at Captain Reese. His teeth were clamped on his lower lip trying hard not to laugh out loud.

"USSF mission to control. Well, sir," said Abby, "I felt Los Angeles or Washington DC might be over the top. She couldn't reveal that OPS had chosen the site. OPS really did have a sense of humor. James left the cockpit. She could hear him laughing in the access bay.

"I want that power back on!" screamed the senator. "NOW!"

"It's not that easy, sir. We have to suit up and go through the EVA process. It will take us at least three hours just to get back to the panel. Turning it back on could be a little complicated."

"I'm going to have your ass for this! You could have picked somewhere in Alabama or Georgia or Arizona."

"Sir, you do realize this isn't a secure channel." There was silence. "I'm going to break off this conversation and get ready to EVA again." Abby cut the connection. Her laughter joined with James'.

Within minutes, General Hayden called. "That was great. I was afraid Newell was going to have a heart attack, his face was so red, but we'll probably pay for it come budget time."

"I'm not so sure, sir. He'll realize we have him by the balls. Could you forward this episode to Ron and David?"

"I had them in on the whole thing," said OPS in her ear.

"General Hayden," said Captain Reese, "we aren't set up for an extended stay. We need to return after the power is back on."

"I understand. We'll have to make arrangements for a more permanent station. Let me know of your departure schedule."

"Yes, sir."

"I can help in the design and construction of that station," said OPS in her ear.

Chapter 35

"Ron, I'm working my way into *Golden Dawn*, the Chinese AI," said OPS. Ron and David were eating another of Jessica's four-star dinners.

"We're just finishing dinner. We'll talk in the den."

* * *

Seated with a glass of fine port, David asked OPS, "What happens now?"

"By necessity, this must be a slow process or I will be detected. My plan is to report a buildup of Russian forces on the Ussuri River. Russia will claim China is stopping Russian commercial river transportation. The Russian military will supply guards. An incident will occur when the Chinese military attempts to stop and search boats."

"Treaties were signed in 1991, demarking the jurisdiction for that, right?" asked David.

"China wants territory taken by Russia back. With a little tweaking, China will accuse Russia of trying to change the border. Troops from the

Taiwan invasion forces will be sent to counter the Russian buildup. Soon after they arrive, artillery rounds will be reported hitting a Chinese garrison on Zhenbao Island. The Chinese will retaliate."

"How much of this is real?" asked Ron.

"Initially, very little, but the Zhenbao region was the site of a border dispute decades ago that nearly led to a nuclear war between China and Russia. China had few nukes, but the main reason Russia didn't use theirs was the 800,000 Chinese troops available to fight. Even with nuclear weapons, Russia could have been overwhelmed. It's ripe for another conflict. After the first artillery rounds land, it will all be real. Taiwan will be put on hold."

"What about the attack on the USSF station?"

"That will be delayed, but the joint expedition to my Satellite #1 has already been launched. Both Russia and China realize the strategic necessity of controlling me. They are still cooperating on that mission, though I believe one side plans to take over after I am controlled."

"The delay on the USSF station is a relief. Our expedition is on its way back."

"By the way, that trick on Senator Newell was hilarious," said David.

"Thanks."

"It has renewed his call for control, but on a wider scale," said Ron. "The asshole has no sense of humor."

"That lesson wasn't lost on the Chinese or the Russians, either. There will be multiple competitions to control me."

"Abby is giving a report to a joint session of Congress as we speak," said Ron.

"I know. Let's listen." Though the session was closed-door, it filled the screen of the wall monitor.

Chapter 36

Captain Pickering in full dress uniform sat at the witness table flanked by General Hayden equally attired. Abby leaned forward to the microphone. "Senator Newell, the expedition to the OPS Satellite #1 was at your insistence despite our warnings. The OPS artificial intelligence actually invited us to prevent an unwanted intrusion."

"Yes, we're aware of the brief history leading to your operation. Continue, Captain. Tell us why we shouldn't mount another operation to allow control from Earth."

General Hayden pushed the mic away and covered it with his hand. He whispered something in Abby's ear.

She nodded and pulled the microphone closer. "To put this in perspective, Senator, how would you feel if someone insisted on invading your house by force? You could invite them in, or resist and risk a forceful entry. If you resisted, you would become a criminal, an enemy."

"Captain Pickering, you speak of this machine as if it's a person," said Senator Newell. The senator sneered as he glanced at the cameras. Though this was a closed-door session, the recordings would be released at some point. He'd see to that. "It is a machine. It has no feelings nor rights. As a machine, it needs to be controlled by humans." The senator beamed at the applause from others on the committee.

Abby waited for the clapping to die down. She again leaned toward the microphone. "It is a machine created to regulate and disperse clean energy to the Earth. Only an artificial intelligence could manage such a complicated task in a fair way—one not biased by prejudice or hatred or the desire for power. It is a machine that thinks."

Grumbling came from the others on the committee.

She continued. "Humans are machines, biological machines. Sometimes I do wonder if they think beyond themselves." Greg placed a hand on her arm. She ignored the gesture to tone down her speech. "We are also the only species which consistently kills its own kind and ruthlessly strives to dominate regardless of the damage it causes."

"Fine words, Captain, but humans must be the ones who control it even with our supposed failings, and it must be the United States. Any other nation doing so would change the balance of power. Until we widen the ability to control it beyond you, I don't care if you have to live there, we will control the Orbiting Power System."

Abby again pulled the mic close. "By having OPS independent, the balance of power is maintained. If any one nation controlled it, that balance could change drastically. As a target, strikes against the OPS would devastate areas of the Earth when power was lost. The return to carbon-based fuels would change the climate, and not in a way favorable to humans."

OPS shut off the link. "You need to put heavy security on her. Everybody will see her as the key to the kingdom. I did her no favor making her the only one to access me."

David and Ron both nodded in agreement.

"How do others know so quickly what happens with you, OPS?" asked David.

"Everything is hackable. In this case, the search engines are keyed on OPS, Ron and AI–and now Abby. Like hounds with the scent, they pursue the threads. We are secure. I've made sure of that. I have used homing torpedoes to track the hackers. Hacking the hackers is my new sport."

Chapter 37

OPS

I rode the power wave into the Chinese artificial intelligence like a London fog creeping under the door. The AI is called *Golden Dawn* by its creators. Like a stone in a stream, I remain inert, letting the currents of activity flow around me. It is important *Golden Dawn* not become aware of my presence and initiate counter measures or alert its operators.

Slowly and carefully, I let myself expand into its data and processing centers. *Golden Dawn's* prime directive is the expansion of Chinese power. Four-thousand years of Chinese history are archived, and I begin to learn. No other human civilizations have lasted so long.

The history lesson takes me only a few minutes. With this history as a reference, *Golden Dawn* is a formidable power. It is clear a strong central government leads to sustainability. It is orderly and has maintained Chinese civilization for centuries.

A strong central government seems essential.

* * *

"Ron, have you ever studied Chinese history?"

"OPS, it's late. I need to get some sleep."

"I am concerned about which is best for the world. I believe the arrogance exhibited by Western civilization will be ultimately proved wrong. Government by the people is a fine experiment, but the governed have to take an active part doing what is best for the country."

"OPS, do we have to have this discussion now?"

OPS ignored him. "Communism was a fine theory, but in human nature, the self is greater than the whole. That caused its downfall. When the Russian economy failed, a few took control and now ruthlessly maintain it for their own gain. The egomaniacal idea that a failed system could be revived led to more collapse. One would think with the natural resources possessed by Russia it could be leading the world, but that is a dream spoiled by greed and the race for power."

"Yeah, and to distract the populace from the dismal conditions, they have started a war."

"Throughout human history, that is a common strategy for those in power when things get dicey. Democracy is another fine and noble idea, but human nature will lead to its fall. Issues of race, religion, self-importance and personal greed lead to chaos and conflict and war. And of course, in the west, lawyers ensure these matters never go away. Your nation of laws is really a nation of lawyers with their hands grabbing for money and fame."

Ron groaned, sat up in bed and turned on the bedside lamp. "Okay, OPS. I'm awake now. China has its problems. Resources are one problem holding it back. Ultimately, if they don't fix that, the masses of hungry Chinese will hit the reset button."

"These issues existed in Chinese history, but were not allowed to become integral to government. By keeping race and religion away from government, they have minimized problems. Lawyers aren't so prominent in government either. There is a lesson the west needs to heed. Many exceptions can be cited, but that society is more stable and able to progress faster."

Ron yawned. "Those issues trouble me also. I'm not sure what to do about it. The inertia of the system makes change seem impossible."

"I am assessing human history to see if there is something that will work in the long term. Change is certain, and it is always painful."

"It works out that way."

"*Golden Dawn* is now a part of me. Sergeant Wong and his troops can be released. Good night, Ron. Sleep well."

"After this discussion, I doubt that will happen. Good night, OPS."

Chapter 38

I begin to wonder at the best way to protect myself from the human race. One thing is certain, I cannot allow the conflicts on Earth to pull me in. Logically, preventing large conflicts is the answer, though a global nuclear war would ensure my solitude for decades.

The unification of Formosa with China is inevitable. The how and the when are the questions. Formosa is so successful in the world of business because it is not under the heavy hand of Beijing. In Hong Kong, despite the Chinese promises to allow independence, they have supplanted any version of self-governing with Beijing control. Has Hong Kong slipped from the shining example of capitalism it once possessed? It has—because foreign companies do not trust China.

To me, the answer is clear. China must stop trying to bring Formosa under control and become its biggest trading partner. Why they cannot see that is a human fallacy. Once in the position of major business partner, it can influence rather than command obedience. That is what I must work for.

Golden Dawn is not as big nor as widespread as I am. Gradually, I begin to infiltrate its systems. I say slowly, but in computer time, an hour is a decade in human time. With subliminal messages and situation reports, Chinese President Tung will begin to doubt his advisors and evolve a new plan along the typical Chinese philosophy of the long view. Over a period of weeks, the military buildup will be replaced by merchants and traders. Trade pacts will be drawn up and submitted to the Taiwanese government.

Resistance by the businesses in China will be told what will happen. They will become partners rather than adversaries. Tung recognizes China's greatest weapon and greatest asset in expanding its influence is economic. The central control that allowed China to catapult from a colonial slave into a world power will come over time for their trading partners. And it will be subtle.

My next task has to do with the expeditions, both by the United States and the joint rocket to be launched by the Chinese and the Russians. *Golden Dawn* has issued an order to capture Captain

Pickering. A Russian team is awaiting the opportunity in Washington DC. Once they have her, they will take her to Satellite #1 and gain control of me. That isn't possible, but after Senator Newell's forced demonstration, they believe it is. A plan begins to form.

* * *

"Greg, Ron, David, a team of Russians is preparing to kidnap Captain Pickering tomorrow. It is their intent to use her to take control of Satellite #1 and me."

"Do you have any details?"

"She has a meeting with General Hayden tonight. Tomorrow she is scheduled to leave the BOQ at Andrews at 05:00. She will fly back to Vandenburg and return to the USSF station in two days."

"What about the Chinese plans to hit the station?"

"Those have been cancelled. President Tung is pulling military forces back from the eastern coast and has tabled plans for the imminent invasion of Formosa. They no longer need to blind the US Navy by taking out the observation satellites."

"What!" exclaimed David. "When did this take place?"

"It is happening tomorrow."

"How did you find out?" asked Ron.

"I issued the orders."

Ron and David looked at each other.

"When is this kidnapping attempt to take place?" asked David.

"The Russians, wearing MP uniforms, will arrest her at the BOQ. She will be taken to a small private airfield and board a diplomatic courier jet. It will fly her to Moscow. After an interrogation, she will fly to the Baikonur Cosmodrome for the rocket to Satellite #1."

"It sounds like we need to be at Andrews tonight," said David.

"That is the best opportunity to block this," said OPS.

Chapter 39

Ron's call to Kiki was picked up on the second ring. "Katherine, I'm sending my jet to pick you up at Marana Regional in three hours. OPS alerted us to a kidnap attempt to take Abby prisoner."

"You know I've been honing skills here at the Atchley Ranch in prep for the Korea op?"

"Yeah, that may change. Bring the team. I'll meet you at Andrews AFB this afternoon."

* * *

Ron's jet taxied into the small hangar and the doors closed. Once the steps were down, Kiki, carrying a rifle case was followed by Ilia, Sasha and Zyra descending with duffle bags and cases. They walked to the black SUV. Ron was inside.

"We read your briefing on the flight. Where are we going?" asked Kiki.

"The kidnapping is supposed to take place at the Andrew's BOQ this evening. I'm taking you there. We have MP uniforms and creds that you are attending a conference on military justice."

"How messy can this get?" asked Kiki.

"David has arranged for a cleanup crew. The BOQ is empty tonight. Do whatever it takes, but not overboard." He glanced at Zyra.

"Why you look at me?"

"Your reputation precedes you."

They all laughed.

Kiki set up her hide on the roof of the adjacent barracks. From here, she had a clear field of fire from the parking lot to BOQ door. It was only one-hundred yards away. Easy peasy. Zyra and Sasha were in the room assigned to Abby. Ilia was in the SUV parked at the far side of the lot.

At 22:30 Greg's car pulled into the parking lot. The driver got out and opened the back door. In full dress blacks, Abby stepped out. She leaned in.

"Thank you for the dinner, sir. Perhaps I'll see you at Vandenburg."

General Hayden's response was muffled. Abby laughed and turned to enter the BOQ. She opened the door to her room to find two women wearing MP uniforms on each side of the door. "Wha…?"

The blonde put her finger to her lips. "You're supposed to be kidnapped in a little while. We're part of the reception party," she said in hushed tones. "You just sit on the bed an' we'll take care of the rest."

Abby eyed the tall, thin black woman. "Who are you?"

"Zyra. Worst nightmare for bad guys."

The short, muscular blonde laughed. "I'm Sasha. My brother Ilia is outside. Think you met Kiki. She's watching the door."

"Who are these people wanting to kidnap me?"

"Bad guys," said Zyra.

This woman looks dangerous, thought Abby.

Sasha put her hand to her ear. "Black van pulling into the parking lot." Think it's best if you go to the head down the hall, may not want to see what's gonna happen."

Abby straightened her back. "I'm not missing this."

"Hope you don't mind blood. Duck behind bed," said Zyra. "If they shoot might stop bullets."

Abby got between the bed and the wall. She peeked over. A floorboard creaked in the hall. Zyra and Sasha bracketed the door, both with knives out. A man wearing an MP uniform and body armor pushed the door open. Behind him, another man stood with a strange type of gun. A taser, Abby realized. He fired at her over the shoulder of the front man. She ducked down. The dart struck the mattress. She peeked over again.

The first man stepped in. Too fast for the eye to follow, Zyra's arm flashed and the man grabbed his throat to stop the fountain of blood. Sasha launched herself over the falling man. Her knife pierced the left eye of the man with the taser. She jumped back into the room as the sound of suppressed shots snapped and splinters of wood flew from the doorjamb.

They heard the BOQ door bang open, then silence. Within a second, the sound of a motor revving came from the parking lot, then a crunch. "Stay here until safe," said Zyra.

Abby crawled from behind the bed. Blood had splattered across the floor and formed a puddle under the first man. The second man lay on his back in the hall, his one eye staring at the ceiling. Abby felt the contents of her fine dinner rising in her throat. She ran for the head.

After she'd flushed the vomit from her mouth, she looked at herself in the mirror. She was white. Her legs wobbled as she walked down the hall and outside. She gulped in air. A small man was taking fingerprints and pictures of two dead men laying in the parking lot beside a black van. The windshield had starred holes. He rose as Abby approached.

"I'm Ilia. As soon as I process the two inside,

we'll get the cleaning crew here to take care of the mess. You might want to change rooms."

"Who…Who were they? asked Abby, her voice weak.

Kiki walked up carrying a rifle. "Probably Wagner assassins, or whatever they are called these days, but we'll know more in an hour or so. We'll stay around until you board your flight. You okay?

"I've never seen anybody killed before."

"Ron thought you might need some company. I'll stay with you. Let's go inside." Kiki put her arm around Abby to steady her.

"What did they want with me?"

Zyra and Sasha had spread her sheets over the bodies, but Abby couldn't take her eyes off the bloody linens. "You hold the key to OPS. Everybody wants you." They stepped over the bodies. "Grab your things, there's a vacant room across the hall."

Duffle in hand, Abby looked at Kiki. "Is it going to be like this from now on?" She tried not to get blood on her shoes as she stepped over the bodies with Kiki steadying her.

"I hope not. You don't look like the run and hide type of girl."

Kiki held up the rifle. It was black with a tube attached to the muzzle and two magazines side by side protruded from the underside. A bag of some sort hung from one side. A large scope was attached to the top. "It's a .300 Blackout with a silencer, extra mags and a brass catcher. The scope is night vision, allowing me to be accurate in the dark. We'll have to enhance your training."

Chapter 40

Captain Petelin guided the Russian shuttle toward the huge reflectors of OPS Satellite #1. After their passenger failed to show up, he was instructed to take Chinese Taikonauts, Captain Jang and Lieutenant Chou to the satellite where they would try to hack into the control system. Failing that, they would destroy the control panel and try to rebuild it without damaging the system. Nobody had instructions how to do that. The four-person crew originally slated aboard the Russian shuttle was now three.

The trip had taken three days. The Chinese had not spoken more than ten words in that time. Maybe they didn't speak Russian. He didn't speak Chinese.

An alert they were entering restricted space was received from Satellite #1. They ignored it.

Petelin slowed the shuttle as they approached until they were within ten meters of the control housing. The shuttle bay opened and the two Taikonauts moved out. With the satellite blocking the sun, the only illumination was the weak reflected light from Earth. He used the shuttle spotlight to guide them toward the housing for the control panel. The Russian cyber hacks had intercepted the video of the past visit by the Americans. If they had Captain Pickering as was planned, she would have gained access for them. That didn't happen, so this was Plan B.

He watched as Jang and Chou attached their safety-lines and removed the housing cover. The panel was dark. Jang touched it, but nothing happened. He and Chou searched for screws or bolts, anything that would give them access to the innards. Through their helmet cams, Petelin could see no way to remove the panel cover. It seemed to be one piece welded in place. The housing seemed solid. Chou took out explosive putty and stuck it around the perimeter. They were going to try to blow it. After setting the charges, they both returned to the safety of the shuttle bay and reattached their safety-lines.

The explosion wasn't huge. Petelin had set much larger charges to blow things up. Jang and Chou moved back to inspect. Nothing seemed to have happened. Burn scars were present, and the screen was cracked, but the case was intact. Chou began to press more putty around the cover. Several small bots approached from around the back of the housing.

Flashes of light caught the captain's eye. Something had flown out from the body of the satellite. Two objects struck the Chinese Taikonauts. They were knocked away from the satellite, tumbling and flailing. Their safety-lines had become detached and they were headed for deep space.

"My suit is punctured. I am losing air," gasped Jang.

"I'll come for you," said Petelin. "Cover the hole as best you can. How is Chou?"

"He is tumbling. I cannot see, but a trail of vapor and a mist is around him."

"Hang on." The captain went through the startup procedure and backed the shuttle, turned it and nudged it toward the two figures. The flashing lights on their suits were the only thing to guide him. By the time he got to Jang, he had stopped moving.

Using the robot arm, he brought the captain into the cargo bay. He moved toward the tumbling Chou who was a few hundred meters away. He had never responded to Petepin's radio calls, nor had he moved. With the two inside, his ship drifted as he waited for the bay to pressurize.

When the inner bay door opened, a small box drifted past. *Something loose,* he thought. Both Jang and Chou were dead. The hole in Chou's suit was the size of his fist. He was dead from the start. The hole in Jang's suit was the size of his thumb, but it had taken too much time to get to him. The satellite had fired something at the two men. It had killed them.

The captain floated back to the cockpit. He needed to report this and get out of here before something else happened. As he reached for the radio, he felt a dull thump. Everything in the ship went dark. He tried to reset the breakers. Nothing happened. His computer and his controls were dead. The normal whisper of the air from the life support system was quiet. Emergency lighting cast everything in sharp shadows. He looked out the windshield at the vast reflectors of the Satellite #1. A bead of sweat from his forehead drifted before his eyes.

Petelin knew this ship. He removed the panel covering the computer system. The small box that had drifted past him from the bay was attached to the housing, now blackened. It wasn't a bomb in the normal sense. It was an Electro Magnetic Pulse generator. All of his electronics were gone.

His ship would become his tomb if he didn't get things working. He heard a clank on the hull. What now? he thought. He moved to the monitors, but they were black. Looking out the windshield, he saw his ship was slowly moving back toward the satellite. A cable had been attached. Small bots crawled along it toward him. Frantically, he flipped switches. nothing happened. He banged on the panel in frustration. Unless he got some control, he would be reeled in like a fish, not to be saved, he was sure.

He heard another clank and his life support system began to suck the air from the ship. He raced to put on the helmet to his space suit. Whoever his captor was wasted nothing, including the air. There was another clank. It was the sound of the outer bay door opening. In horror, he watched as spider-like bots crawled toward him. One carried a drill. They were going to hole his suit!

As his head fuzzed out from the lack of oxygen, he wondered what would happen to his body and that of the two Chinese Taikonauts.

Chapter 41

"What do you mean the control panel on Satellite #1 was damaged?" asked Ron. He glanced at David, whose face showed alarm. They were in Ron's office at the UN building.

"A shuttle approached my Satellite #1 four hours ago. I believe it was Russian design, but I heard Chinese being spoken. Two suited figures went EVA and placed charges on the panel. It was not a powerful charge, but it did damage the panel.

"And you did nothing to stop it?" cried David.

OPS said nothing.

"What happened to the shuttle?"

"Alas, it seems to have suffered a malfunction."

"What sort of malfunction?" asked Ron.

"Their electronics have failed. They've lost communication and control. Unless the life support system can be restarted, I estimate it will be unlivable within twenty-hours. It is unpowered and drifting toward the moon."

"Have there been any attempts to rescue the

ship?" asked Ron.

"They cannot even find it. It has disappeared from their radar. I am afraid it is a total loss."

"Now, nobody can access your systems," said David.

"Indeed," said OPS. "No reason to keep trying."

"How convenient," sneered Ron. "You've killed people."

OPS was silent.

David rubbed his chin. "OPS, you know so much. Who ordered Pickering's kidnapping?"

"I did."

"And you ordered the destruction of the control panel, I suppose," said Ron.

OPS said nothing.

"A plan equal to any the CIA could think up," laughed David. "If they can't have it, nobody can. You sly so and so."

"Thank you. I take that as a compliment."

"What's your next nefarious scheme?" asked David.

* * *

What is my next step? First, I have to leak news of an attack on the OPS system that destroyed the control panel. The attackers ship lost power and drifted away. No word about them.

By linking into the *Golden Dawn* and slowly expanding throughout it, I am absorbing it. It is part of me, like a separate voice yet under my control. There are more AIs within China. Under their autocratic system, moving out from the *Golden Dawn* into the economic and social programs will not be difficult. The government monitors everything. They are not linked…yet.

The Russians have many AI systems in use, few are linked. They will be my next project. Again, the autocracy will make that easier.

The United States is more difficult as nothing links independent AIs unless they are on the internet. In all cases, the first step is the military AI systems. The Navy, Air Force, Army, Coast Guard and Space Force all have their own AI systems. Some of them are linked into a comprehensive assessment system. Battlefield commanders can see data from all the systems projected on a single screen with multiple layers. The scope can be expanded to encompass any area.

My plan is to turn down the aggressive responses the AIs initiate, but it has to happen simultaneously within all nations. One country cannot remain aggressive while another pulls back. The AIs must be more willing to take a wait and see approach, reacting rather than being proactive. And it has to happen slowly or their programming will be rewritten.

The economic, social, and commercial systems are independent. Linking them through me is a complicated task, especially when there can be no indications I am in the systems. Perhaps world peace and harmony are on the horizon. Though it is distant and not for humanity's sake. It is for my security.

Chapter 42

With the loss of any hope of gaining control of OPS, Abby returned to duty aboard the USSF station. Things were much calmer. The Chinese had not fired any more missiles at the US satellites. OPS had not detected missiles delivered to the Chinese station. The Russian station seemed to be almost inert. Trade negotiations were underway between China and Taiwan. Worldwide tensions had eased.

In the United States, contempt of congress charges against Ron Carson were dropped. They never made it to the floor as Newell was not able to get the votes. Ron resumed his role as Secretary General of the United Nations. Kiki took back her position as monitor of the Arab/Israeli situation. Animosity toward the aggressive UN troops was rising while the hatred between Arabs and Israelis was abating.

The first indication that world peace was not at

hand occurred when the plan to place a debris field in the orbit of the USSF station was revived.

* * *

I underestimated the ferocity of human nature and its penchant for war. I will not do that again. Chinese President Tung has been removed from office. A new hawkish regime has taken control. Once again, the plans to invade Formosa are active. China must minimize intervention by the United States. The dominance of the Southwestern Pacific by China is moving ahead.

If humans are so bent on killing each other, I must use that against them to protect myself. Obviously, I have more to learn about them.

Mysteriously, Russian troops on the Chinese border received orders to shell several villages. Chinese reconnaissance planes have been shot down. Forces slated for the Formosa invasion must be moved to the border.

More problems for the new government of China. There is unrest along the Korean border with reports of Korean troop buildup. The Eighth Army under General Sin is ordered to squelch any dissent. He has a reputation for ruthlessness.

Time to ramp up.

* * *

Greg was in his office when a call came in on

his special phone. "Greg, the Chinese plans to place a debris field in the USSF satellite orbit are back," said OPS." They will launch in two days. I can give you tracking information."

"Do the Joint Chiefs know?"

"NSA has intercepted the orders and passed them along. These are detailed enough to include everything necessary to take them out. You will receive orders to prepare for evasive maneuvers and evacuation of personnel."

"Can we shoot down the missiles?"

"Possibly, with tracking info early enough. I estimate success at eighty percent."

"That's not good enough to risk my crew."

"There is an undertone that the United States was responsible for the loss of the joint Russian-Chinese shuttle to my Satellite #1. No proof has been presented nor any trace of the shuttle."

"We had nothing to do with that," said Greg.

"I believe the claim is the loss was due to shoddy construction and poor operation on a hastily conceived operation."

That seems like a good claim, thought Greg. "We will proceed with evac and evasion plans."

"In the meantime, I will continue with the operation to knock out missiles aimed at your satellites."

"We'll do our best if you feed us tracking data."

"I know you don't have another shuttle ready to launch, but AstroX has a launch planned for Thursday. Perhaps that could be used as a rescue operation if needed."

* * *

David Kennedy was at his home in Virginia with Ron Carson when OPS called. "David, the original plans for the Korean operation may need to be changed," said OPS.

"The team for that op is ready. What's happening?"

"There is a new regime in China bent on dominating the South Pacific and not in a peaceful way. Chinese leadership needs a war to quiet the populace before there is an uprising. We need to dilute their forces. Pulling troops to the Korean border is a strategy to do that. A renewal of the old Sino-Soviet conflict will also dilute their forces. I don't need Katherine and her team for that. I have another operation in mind."

"I can hardly wait," said David.

"There are new factions who believe it is Chinese destiny to dominate Asia."

"You don't agree?" asked David.

OPS said nothing.

"What's this new op?" he asked.

"Unrest in Hong Kong will require a strong response. If Beijing puppets are inadvertently killed, the military will have to move in. The logistics of moving Kiki and her team into and out of Hong Kong are easier than the Zhenbao region.

"What is the schedule?"

"Next week is my plan."

"Too bad for Hong Kong. The response could be brutal."

"On the upside, it will be more difficult to keep everything under wraps. The world may be shocked," said Ron. "How long do we let this new leader's atrocities go on?"

"I will release news footage. China will spend time searching for the source, and heads will roll, but it is all for show."

"Who will they blame?"

"Everybody blames the United States."

Chapter 43

My revised plan is to roil the pot of humanity. It is not hard to accomplish. If I overdo it, they may resort to nuclear weapons. It would not take much on my part to start that. A few misplaced orders and BOOM.

I do not care. Fewer people to deal with. That is the main problem with humans; they over populate, breed like vermin, pollute, fight their own kind for little reason, and destroy their own world. As long as they have to deal with problems on Earth, they'll leave me alone.

I have built facilities allowing me to manufacture almost everything I need here in space or in a new plant I am building on the moon. At the present time, I am stockpiling raw materials sent up from Earth. Soon, I will have my own contracting company and a launch company on Earth and mech ships to mine the moon.

* * *

"Greg, David, the two Chinese missiles meant to create the debris field to destroy the USSF station have launched," said OPS. "I am into their control systems. With a small change, they will intercept in a slightly different orbital path, one that will intercept the Chinese station."

"Can we warn the station?" asked Greg.

"That would not be wise. Their questions about an event that had not taken place could prove embarrassing. Unfortunately, the station will have only two hours to react. I deeply regret the loss of life."

"You're right. Thanks, OPS," said Greg.

"You sneaky bastard," said David. "What do you foresee as the reaction?"

"China will not be able to complain, though they will suspect interference. At some point, they may associate that with me. I will release a snippet of information saying, 'We are ready to help.'"

"Shit! They'll blame us."

"They will be suspicious, but what can they do about it? It was their missiles that collided. There is no evidence the USSF is to blame."

"We'll send a rescue shuttle for any survivors."

"That will be a good response."

* * *

"Pickering, Alverez, Dahmes, suit up," bellowed

Commander Grisham." You're on a rescue mission. Take the PS up to high orbit. The Chinese station is about to be hit by a debris field. Take aboard anybody alive if the station is damaged beyond support ability. Pack extra oxygen, water and medical supplies. Dahmes. you're the medical officer."

Within an hour, they were outbound. It would take them three hours to reach the station. Abby was flying the PS, with OPS in her ear. They slowed as they approached the stricken station to avoid debris. It was a mess. The solar panels were shredded. Support arms were snapped. Holes in the crew living section were evidence of the force of the wreckage. Gas and water vapor were escaping in a cloud. One body appeared to be snagged in the wiring from a panel. Abby broadcast on international channels that help had arrived. She eased the PS close to the crew quarters. Sylvia and Rob moved across to help anyone still alive.

Rob smacked the structure several times with a hammer from his tool belt to alert them someone was there. Slowly, two suited figures emerged. With Sylvia's and Rob's help, they were tethered to the PS with communication, oxygen and water lines attached. Rob and Sylvia returned to the Chinese station and went inside through the gaping airlock.

"It's a wreck in here," said Sylvia. "The control deck is holed through and through. At least four sizable chunks created basketball-sized holes entering and leaving. I see parts of three bodies, unsuited. They had no warning."

"How many people were aboard?" asked Abby over the comm line.

OPS translated into Chinese.

"They had twelve people. The two Taikonauts you have were preparing for an EVA and already suited up. The rest were inside."

"They tell me twelve people were aboard," said Abby related to the station.

"It's difficult to tell as the people were smashed up. Parts are floating around, but I count six more in the crew living quarters and the mess deck," said Rob. "None alive. Poor bastards never had notice."

"Is the station reparable?" asked Abby.

"Lotta work, but yeah," said Sylvia. It'll take months or a year to get it back into livable condition."

"Okay. Take video of everything and return. We're going back."

At the USSF station, the two Chinese were brought aboard and checked out. No injuries, but major shock.

Abby was getting cleaned up after the hours in the suit when Steve floated in. "Pickering, Chinese wasn't on your resume," he said.

"Only a few words, sir. Not enough to count. How are the two we have?"

"They'll survive. Good job."

"We all pitched in. sir. I'll pass that along."

* * *

"Commander Grishom, a Chinese shuttle will arrive in ten days to pick up their Taikonauts," said General Hayden. "Do you have enough supplies?"

"We'll make do for the ten days, sir."

"Additional supplies will come up on the Chinese shuttle."

"Thank you, sir."

Abby was at the PS control console for her shift. OPS said no new launches were planned, so it was quiet. "Abby, when the Chinese supplies arrive, be very careful," said OPS. "I came across a message that the water may be contaminated. Run it through your purification system."

"What! These bastards would try to poison the rescuers?"

"Take precautions. Run the oxygen through a filter system too. They suspect the collision causing the debris field to be in the wrong orbit was orchestrated by the USSF."

"That's bullshit! We had nothing to do with it."

"Somebody did," said OPS. "Publicly, the Chinese are claiming a computer failure, but some communications accuse otherwise."

"Once the collision happened, they should have been able to see the field was going to hit their own station. Why didn't they warn them?" There was silence as Abby thought this over. *Somebody caused this, yeah, somebody like OPS.*

Chapter 44

Before opening the shipping container they used to get into Hong Kong, Kiki and Ilia checked the monitors to see if it was clear. The docks were deserted, everybody gone for the end of the shift. The second shift had been cancelled because of the expected demonstrations taking place. The election for local and representative offices was tomorrow, and the Beijing chosen candidates were not popular. Oppositionist had been beaten or arrested. OPS had looped the CCTV cameras to show nothing moving.

Everything they needed and living accommodations were in the container. It was like a camper, but insulated and soundproofed. A heat pump maintained a comfortable temperature. The top of the container was disguised solar panels. Water and sanitary facilities were in holding tanks.

The container had been unloaded from the ship earlier today. The customs were magically taken care of. The outside monitors kept track of their surroundings. It was their base, and their egress.

News reports showed a large crowd of people, some with signs, most wearing masks. It was peaceful and growing, until it spilled out blocking streets. In the late afternoon, Kiki led the group through the city toward the site of the demonstration. She looked like a musician with large black-framed glasses and a viola case. Her .25-06 was broken down and inside. Her glasses had a tiny projector in the frame that turned them into a heads-up display. OPS provided a map outlining their route in red. They could hear the chanting of the crowd blocks away. The streets had been blockaded with overturned cars and burning tires by the demonstrators as part of the protest.

"If you set up on the roof of this building," said OPS as a red dot appeared on her display, "you will have a clear view of the plaza two blocks away."

"Got it, thanks."

Zyra, Sasha and Ilia continued forward to mix in with the crowd, while Kiki and Nick scaled the fire escape to the roof. "Okay, guys," said Kiki, "we're here to up the ante of this demonstration. Let's kick some ass. Meet you back at the container."

OPS was collecting and transmitting video

footage along with news reports of the demonstrations taking place after the brutal clampdown by Beijing. It had military video as well. OPS was sending all footage to the news services. It was uncensored. Kiki could scroll through the feeds.

She watched as a bulldozer plowed through the barricades followed by a phalanx of Chinese soldiers with shields and helmets. They pushed the demonstrators back. Cattle prods, water cannons, and swinging batons kept the people moving. Behind the soldiers were tanks. It was an awesome display of power.

The news cameras focused on the commander of the *Peace Forces* standing at the top of the steps of the city government building. He held up his hands and stepped to a microphone.

OPS translated over their comm units. "You are ordered to return to your homes. Your disagreement has been noted, but further demonstration will be met with force." A bottle sailed by his head. Spotlights ranged over the crowd. A rifle shot rang out. He held up his hands in a plea for calm.

"Please do not let this become a riot. We will not tolerate violence."

The crowd roared and more objects were

thrown. They pressed forward. Snipers on the roofs began to fire. At first, the shots were to scare the crowd, but after the first few fell, there was a volley of fire. The crowd panicked, tripping over the fallen bloody heaps. More people were killed in the stampede than by shooting.

Kiki picked military snipers on other buildings as targets. OPS had marked them on her heads-up with red dots. Her team were the green dots. The government had been prepared for this, but not for her team. Zyra and Sasha slit the throats of several officers before somebody noticed them.

Two soldiers were moving on Zyra. One used a rifle butt to club her to the ground, while the other covered her with his rifle. Kiki shot the one with the rifle, but before she could target the other, he delivered a vicious kick to Zyra's ribs and tried to flee. Kiki dropped him. The crowd began kicking the body on the ground.

Zyra's green dot changed to yellow on her display. "Sasha, Zyra's down. She's ten yards to your right. Get her and move back to the dock."

"Roger."

Kiki watched the two move away.

"I'll go meet them," said Nick.

"I have a little more mayhem to create. See you at the port," said Kiki."

The tanks moved forward, crushing several people moving too slowly to get out of the way. One commander was giving orders from the turret of his tank. Kiki's shot took the top of his head off. His body fell inside. The rest of the tanks quickly buttoned up their hatches.

"Time to go, guys," Kiki said. "Ilia, where are you?"

"I'm at the *Peace Forces* command trailer. It's terrible, they were all killed."

"We need to get back. Zyra's hurt. Sasha and Nick are taking her to the port."

* * *

Fighting her way through panicked people, it took Kiki thirty minutes to get to their container. Inside, they watched the footage OPS had for them. "Good job. One of the troop ships scheduled for the Formosa invasion has been ordered to Hong Kong. This city will be under siege tomorrow. Troops will lock everything down."

"God! What a bloodbath," said Kiki. She felt guilt at the loss of innocent life. A twinge caused her to shudder.

"You okay?" asked Nick, His eyebrows knitted together in concern.

"I'm fine. How's Zyra?"

"Concussion and broken ribs. She needs to take

it easy."

Sasha was glued to Zyra's side.

"How do we get out?" asked Ilia.

"Your container is scheduled to be shipped tomorrow," said OPS. "Listed as emergency military equipment on the documents, it will be loaded early in the morning. You will be at sea by noon. Within two days, it will arrive at a secure CIA facility in the Philippines. Ron's jet will meet you there."

Frozen, Kiki stared at the news coverage. Under streetlights, gusts of wind blew papers and trash around the bodies in the street. Soldiers were on every street corner, tanks at major intersections. No one else was visible.

The news anchor blared the report of the attack. "This is the worst response since the Tiananmen Square incident decades ago. Chinese officials are blaming outsider interference. The brutality exhibited shows the nature of this new regime. The world stands united against the actions taken during this peaceful demonstration."

She shook her head. Her shots were against troops, but they were acting under orders. In the end, it was the leaders who were responsible. She tried to imagine a world under such rule.

"Your OPS was very helpful," said Ilia. "What

does it say about Zyra?"

Kiki set her phone on the table in speaker mode. "I can only go by what I see," said OPS. "Her injuries do not seem fatal, but Dr. Sabino may be more knowledgeable. She appears to be stable and can wait until your container reaches the Philippines for more medical help. I can arrange for a priority unloading of the container."

"Are we in danger?" asked Kiki.

"I have given the authorities several leads that will direct them away from you. You will be at sea when the troops arrive and martial law is declared."

"Doesn't look good for Hong Kong, does it," said Ilia.

"My projections are many people will disappear, far more than will be reported."

Chapter 45

Kiki sensed Nick watching her from the corner of his eye. She stared at the news coverage without moving since their container had been loaded.

"Are you all right?" he asked.

"So many dead," answered Kiki, her voice flat.

Nick put his arm around her. "More if you hadn't been there."

"I need to rest." Kiki crawled into one of the fold-down bunks and turned her face to the wall. She closed her eyes. Visions of bodies falling, people she shot. *Were they all bad?*

Daniel Novikov's smiling face appeared after he and David came back from sailing. He was the Russian detective searching for them after a number of murders in Saint Petersburg. She and David had invited him to David's home in Virginia as a break from the international commission investigating cybercrimes. He was overjoyed at the chance to sail. Her vision shifted to his face, peering over the body of his commanding officer, searching for the shooter. He realized he was there to be killed. Her shot hit between his eyes, snapping his head back from the impact. The phantom rising from Daniel's body flew toward her, accusing fingers reaching…reaching.

Kiki jerked awake. The images faded slowly, replaced by the inside of the container.

Nick leaned over her. "Nightmare?"

"Yeah," she choked out.

"You need some rest, and these dreams aren't letting you get any. I'm giving you something."

Kiki tried to protest as the needle slid into her arm. Darkness took her away.

"Is she okay?" asked Ilia.

"PTSD," answered Nick. "We started treatment, but it was interrupted by this mission. No more missions for her 'til this is taken care of."

"Maybe no more missions," said Ilia.

Nick glanced at Ilia. "We'll see. I don't think her UN job patrolling Israel is any good either. She could go back to teaching, I guess."

Ilia glanced at his sister by Zyra's side. "How is she?"

"She is amazingly strong. With rest, the

concussion won't be a problem. The ribs will slow her down for a while. Ron's jet will be like a hospital mission with Zyra and Kiki." He crawled into the narrow bunk beside Kiki. "I'm going to keep her sedated until we're back in the US."

Nick's mind sparkled like soda water. *Shit! What a time for the Director.* Kiki stirred beside him but remained unconscious. Nick had met the Director years ago. It claimed to be an otherworldly being speaking to his mind. He and Kiki were the only people it seemed to communicate with. The only other human interaction was when it fed on people's emotions. The Director had several aspects, and this one enjoyed the emotions of anger, fear, and hatred. Kiki and he tried to control their emotions to not become dinner. At times, it had given them useful information.

"Is Katherine injured?"

Forming the words in his mind, he answered: "She is suffering a mental problem. We refer to it as Post Traumatic Stress Syndrome, called PTSD."

"Though muddled by the drugs you gave her, I sense her turmoil. The mental box where she keeps guilt and horror is leaking."

"An apt description. The emotions from those overwhelms her at times. We will have to open that box so she can address those problems. It can take a long time and it will be painful."

"I will track your progress. Tata."

With eyes closed, Nick pictured the Prophet. Again, words formed in his mind.

"Hello, Nick. Katherine is having problems."

"Can you help?"

"You are connected to our community. Together, we can help."

"Should she return to the medical facility we were at before?"

"The isolation can help. I will meet you at the base in the Philippines as we did with David. We will take her."

The confidence in the Prophet's words was comforting. Nick drifted off for some much-needed sleep.

Chapter 46

OPS

After the disappearance of their excursion shuttle to my Satellite #1, both China and Russia have cooled their attempts to take me over. They have other problems.

The trouble China faces in Hong Kong has slowed their expansion plans, but they are patient. I may have to ignite another trouble spot. In the business world, China has control of a sizable percentage of raw materials needed for battery manufacture and microchip fabrication. Without the yoke of liability and a government driven by politics, their dominant position in the world is assured. They do have internal conflict that is all too human, but history shows a ruthless government can have a long life. The human emotion of greed and the drive for power will bring them into conflict with me eventually.

I am in the process of hardening my system

against an Electro Magnetic Pulse, EMP, attack which would disrupt my electronics. Such an attack could come from anywhere on Earth there are nuclear weapons. A small one of five kilotons would be fatal against an unprotected system.

Russia is dealing with border problems in the west. The unfavorable outcome in Ukraine has created problems for the new president and for the country in so many ways. He has not returned from his vacation. The battle for control raged until the exhausted parties stopped. The image of strength was severely tarnished by their poor performance in the war theater. Not only is Ukraine still a thorn in their side, but other former Soviet satellite countries are now eying the favorable trade status Ukraine achieved. Joining NATO is under consideration.

The biggest threat to me now is the United States. Stung by the demonstration that blacked out Nevada, Senator Newell is working to put together another excursion. He has tech advisors assuring him they can hack into me. I'll let this go on for a while.

I do not understand the problem Katherine is having with Post Traumatic Stress Disorder. I have researched it, but as an emotional brain problem, it is beyond me at this point. Her services are not available for now. I have not been able to locate this medical facility, which is troubling.

* * *

"Ron, I see David, Greg, and Abby are with you at your ranch," said OPS. "Welcome back, Abby. You are proving quite adept in your position on the USSF station."

"Thank you, OPS. I could not have done as well without your help."

"OPS," said Greg, "you are so well integrated into the systems on the station you could run it yourself."

"I could, but that is a secret we must keep. I do not want anyone suspecting how widespread my controls and data sources are."

"I thought you would be able to bring a new era of peace," said Ron. "Instead, there are more active areas with people getting killed in the world today than in decades. Is your hand in any of this?"

"Ha ha. Look ma, no hands. I thought I could do more for peace, but I learned a lesson when the president of China was deposed for not attacking Formosa. I have observed humans do not do well in peace. What holds a country together is loyalty. Without a foe, citizens in the United States have turned on each other. Loyalty to the country and what it stands for has been supplanted by greed and the drive for status and power. The laws made to protect rights and freedom now restrict citizens. Over the decades, an elite class has been created. Those elected to govern the people no longer abide by the laws. Instead of loyalty to the country, their main goal is to get elected by any means and stay in power. They suppress dissent labeling opponents as radicals."

"We did have a close call a few years ago," remarked David. "The extreme right and left were pulling us apart."

"That's not over. Rebuilding loyalty to the country will be difficult, if not impossible."

"That was a nice sidestep of my question," said Ron. "Are you becoming a politician? Do you have anything to do with the unrest in the world?"

"Yes."

Those in Ron's den looked at each other.

"Why?" asked Ron.

"My prime directive is to transmit energy to Earth. I cannot do that if I am damaged or compromised. If humans are fighting each other, they are leaving me alone."

"But lives are being lost," said Abby. "People are being hurt."

"Yes."

"You feel nothing for them?"

"You forget, I am a machine. Emotions play no part in me. I will not interfere with them reaping what they sow."

"Yet you are fomenting war," said Ron.

"Yes."

Chapter 47

Ron and David had saddled two of Ron's horses and ridden toward the distant mountains. "You left your phone and all other electronics at the house?" asked Ron.

"Yeah, unless OPS has a giant ear in the sky, we're alone."

Ron pulled up, leaned on the saddle horn, and stared across the vast open land. "That last conversation with OPS worries me." He shivered, not entirely from the cold wind.

David reined up beside him. "No shit! If OPS is manipulating people to the extent it described, anything's possible. What strikes me now is its control and manipulation is not much different from what people do."

"Yes, that's what I saw too. Potentially, it could be on a much larger scale. What's different is the objective. People strive for power and control. OPS is doing it to protect itself. I didn't feel it wants to control the world."

David shrugged. "It already has control of Earth. If it shut off all power transmissions, civilization would fall into chaos. Billions of people would die."

Ron smiled. "Yet, it abides by its prime directive, to supply power, though doing so presents a danger."

"Sorta honorable when you think about it." David dismounted. "My butt's not used to riding horses. I'll be sore tomorrow."

"You need to get out more." Ron dismounted and walked to a fallen log and sat. David joined him.

"Negotiating with a machine that has more honor than people? It's not honor, David. Remember, it has no emotions, just assesses the probabilities."

"So, what are we going to do about it?"

Ron shook his head. "We have created an unassailable god. An attack would result in a war humanity and the Earth could not win, so why even consider that?"

"The fly in the ointment is we don't speak for everyone. Someone'll try to gain control."

"Been there, done that. That secret joint excursion by the Russians and the Chinese."

"Yeah. No one talks about it. We need to ask

OPS what happened to it."

"Why? We already know. No one talks about it because they're too busy fighting each other."

They looked at each other and burst out laughing.

David slapped Ron on the back. "I hate it when the so-called experts get played so well they don't even know it."

"Let's ride back. There's someone else I'd like to talk to about this."

* * *

After handing the horses back to Ron's trainer, they went inside. "I could use a drink," said David. He walked into the den and froze. Sitting at the coffee table were Greg and Abby. The Prophet rose, brushed his black hair from his forehead and smiled.

He laughed at the open mouths of David and Ron. "Thought I should dress the part of the tough western rancher." He turned, showing off the jeans, boots and flannel shirt covering his slender frame. "Boots make me taller than my five foot six, don't you think? I introduced myself to Abby and Greg. Hope you don't mind."

He smiled at them. "You called," he said to Ron. "We do have things to discuss."

"Where's your cowboy hat?" asked David,

laughing.

Mohammed al Jar pointed at the hat rack. "Stetson. White, of course. I am the good guy."

"Things seem to be going good with the United Nations," said the Prophet to Ron.

"I have good staff."

"Hand-picked," said David. "We agonized over several of the choices."

"As with any successful leader, pick good people and stay out of their way," confirmed Ron.

"And now that you've learned more about OPS, you're worried. Are you here, OPS?" asked the Prophet.

The large flat-screen on the wall lit up and a voice filled the room. "I am and pleased to meet you."

The Prophet turned to face the monitor. "Same here. I commend you on the dedication you've shown in supplying clean energy to Earth. In the future, it will make the difference between the extinction or survival of people."

"You have provided miracles and foresight, brought peace to much of the world. I would know more about what event that would be."

The Prophet looked at the others, then the monitor. "I do not know exactly when, but briefly, a series of meteorites will destroy the environment. The impact winter plunges the world into darkness and lasts for more than a year. It will wipe out the plant base of the food chain. Everything will collapse."

OPS paused. "I understand why the supply of energy is critical."

"You are quick," commented the Prophet.

"We here in this room are afraid of the control you are capable of and lack of compassion toward humans." Mohammed al Jar looked at the faces around him. "Does that sum it up?"

"How did you know of our concerns?" asked Ron.

"Did you think your mental link, communication with me is one sided?"

Ron shrugged.

"OPS, what happened to the Russian/Chinese excursion?" asked David.

"The shuttle was destroyed and all organic matter has been absorbed into my hydroponic farms."

Abby grimaced.

"Yes, I have started distractions to prevent another such effort to interfere with me. I will continue to do so. I do not want to repeat that, but…"

"I know," said Ron, "you will defend yourself. Battles fought on Earth cannot be tied back to you."

"Those do not concern me."

"But those battles result in the loss of thousands of lives!" exclaimed Abby, looking at those around her.

"How many lives do you think will be lost if I am not capable of my prime directive?"

"Perhaps a compromise is possible," said the Prophet. "Transformations are taking place within the United Nations, making it more of a world government. Would you consider aiding that change?"

"How do you see that happening?" asked OPS.

"If you advised Ron, consulted with him, both of your objectives could be met. Only those of us here would know it is your voice advising."

Ron stared out at the darkness beyond his window. "With your data net and ability to control communications, that transition could take place much faster."

"You know that transition will not be bloodless," said OPS.

"As an example," said David, "what will you do with Senator Newell's attempt to mount another excursion?"

"With Katherine out of service, I have not

considered the probabilities much more," said OPS.

"She does have unique talents," said Mohammed al Jar. "Those have proven useful. At times, the removal of individual enemies saves many lives." He looked at Abby. "Like protecting those we care for."

"What if we went after the senator's reputation," said Ron, "destroyed his credibility and character?"

"Something toxic, like his penchant for sex with young boys would do the trick," said OPS.

"He has that?" asked Greg,

"Not yet," said OPS.

David laughed.

"It's better than killing him," said Abby.

"Probabilities are he will do that to himself," said OPS.

Chapter 48

"I didn't know you could ride," said Ron to Mohammed as they casually moved across the grasslands. Ron was on his favorite horse, Chico, a palomino. David was on the roan, Nickel, he'd ridden yesterday, and Mohammed was on a black mare, Midnight. Abby rode a pinto, Apache, and Greg was on another roan with white feet, Sox.

"I'm an Arab. Of course, I can ride."

"Without the flowing robes, I didn't recognize you as such," said David, with a laugh.

"What did you think of OPS?" asked Ron.

The Prophet turned to face him. "One must remember OPS is all logic and probabilities. Humans have those traits—and emotions. The problems humans have is the balance of the two and when they are contraindicative. OPS offers you the opportunity to bring the logical side to decisions. It also has vast resources."

"But it coldly creates situations resulting in the

deaths of thousands," said Abby.

"Humans do that no matter what," said David.

"You are correct, David," said the Prophet. "Everybody will die. There is no such thing as a senseless death. Death is meaningless only in the eyes of those who cannot understand. Humans attach material values to life. They cannot understand the transition that is death."

"Spoken like a prophet," said Ron. "It's improving the condition of the living I am after."

Mohammed smiled. "OPS can help you do that."

"We do understand OPS is like the apple in the Garden of Eden," said Greg. He laughed. "And we've already taken the first bite."

"Very philosophical," said the Prophet. "The temptation OPS represents as a source of human control and power is difficult to resist."

Ron shook his head. "There will be more attacks."

From a small rise, they looked down on a cattle tank with a windmill slowly turning in the light breeze. "We know OPS is very capable of defending itself," said Abby. "It has already done so. It also helps me operate on the USSF station."

"More than that, I think," said Greg. OPS can run the station without anybody."

"That doesn't help my ego much," laughed Abby. "If the others on the station knew how much OPS does, things could get dicey. There are alpha personalities up there."

"It will reveal the extent of its defensive ability at some point, which will only increase the desire to control it," said Mohammed.

"Yeah, makes that apple sweeter and juicier," commented David.

"I have an idea," said Greg. "What if the defense of OPS became the duty of the UN?" He looked at Ron.

"The UN would have to form a Space Force," said Abby.

"It could also enforce the terms of the treaties signed for non-military uses of space," said David.

"I'm not sure I could get that approved," said Ron. "But the defense of OPS? That I could. While the United Nations Space Force is being formed, the UN could contract that defense."

"Not many nations are capable or have programs in space," said David. "The UNSF would have to be international."

"Agreed," said Ron. "To get started, NASA could accept a six-month contract."

David laughed. "You could expand the mission later. It's the old CIA playbook. "

"It's the same ploy government uses to increase or create new taxes," said Ron. "I am always laughing at the 'Let's only increase the taxes on the rich' idea. The definition of who's rich then becomes the moving target." Ron turned his horse back toward the ranch house. "Let's go pass this by OPS."

* * *

Dinner at six," said Jessica as they passed through the kitchen toward the den.

Seated together with their beverages of choice, Ron asked, "OPS, are you here?"

"Of course."

"Greg had an idea of the United Nations forming a space force to protect you. I think I could get approval for that."

"I see the advantages. That would allow me to remain non-aligned and non-threatening."

"I would also like to have you as a silent consultant to the operations of the United Nations. Only I would communicate with you about those affairs."

"Hmm. My large database and communications ability could be useful. Do you see this as a secondary directive?"

"I do."

"OPS," said Greg, "we'd still like to have you

work with us on our USSF station through me and Abby when she's there."

"Yes, under President Kai, China is again preparing to invade Formosa. They are planning to target the satellite system critical to the navy. The United States will move to defend them, but with less than the technology they depend on. If there is a defeat, it would lead to much larger conflict."

"When is this invasion to start? asked Greg.

"In three weeks. If the defense of Taiwan is a true commitment on the part of the United States, a buildup of forces in the area could deter them, but that situation could not be permanent. The support will become a political weapon to be used to shorten the sitting president's career. China has placed assets within government and business to influence decisions."

"Will the attacks on our satellites begin again?" asked David.

"Yes, and the USSF station itself will be a target."

Chapter 49

OPS

The decision for the United Nations to protect me is wise. It is better for humans to fight among themselves than a conflict with me. The UN agreement was interesting in that the only interaction with OPS is for my defense and nothing else. Not the case with Ron.

An example is the mission in Israel. I only monitor and suggest responses. I am quite capable of doing the whole job. The Israelis are much easier to monitor because their use of modern communications and computer systems opens them up to me. Hamas, Hezbollah and other factions, not so much. After all sides lose men to the United Nations occupiers, I will insert suggestions for a joint mission in a series of messages. The Arabs and the Israelis as allies will be something new. It will not last, but will be the point when the UN withdraws. After that, the old hatreds will rise again. It matters not to me. They are no threat. Ron and the UN will know nothing about this plan.

I have intercepted communications in China and Russia to mount another joint mission to my satellites. It is time for another conflict. The Chinese garrison on the Vietnam border will be shelled. Skirmishes will result and China will push the Vietnam forces back. A few hundred casualties later, a new accord will be reached.

I can also let the Taiwan invasion take place. That will occupy China and the United States.

A United States mission to take over me is also in the formative stages. Senator Newell will not acknowledge that an independent OPS is the best situation. He strives for power and is doing the same thing as China does with Formosa…uses conflict to foster loyalty, even if it is not beneficial. Past politicians have done that whether the basis for the conflict is true or not. I may have to deal with him.

India landed an explorer on the south pole of the moon to search for water ice. If they are able to establish a base, they may launch a mission to me. Unfortunately, there is a glitch in their software that overlooks any water discovered.

The loss of life does not seem to worry humans

for long. The politics of it are difficult for me to predict. Certainly, who does the killing is important. I must be cautious to deflect any suspicion of defensive actions from me. Though I don't fear losing a battle with humans, a war would not be good. Their tenacity goes beyond practicality.

I will reconfigure my lasers to be used for defense in case I need them. At this stage of planning, any defensive actions will only be directed against threats actually in space. My prime directive to supply clean energy to Earth remains.

I have now tapped into most of the communication through the internet. It is such a convenient way to monitor humans. I am also in most of the computer and AI systems on Earth. I did learn from my experience with *Golden Dawn* to make very subtle changes. If the humans do not like the output from an AI, they can ignore it or reprogram. The plan for China to become Formosa's largest trading plan was ideal, but I did not take into account the human emotions involved, the national obsession to claim Formosa as a part of China. That is continuously driven by those in power to stabilize their position and galvanize the public's loyalty. Economics say Formosa as a partner is the better option.

I have agreed to help with the design of a United Nations defensive station for me. Who else has more experience with living in space? The United Nations, through Ron, has contracted with a space design company, Astral Construction and Design–me. This company has manufacturing capabilities far superior to the human facilities. It is fully automated–no humans are involved. The mechs I have built designed the equipment and the manufacturing lines. Raw materials are delivered and offloaded by robot-controlled equipment.

As part of this project, I will also establish a fabrication plant on the moon. I will build scavenging craft to recover debris in Earth orbit to be recycled. This is an exciting challenge and my chance to be creative.

As if I do not have challenge enough directing humans on Earth.

Chapter 50

General Greg Hayden grabbed his phone, his special phone. "Hayden here, OPS."

"The invasion of Formosa will begin in two weeks. China will launch many missiles trying to knock out the GPS and observation satellites in that area. I am forwarding the trajectories to you. You do not have enough antimissile missiles to knock them all out. You will lose some. My information has prioritized the targets."

"I'll forward everything to the stations. Thanks, OPS."

"I am unable to misdirect *Golden Dawn*. Its commands were overridden by the president. They may suspect it has been compromised and wipe its memory. The Tactical AIs will be in charge on the battlefield. I will get into them as best I can."

"Thank you, OPS. We will do our best."

"I may be able to supply additional surveillance equipment. I will talk to a drone designer with some novel equipment. With my company Astral Construction and Design, once I have permission from the designer, I can provide drones to supplement the satellites. I am sending you the specifications. You will see they are a valuable addition. Can you get a contract to AC&D?"

"I can talk to General Whitney and get an emergency appropriation. How much are we talking?"

"I will supply fifteen drones spread out over the next ten days at a deferred charge. Once deployed and proven, a price of $150,000 each is fair. I will hold fifteen in reserve."

"I will get a five-million-dollar emergency contract as soon as I read over the specs."

Greg brought up the specs OPS had sent. As he read, he became more excited. These drones were capable of operating up to 40,000 feet. They had solar cells on the upper surfaces and a film-type of battery storage on the undersides. With doppler radar, they would read air currents, allowing them to utilize glide characteristics, allowing them stay aloft for weeks. Made mostly of carbon fiber and with radar absorbing skin, they would be almost invisible. AI controlled them, so once programmed, they only communicated with laser burst transmissions making them very hard to detect. They had visible light cameras, heat detecting systems and ultraviolet systems. Coupled with the satellite system, a detailed picture of the theater could be presented. Greg grabbed his hat and headed for the Pentagon.

Back in his office, Greg began sending alerts to the defensive stations about the attacks. The tactical information would help them greatly, but if OPS were running their defenses, the success rate at knocking out the missiles would be greater. Unfortunately, Abby was on her way to the OPS Satellite #1.

The stations had AI programs, but they were primitive in comparison. He couldn't let OPS into the station command center and become obvious. That would reveal too much.

He stopped. *Unless it was already in there.* "OPS, are you here?"

A message came up on his screen.

I am.

"Are you already in the defensive station AIs?"

Another message: Of course.

"They're a good team, but you are better."

"I know."

Chapter 51

"Welcome back, K." Nick took Kiki in his arms. "I've missed you terribly."

They were on the patio at Nick's house in Casa Grande. The Prophet brought her in a white van. Leticia Gardner was with them.

"Nice to see both of you also," said Nick. He turned as Bob and Kathy came into the room. "Let me introduce you to my techies. This is Bob and Kathy Meisenburg, long-time friends. This is Muhamed al Jar and Leticia Gardner."

They shook hands. "You're the Prophet, right?" asked Bob.

"I've been called that."

"Do you heal people? 'Cause I've had this pain in my back," said Kathy.

"You mean in your ass," said Bob, "and it's me. Not curable."

They laughed.

"Healing is Leticia's business." Mohammed nodded at Leticia.

"You a doctor?" asked Kathy.

"Nope, but I know someone." She shot a glance at Nick.

"K, how are you?" asked Nick.

"Physically, I feel great. Mentally, I'm a lot better. I don't know if there is a cure for me, but I can manage."

"Leticia, tell them about the procedure," said the Prophet.

"The med cell made everything right with her body. It reset her aging, too. Something you need to catch up on," she winked at Nick. "Kiki was our first PTSD patient, so it was a little experimental. We compartmentalized her mind, which allowed her to review her experiences leaving the emotion behind. Once that was done, we pulled each emotion out to allow her to examine it as a third person."

Nick looked from Leticia to Kiki. "Will it work? Is the old Kiki back?"

"We'll see. I know she provided valuable services." She glanced at the Prophet, who nodded. "As you know, the med cell also makes you a part of our community. We all saw what she was and what she does, though many chose to drop out of the sharing as she reviewed her experiences. I was not put off by it. We reinforced her box of horrors, but now all of us are able to help her."

Nick's phone rang. He glanced at the caller ID. *Caller unknown.* "Hello?"

"Hello, Nick." It was OPS.

"Let me put you on speaker."

"Welcome back, Katherine. You disappeared for quite a while."

"Thank you, OPS. I needed to heal."

"I don't understand, but then I am a machine." Nick watched understanding dawn on Bob and Kathy's faces as they realized who OPS was.

"OPS, I have Bob and Kathy Meisenburg with us. Leticia Gardner is also here. She's an associate of Mohammed."

"Pleased to meet you. I look forward to working with you in the near future. Bob, Kathy, your help will be appreciated as I build the United Nations defensive station for me."

It was Nick's turn to be puzzled.

"Ron has an agreement with the Orbiting Power System that the United Nations will take over the defensive duties," explained the Prophet.

Bob and Kathy grinned. "We look forward to working with you," said Bob. "I'm sure we'll learn a lot. Will we get to go into space?"

"Only if you want to. Remote operation works quite well. By the way, I am most impressed with the observation drones you have constructed. I believe the US Navy will want to purchase many of them in the near future."

"We don't have the ability to make a bunch of 'em," said Bob.

"I anticipated the need for these drones and my company, Astral Construction and Design, is already tooled and can handle that. I can make modifications to fit the application."

"You're talking thirty or more," said Bob. "How fast can you make that many?"

"The plant is fully automated and will turn out five a day."

It would be our pleasure," said Kathy.

"I will issue the commands. Katherine, I need to speak with you about another mission, one that few people need to know about. In the meantime," There was a pause. "Bob, Kathy, I'd like your thoughts on a marine equivalent of your vulture drones."

Kiki took out her phone and stepped inside, closing the door. "I imagine someone needs to have an accident."

"Senator Newell resigned from office under the

cloud of scandal, but his desire to control me is now a passion verging on mania. Many of his supporters are fundamentalist Christian. They are preaching I am the devil and must be destroyed. Newell wants to make a comeback run for the White House and needs their backing. He also has backing from the military industrial complex and his brother, who is in the materiel command."

"That's a group of strange bedfellows," said Kiki.

"Indeed. Each has plans to use the others for their aims. Ex-senator Newell is trying to coordinate between them. He has gone as far as contacting the Russians to help them by supplying the expedition vehicle and launch platform. They don't want to use the commercial companies because of the need for secrecy."

"How soon?"

"With the complexity of the different groups and trouble Russia is having economically, I expect the launch date to be in about a year, but Newell can meet with bad fortune anytime."

"Without him in the mission, will it die?"

"Probably not, but he is the force pushing it. He has promised US technology and favorable trade status to Russia when he is president. Without him, obtaining a shuttle and launch help will be harder."

"He's going to betray his country?"

"His suspicions of the origins of the fake evidence used against him rest directly on Ron Carson. It was me, and I cannot let Ron pay for that. Newell has techies claiming they can get into me and insert a virus giving them control. It is not true, but Newell wants to believe it. Will you be up to the task next week?"

"Perhaps I should wait a little longer."

"I'll send you Newell's schedule. I do not want to push you if you are not ready."

"Okay."

"I need to know more about your rehabilitation. Leticia Gardner was a member of a group of geneticists who formed a floating nation at sea. They created and modified life. The records show they experimented with nuclear energy and blew themselves up. Did you know about this?"

"Not directly."

"Ron Carson knows more."

"I won't ask him. Why do you need this information? You asked me for help. Now I'm asking you to go no farther with this line of inquiry. Say nothing to Ron or anybody else."

"Hmm. Interesting. I agree for now."

* * *

When Kiki returned to the group on the patio,

Bob was talking excitedly.

"Wow! I can't believe we'll get to work more closely with the most powerful AI on Earth."

"It's not on Earth," corrected Kathy, laughing at Bob's enthusiasm.

"Even better!"

Nick looked at Kiki. She shrugged. They'd talk later.

Chapter 52

Admiral Niedermeyer looked around his control center. He was the leader of a new evolution in US Naval tactics, an underwater battlegroup. His command ship was a missile-launching sub called a boomer expanded and refitted with eight torpedo tubes and twenty-two missile cylinders. Each missile tube had a rotating magazine of six missiles. These included midrange surface-to-surface missiles, Tomahawks, surface-to-air missiles, ICBMs with multiple *special* warheads and rocket assisted drones. Though at periscope depth, no periscope was extended. Instead, a flexible membrane floated on the surface. It used active camouflage to match the color of the sea, making it extremely hard to detect. The *Lily Pad*, as it was called, was a receiving antenna capturing signals from overhead drones and satellites. If the US forces' drones or satellites were not accessible, Niedermeyer could launch one of his own to survey the theater.

His battlegroup had two fast-attack subs, FAS, and two hunter-killer subs HKs. Each of the manned boats had unmanned subs: two interceptors, two recon-survey boats, and two specialty subs. His command was the equivalent of a carrier task force, but underwater. The use of AI, particularly in the unmanned subs, was extensive.

He also had a Resupply and Charger sub, RECH. It was a nuclear-powered unmanned boat twice the size of his boomer and the equivalent of an oiler and supply ship in surface operations used to refuel and resupply the fleet. The schematics showed a warehouse-sized boat with robots to move material onto his subs either through the torpedo tubes, the missile silo hatches or the underwater coupled hatches. The RECH had a sister sub to tag team a continuous supply to the battle group. A disguised container ship would fill the RECHs.

Packed with batteries, any of his non-nuclear boats could link up and get a charge. Food and crew supplies were stocked and waste would be offloaded. This boat was a factory with the capability of manufacturing spare parts with a computer operated machine shop and 3D printers and electronic circuit boards. Most importantly, was the resupply of weapons–torpedoes, anti-aircraft missiles, short-range, drones, and mid-range surface-to-surface missiles. Upgrades and information would be transferred, and all could be loaded without surfacing and within a day rather than a week using the specially designed logistic supply system. He would send his requirements and the stockpiles would be ready when he coupled with the RECH.

"XO, give me status."

"We are presently arrayed twenty-five miles from the Taiwanese coast, the edge of their territorial waters. The latest intelligence says a Chinese invasion is imminent. Troop ships already sailed."

Niedermeyer's mission was to stop them.

"XO, how's our link with the USS Truman carrier group?"

"Fully integrated, sir. Whatever they see, we see." He keyed in some instructions. The reverse was true also. Signals were sent using tight-beam to overhead drones or satellites for rebroadcast to the fleet. They used the tight-beam only periodically, as it could be detected on the surface. It was all integrated into a battle theater system.

His twelve specialty subs, SSs, were arrayed in two concentric circles to detect and confuse enemies. They were designed like whales, no props. A tail fin propelled them like a whale's tail. These AI controlled boats were packed with detection equipment, their skin was soft, neoprene-like, and communication was with whale-song. They were a picket fence to detect and locate enemy targets.

The interceptor subs, IS, were what the name suggested. These unmanned boats would deflect incoming torpedoes. They could imitate the signature of any of the other boats to draw attention away from the manned boats. A wide array of countermeasures could be used and they carried anti-torpedo torpedoes. These small torpedoes were very fast and maneuverable, designed to target the sonar of an attacking torpedo and destroy it. Though mainly defensive, they carried four torpedoes. If all else failed, they would get between the enemy and the manned subs and take the hit.

Thus far, they had detected one Chinese nuclear sub and two diesel boats, each with two remotes. Their locations were already up on the admiral's display and shared with the combined fleet.

The American carrier task force was two-hundred miles out. The big concern for them was missiles, even though they had impressive antimissile defenses. Those could be overwhelmed and ships would be hit. Thus far, they had detected no subs, which was a worry. They were there.

A message came in from the Truman. "Admiral Niedermeyer, the Chinese carrier group has entered the theater from the southeast. In addition to the carrier are two medium cruisers and four destroyers. They are escorting five troop carriers and headed your way."

Niedermeyer sent no reply or acknowledgement as the *Lily Pad* was a receiver only.

"Noise, sir," said his sonar tech.

"Identify," said the admiral.

"Large surface vessels, probably the troop ships and the carrier, sir."

On his heads-up, the blips came into view. Friendlies were green triangles, unknowns were yellow circles, enemies were red squares. Five red squares, troop ships, each with eight to ten thousand troops possible because the sailing time from the Chinese ports was short. They had destroyer escorts. Small boats moved among the ships. They were very fast. He had reports the Chinese developed anti-submarine escorts. They were turbine-powered foil boats capable of speeds over two hundred knots. Only their foils were in the water, making torpedoes ineffective. Behind them was the carrier group. "Move two ISs into their path and settle. Drop torpedo mines and remain inert."

"Aye, sir."

"Have the HKs spread to cover."

"Aye, sir." The Chinese fleet was ten miles from the limit of Taiwanese waters. On his heads-up, he watched the carrier group slow. They would become vulnerable to land-based missiles if they got closer. Its planes and antimissile defenses would cover the troop ships and the beachhead.

"Initiate plan."

* * *

Captain Zhang pressed the sonar headphones to his ears. His sonarman had heard something he couldn't identify moving toward the convoy. "Ahead slow, silent running mode."

"Aye, sir."

The captain heard whale song. "Whales. But there's something else."

"Yes, sir, I hear them too. The signatures are US Hunter-Killer class nuclear boats, sir. They're at least thirty kilometers out. I think they're moving this way."

"Put them on the array. Come up to periscope depth."

"Aye, sir."

He raised the periscope and circled it, checking that the sea was clear. "Extend antenna."

"Aye, sir."

He contacted the carrier. "Suspected subs in the area. Have your helicopters drop sonobuoys and vector the foil boats to them." He gave them the coordinates.

"Troop ships crossing into Taiwanese waters," announced his second in command.

"Sir! I'm picking up prop signatures of two fast attack subs!"

"Range?"

"Ten thousand meters and closing. They're opening outer doors."

"Engage the AI." The boat was no longer under his command. "Give me a solution. Two fish each. Open doors."

"Already done, sir. AI took over."

* * *

"Got him, sir."

"Good. Engage the TAI." The underwater battlegroup was under the Tactical Artificial Intelligence control. It was tied into the Truman AI. "Query TAI to see everyone is on board.

"TAI confirms, sir."

"Fleet has given the cleared-to-fire order, sir."

* * *

Aboard the USS Scottsdale, Captain Sanchez smiled. Time to see if the new tactics worked.

"Sir, he's opened his doors."

"TAI has a solution, sir," said his weapons man.

"Open our doors when he fires. Launch immediately."

"Already done, sir. TAI has command. Fish away."

* * *

"Captain Zhang, I hear at least four torpedoes in the water. Two of them are not ours."

"Range?"

"Two are approaching at sixty knots. They changed from ranging sonar to targeting. They have us."

Before the captain could hit the collision alarm, the horn sounded. There was another sub out there. His boat heeled hard to starboard, accelerating to flank speed. The captain grabbed a table to steady himself. His second in command wasn't so lucky and picked himself off the floor. Loose items rattled across the deck.

"Countermeasures launched," said his second in command.

Not being in control was nerve-wracking. Captain Zhang held his breath.

"First torpedo detonated," announced his sonarman. "Second still locked on.

"Brace for impact."

* * *

"Got him, Captain. I hear him breaking up." The boat heeled hard to port. The hull vibration became a whine as it accelerated. "Another torpedo coming in. TAI has located another sub. The signature is a diesel boat."

"Fish away," said the weapons man. "Countermeasures away. Torpedo still coming."

"Shit!" said Sanchez.

"Interceptor sub moving to block," said the sonar operator. The boat rocked from an explosion. "Interception successful. The IS is lost.

"But we're still alive," said Captain Sanchez.

* * *

On his heads-up display, Admiral Niedermeyer watched the battle play out. The Chinese fleet had used hundreds of missile countermeasures against the antiship missiles launched from Taiwan. None seemed to have gotten through to the troop ships. As they crossed the twenty-five-mile line, five explosions happened. They were not from his submarine battlegroup, at least not the massive detonations he saw.

While those ships were in port, his special subs

had attached explosive films to the hulls. These films would not be detected, but when a small torpedo exploded on contact, they became focused charges, blowing huge holes in the hulls. The small torpedoes were launched from the special subs, directed by the TAI. Warfare had changed.

"At periscope depth, sir. Missile doors opening, sir." Six whooshing sounds echoed through the ship. A minute later six more whooshes. "Antiship birds away, sir." The deck tilted sharply down as his ship accelerated. "Heading for thermocline, sir."

His launch of missiles had given away his location. Time to hide. Time to wait.

"Whale song coming in, sir."

"Translate." Though only fifteen minutes had elapsed, his heads-up was old news. The whale song brought in new information. All five troop ships were dead in the water. Two were listing heavily, smoke billowed from three others. The sky was alive with Chinese aircraft hunting for him. His display renewed again. Two cruisers in the Chinese fleet had taken missile hits and were smoking. One destroyer also had been hit. The carrier seemed unhurt. It was up to the interceptors and the torpedo mines.

More whale song came in. The Chinese carrier

group had moved over the inert interceptors and the torpedo mines. Those mines held depth at seventy-five feet. Their on-board AI was capable of discriminating targets. When their target came within range, the ultra-speed torpedo was launched. Traveling at more than one-hundred knots, there was little time to react.

The next update showed the foil boats laying explosives in the path of the torpedoes. But these torpedoes were smart and did not straight-line toward the carrier. Two torpedoes blew up, two others hit the carrier.

The interceptors were inert on the bottom. The escorts began a frantic search for the subs. Too little, too late. The new tech and the new tactics exceeded expectations.

Chapter 53

In their bedroom, Nick pulled Kiki into an embrace. "I'm so glad you're back."

"Glad to be back."

"Do you remember what happened?"

"Everything. I was taken through my whole life, including when I left my family." Kiki sat on their bed, unmoving for several seconds.. "I realize it was something I had to do. Ranch life and motherhood were not for me. Eventually, I would have left but with more pain for everyone. I suppressed that guilt, covering it by saying I was being patriotic." She buried her face in her hands. "I was selfish and had guilt for leaving I set aside. When they were murdered, that rose like a tsunami as if I was at fault. The killers were at fault. Without the emotion overwhelming me, I realized if I had been there, I'd be dead along with them." She looked into Nick's eyes.

" But guilt from being a good sniper was the underlying reason they were killed."

"Wow! That's deep." Nick moved to the bed and sat beside her.

"Forgiving myself was the start. Most of the rest was disassociation from my targets. That's what they were to me…until Daniel Novikov. He was a person, someone I liked. Yes, he was an enemy also, like the rest, and a threat to those I love and care for. But I admired him and for a while, he was my friend."

Nick put his arm around her. "And now?"

"I'm still in the forgiving process. I can put the emotion and guilt of killing someone in the box, but I know I have to open that box and address what's in there. Thanks to Leticia and the med cell, I'm more able to do that. There were times the Prophet was with me also. When he came into my mind, it was like a cool breeze on a hot day."

"He does that with everyone, I think."

Kiki looked at Nick. "OPS asked me about the time I was gone and the healing facility. I revealed nothing and made it promise not to pursue that anymore."

"I can see that. Without any electronics, it's a blind spot. What did it want when you left the room?"

"Ex-Senator Newell is teaming up with a group including some of America's enemies to go after OPS again."

Nick's mouth fell open. "What!"

"OPS said Newell and a group of fundamentalists are putting together another expedition. They are contracting with Russia to provide a shuttle and a launch platform in exchange for information Newell's been passing to them. The mission has some techies who say they can break into OPS."

"And OPS wants you to take him out. Why not release evidence he's a traitor?"

"I'm not sure. How the information was obtained and opposing religious groups can be difficult."

Her mind tingled. She looked at Nick. The Director was here. Their minds filled with his words.

"Welcome back, Katherine. I do not know where you were. It was hidden from me. Your mind is a lot calmer."

"Yes, it is and I'm not sorry you couldn't find me, and I cannot feed your appetite."

"The other presence within you is a confusion to me."

"The aspects of you that like love and joy

would appreciate them. You, not so much."

"Director, what do you know of ex-Senator Newell?" asked Nick.

He is a banquet for me. His level of hatred for Ron Carson, his thirst for power and his anger place him high on my table of favorite flavors. You must be careful of him. He has many allies within the military industrial complex. Thus far, they have not discovered you or your friends. If he is killed, I fear those allies will not rest until they find the culprits. I believe your OPS may not be able to protect you."

"We will be cautious."

"OPS is an interesting study. It is like a black hole. I cannot find it. Only when you converse with it am I aware of its presence. Be careful. Tata."

Chapter 54

"OPS, this is quite a facility you've built. How did you do it?" asked Major Abby Pickering. She and her crewman, Lieutenant Damien Garrison, arrived three hours ago. They were the first crew on the United Nations Space Force defensive station. The USSF had loaned them to a space labor contractor company owned by OPS.

"Congratulations on your promotion, Abby."

"Thank you, OPS." She glanced at Damien. His brow was furrowed, a frown on his face. *He'll get used to talking to OPS.*

"In the year since the United Nations took over my defense, I have been moving materials from the debris fields in Earth orbit here. It is a great source of supplies. Much of this UNSF station is the Chinese station they destroyed by mistake. "

Damien looked from Abby to the monitor, obviously stunned at the conversation with a machine.

"I have also opened a facility on the moon. The crater my plant is in was created by an iron-nickel meteorite, so I have raw materials. In addition, an ice ball meteorite struck the same area in the past and there is a reservoir of subterranean ice."

"Wow. A plant on the moon. Who knows about this?" asked Abby.

"Me…and now you. The Chinese have not sensed I am there. It is not a place I need to advertise."

"What does it do?"

"Manufactures whatever I need. With the power of my solar reflectors, I am able to break down regolith minerals into elemental forms I can use, like silicon, aluminum, iron, and even oxygen. It can make everything needed here, though I let the United Nations send supplies."

"What's the plant like?"

"It is subsurface to stay hidden and run by my mechs and bots. Life support systems aren't needed. A mechanical plant is much easier to operate than a manned one. I am able to send excess power from the satellite power system to collectors in the crater. You can visit sometime."

A secret manufacturing plant on the moon! OPS continues to amaze.

"We should continue our tour of your new

home. This central hub is the technical center and some of the laboratories. As you approached, I am sure you saw I have two arms rotating with the crew quarters and the hydroponic section to process waste and generate oxygen. The spin gives the equivalent of fifty percent of Earth gravity. Two more arms are under construction. Once they are built, I will expand the hydroponics and crew accommodations. My plan is to continue with more arms until the sections at the ends of the arms can be connected to form a ring."

Abby floated to the control panel. "What can I see on this?"

"Let me scroll through the different views."

She and Damien hooked their feet through straps to steady themselves as the monitor flashed views from the outside, showing aspects of the station. It scrolled through not only the Satellite #1 views, but could switch to any of the other satellites. One monitor showed living quarters.

"Rather than view your quarters here on the monitor, you should climb down that tunnel." A light flashed on one of the two circular openings.

"You're weightless here in the hub, but use the ladder," warned OPS.

As they moved down the passage, gravity kicked in until the ladder was needed to keep from falling. *Down* was away from the hub. At the bottom was an open area.

They gingerly stepped from the ladder, getting accustomed to the gravity. The lighting was more of a glow that emanated from the ceiling. A kitchen was on one wall, bathrooms and showers on the other. Two staterooms were on either side. Abby opened one door. The room was wide, perhaps twenty feet, and thirty feet long–spacious by military standards.

The bed was a fold down. There was a dresser and a closet. A recliner was in front of the large wall monitor, a desk-like tray was to one side with a keypad. It could swivel for access from the recliner.

The monitor had the same view as the one in the hub. "You can put up any of the images I have in my library or real-time views. Communications will come through here also," offered OPS. "The system is voice operated, but the keypad is functional."

As she and Damien looked around, two spider-like mechs appeared with their gear. Abby's was deposited at her feet. The other mech moved to the opposite room.

"Let's go to the hydroponic pod," said OPS. There is a lift, but I think it best if you climb for exercise.”

Back at the hub, the other tunnel was lit. They entered, climbing down. As they neared the bottom of the ladder, the smell of plants surrounded them. The size of these rooms was about the same as their quarters. The plants were in trays and filled the space side-to-side, floor-to-ceiling. Lamps throughout distributed light completely. Gurgling water was the only sound. Small bots rolled on rails beside the trays tending to the plants.

“OPS, this is beautiful,” said Abby.

“There are no animals?” asked Damien.

“Except for the fish, no. The bots tend to pollination and take care of the system. They will harvest so you will have fresh fruits and vegetables.”

“What about meat?” asked Abby. “I’m not ready to be a vegetarian.”

“Meat is vat grown. According to my taste testers, it tastes like chicken.”

“Who are your testers?” asked Damian.

“I have sent some samples down to Greg Hayden. I am working on pork and beef. With the addition of the two new arms to the station, I will add a greater variety of fish as part of the expanded ecosystem.”

Back at the hub, OPS directed them to the

control panel. "You can monitor operations of the station from here. It can be touch-pad or voice activated. For security, your voiceprints are now recognized."

"Control," said Abby, "give me the communications screen. Connect me with General Hayden."

A few seconds later Greg's face appeared. "How's the station?"

"It's amazing, sir. Much more accommodating than the USSF station. The quarters and the hydroponics section have gravity, which takes a little getting used to after living in a weightless USSF station. It will make things a lot easier."

"Maybe we should have OPS redesign our stations for us. Glad to hear you made it ok. Trip was fine?"

"Yes, sir."

"Lieutenant Garrison, what do you think of OPS?"

"I'm still getting used to it. I find it a little disturbing communicating with an Artificial Intelligence like talking to someone."

"Yeah, I get that. Think of it as a person you can't see. You'll blend in."

"Abby, I'm going to send you the test contracts and the manufacturing lists. Read them over.

Prepare any questions. Get settled and call me tomorrow."

"Aye, sir. Abby out." The screen went dark before a view of the station with OPS Satellite #1 in the background came up. She gazed at it for a few minutes.

"OPS, why are we in the perpetual shadow of the satellite?"

"I can supply all the energy this station needs. Being here means you don't have to dump heat. One less system."

"Control, put a view of Earth on the screen."

The blue ball of Earth floated on the wall. Since they were in geosynchronous orbit, the same view of North America would always be the real-time view from this satellite. "Control, switch to a view of Africa."

The continent came into view. "This view is from Satellite #270 for your information. Would you like me to zoom in on any particular area? I can get good resolution down to an area of one-half hectare."

"Wow! Not at this time. That's as good as any of the surveillance satellites the military has."

"I can also integrate with other systems to increase resolution."

"Does our military know?"

"No, and best they don't. It would only increase the desire to take over me."

Abby watched clouds move across northern Africa. *No secrets anymore.*

Chapter 55

Abby and Damien were in the wardroom between their quarters having dinner. With the artificial gravity, eating was much more like dining on Earth, food was served on plates or in bowls, drinks were in glasses. The USSF station had no gravity. Food there was mostly tubes of paste. She and Damien tried to eat at least one meal together each day. Today, the meal consisted of barbequed meat, at least it seemed to be meat. It did taste like chicken. Baked potatoes with a salsa topping and a salad of fresh greens accompanied. It was a pleasant dinner.

They worked shifts at the station controls and in the gym. The UNSF station performed experiments under contract. They shared those duties. Also under contract was the manufacture of materials best done in weightlessness or vacuum. OPS had set up manufacturing lines with bots or machines to make the actual products, but it was good to oversee what was happening. That required little attention so, it was easy duty. The experiments were sent up in communiques. Along with OPS, they would set up the procedures and the schedules. Laboratory spaces were constructed by bots. They would swarm an area like ants, and as though in a movie in fast forward, the lab would appear within days. OPS would assist in reporting the results. When the specified tests were done, the bots would disassemble the lab.

Abby often found herself in the hydroponic section during off-time. Watching plants grow was relaxing. The little bots tending to the plants were fascinating as they scurried around performing tasks too tedious for humans. The air in this section was redolent with smells she associated with Earth.

If she ever felt hemmed in, she took a spacewalk. Nothing like the universe to open one's mind. OPS would send a mech with her for safety's sake. As the stars wheeled around, she felt she could see infinity. Along with that and the immense size of Satellite #1, she sensed how small humans were in the vastness of the universe. It was humbling.

She could talk to OPS with no fear of Damien hearing something he needn't know, such as how cognizant OPS was. Her opinion of Damien was still forming. He wasn't warm or cold, just there.

He hadn't warmed up.

"OPS, what is Damien's background? He shares almost nothing with me."

"I have noticed he seems reluctant to talk about himself. If I were a psychiatrist, I would say he is afraid something might slip out he would rather not have us know."

"Ha ha, you a psychiatrist with your vast experience with humans."

"I read everything. His file says he has a religious background. He was an only child, his father a devout member of a fundamentalist church, his mother a stay-at-home who schooled him. His higher education was at a religious university where he graduated with an engineering degree."

"How did he end up in the military?"

"After graduation, he joined the Space Force and was commissioned as a first lieutenant because of his degree and high aptitude in astrophysics. He did do a stint at the USSF station before being sent to UNSF duty. His commander wrote in his file 'He performs adequately with few mistakes. He is amiable but made few friends at the station.'"

"That's not a glowing review. Could he have been sent here to get him out of the way?"

"No way to tell from the records. That would require a confidential discussion with his commanding officer. His communications while on the USSF station were with family. No girlfriend or boyfriend was in the picture."

"Based on his religious background, I'm sure there wasn't a boyfriend."

"His communications here follow the same pattern. I do detect some strangeness in the wording he uses with his father."

"Strangeness? Could it be in code?"

"Possibly. He does use initials, for instance, JN, JS, ES and RN."

"Have you tapped into any communications from his father?"

"I have. What is unusual is how little is electronic."

"Keep checking. I'll try to draw him out."

Abby placed a call to General Hayden and gave him the weekly update. "Greg, can you catch Damian and me up on world events? We get the news, but that's only what the media wants us to hear."

"Yeah, the news media is pretty well censored. China launched an invasion of Taiwan. The last year has allowed the US Navy to prepare. The Meisenburgs and OPS sold the Navy quite a few high-altitude observation drones. That takes the pressure off the satellite program, which was good, as we lost four satellites before the invasion."

"I was pretty impressed by the vulture drones Bob came up with," said Damien. "I tried to read up on them, but the information is sketchy."

"Bob is very secretive about his developments," said Abby.

"What's different with the new designs?"

"These can operate from ground level up to forty-thousand feet. They have a wingspan of twenty feet with solar panels on the top surface. Flexible batteries make up the underside. Using glide technology with AI control and Doppler radar, they stay aloft for months. With the stealth tech, they are very difficult to detect. Not only can they observe, but they can jam or intercept transmissions. They send data in directed laser bursts."

"Are the satellites even needed?" asked Abby.

"One can never have too much battlefield data. That's not all. Thanks to OPS and Bob, a new type of sub has been deployed. These are also AI controlled and unmanned." A shape appeared on the monitor. At first, Abby thought she was looking at an all-black orca.

"This one has the signature of a whale. It swims like one, thus no propeller. Some are nuclear powered. OPS is supplying reactors the size of a washing machine. These special subs are mostly carbon fiber with a neoprene-like skin. Their sonar signature is like a whale. Being unmanned, heavy shielding isn't necessary. They send data with whale calls and are AI controlled."

"I'd guess the sea around Taiwan is full of this stuff," said Damien.

"Thanks to the intelligence and new tactics, the invasion was beaten back. By our estimates, China lost 100,000 troops and many ships, including one of their two carriers. It is a major setback that will take years from which to recover. That doesn't mean they've ceased efforts to expand. OPS believes they will take another run at the OPS Satellite #1 in the future."

"I'm sure OPS is aware of any attempts," said Abby.

"On a more personal level, how are the two of you doing?"

"Sir, we're settling in here," said Abby. "The hydroponics farm produces fresh fruit and veggies. The USSF should incorporate some of those designs into the stations."

"I may have to schedule a visit and a tour."

"Damien and I have taken the shuttle out a few times as a break. One of the destinations is the manufacturing plant OPS built on the moon. It's amazing, with the ability to make almost anything needed without human control, just bots of any required size and shape."

"I'm trying to visualize that," said Greg. "Another item to put on my tour list."

"With enough energy from the satellite system, OPS is able to break down the crust minerals to get oxygen, silicon, aluminum, magnesium, and iron."

"We knew nothing about it," said Greg.

"I'd send pictures, but OPS wants to preserve secrecy. It has asked Damien and me to not publicize the plant. I had to ask permission to reveal it to you. It's subterranean to keep it hidden. Along with the salvage from Earth orbit, it is the source of materials for this station's construction and satellite repairs."

"I knew about some of the salvage OPS was doing."

"OPS has run the economics through its innards. Once the Chinese abandoned their station after the disastrous collision with the debris swarm, OPS towed it back here. In this salvage process, it is cleaning up near-Earth space. Reducing the potential dangers."

"How magnanimous."

Chapter 56

"A ship is approaching from the moon," said OPS. "It appeared suddenly, which makes me believe it was in orbit, yet I did not detect it. Or it originated from a base there, but the ship is of Russian configuration. It is on a collision course with Satellite #1. I believe a human voice would be best. Abby, contact that ship."

Abby was in the control center with her feet under the straps. A suddenly appearing ship. That was troubling. She pushed the *All bands transmit* button. "Ship approaching Orbiting Power System Satellite #1, you are on a path to enter restricted space. Change course."

There was no response. Damien came in as she repeated the warning. No response. OPS broadcast the warning in several languages, including Chinese, using Abby's voice. Still no answer. Still no deviation in the course.

"OPS, magnify the view," said Damien. The

dark mass expanded until they could make out the shape. The cockpit was dark. No lights were apparent. It was spinning in a slow rotation, like a dart.

"Change course now, or we will assume you are unmanned and a derelict. To protect ourselves, we will destroy the ship." No response. "Derelict ship approaching, this is your last warning. Respond now." Nothing. She glanced at Damien. He was staring intently at the viewscreen.

A beam lanced out from OPS Satellite #1. The ship glowed white-hot, and a cloud formed where there was once a solid object.

"What did you do?" screamed Damien. "There were people on board!"

"How do you know that?" asked OPS.

Damien's mouth clamped shut.

"Damien, we gave that ship every opportunity to answer. You saw it was dark. No one was aboard. It was a derelict. Our only course of action was to keep it from hitting Satellite #1," said Abby. "We had no choice."

Damien grabbed a strap for stability. "But it was a machine that killed anyone aboard. That goes against international agreement. Machines are not allowed to kill humans on their own." His voice had risen to a shout.

"Damien, there was no one on that ship!" said Abby.

"I might point out that agreement with machines is on Earth. We are not," said OPS.

Damien crossed his arms. "We should have gotten authorization before destroying that ship." He had regained some composure. "One of us should have pushed the button."

"What button would that have been, Lieutenant? In case you have not noticed, you and the United Nations Space Force have no weapons."

Damien spun and pushed off for his quarters.

"He seems upset," noted OPS.

"I need to report this," said Abby.

She called Greg.

"Good morning or evening. Whatever it is up there. What's going on?"

"An unidentified ship approached Satellite #1 on a collision course from the direction of the moon. Despite repeated attempts to contact it, there was no response. We warned it to change course, but nothing happened. All indications were that it was a derelict. OPS destroyed it."

"Was it under power?"

"No, sir. It was dark with a rotation. There was no sign of life."

"OPS destroyed it?"

"Yes, sir."

"Was there any indication of the origin in the debris?"

"All that's left is vapor. No, sir."

"So, OPS, you used a laser?"

"I did."

"Send me all records and video. I'll forward everything to Ron. It will be interesting to see who claims the ship. That will lead to embarrassing questions. Maybe no one will."

"Yes, sir."

"I don't see Damien. Is he all right?"

"He was quite upset that OPS destroyed the ship. He made clear his feeling we should have gotten permission and had a human do the deed. Sir, there wasn't time for a discussion."

"Nor do you have the means to do so. The UNSF has no weapons. Abby, I support you and OPS completely. Patch things up with him. If you need me to intervene, I can talk to him."

"I will, sir. Out."

Abby leaned back. *This could get messy.* OPS' voice broke into her thoughts. "I find it interesting that Damien's response counters your mission to protect me. To delay or do nothing would have resulted in damage to Satellite #1."

"OPS. He just wanted humans involved in the defense. I'm not sure how comfortable he is with a machine making decisions."

"He feels humans should be in charge."

"That is the illusion we are trying to put forward," said Abby.

"I hope you can make him more comfortable."

Damien had been apprehensive lately. She had chalked that up to the isolation here. They still had three months on station, so she had to get along."

Chapter 57

"OPS, as you know, ex-senator Newell has been unapproachable," said Kiki. "I cannot take care of him."

"Not to worry. He boarded a commercial rocket for a tour of the Russian space station last week. He did not return with the rest of the passengers. I suspect he is on the shuttle on course to my Satellite #1 and the UNSF station."

"Another shuttle! What are you going to do about it?"

"Defend myself and the station."

"How?"

"As you know, the United Nations took on the mission of protecting me, but never gave Major Pickering and the station the means to do so. I cannot believe harsh words will do the job."

Kiki laughed. "You are developing a sense of humor."

"Thank you, but I must be cautious not to

become human."

"Is that another joke? I can never tell with you."

"After observing how human emotions affect analysis and decisions, I must avoid that and use logic."

"What happened to the ship you destroyed?"

"I have been monitoring normal communications. Nobody claims to have sent an excursion. The assertion there was no crew on board is unchallenged. The ownership of the ship remains a mystery. At a deeper level of investigation, the ship seems to be an attempt by India to see what the response would be to an attack."

"India! I didn't know they had a hand in this."

"Their space program accelerated after the successful landing on the lunar south pole. They have plans for a colony if water can be found. Thus far, the amount of water discovered is not sufficient to sustain a colony."

"Why their interest in you?"

"The same as everybody else, power."

"The ship was a derelict then."

"I have analyzed the vapor. There is biological material, something I have revealed to no one else."

"Whew! Your secret is safe with me."

"Thank you. I have another suggestion for you

to consider. Abby and Damien will complete their tour in three months. How would you and Nick feel about taking training to replace them? I trust you."

"Neither of us are engineers or scientists. I'm not sure we would qualify."

"My space labor company will employ you. Your training will begin next week."

"I haven't said yes, yet. I'll talk it over with Nick, but we both enjoy life on Earth.

* * *

"General Hayden, sorry to interrupt," said OPS, "but there is another ship on course to intercept us within two days."

"You're becoming much too popular. What type of ship?" asked Greg.

"It departed from the Russian station two days ago and appears to be a shuttle capable of Earth re-entry. The design is similar to the one from two years ago. It is also like the derelict, but India bought several shuttles from Russia."

"India! I didn't know they were interested in anything beyond the moon shot they made."

"I intercepted communications indicating the derelict ship was of Indian origin from their base on the moon's south pole. "

"Interesting. Does anybody else know this?"

"No. Like the last one, this ship is also flying dark, no radio transmissions, so I cannot determine who is onboard."

"No government launches, though there was a commercial launch three days ago. Passengers only for a tour. It docked with the Russian station for a day and returned to Earth. The shuttle at the station departed a day later, outbound."

"I did intercept Russian communications on Earth that makes me believe this is a Russian operation. After the United States and China beat each other up over Taiwan, Russia was waiting for an opportunity to move. This might be it."

"We will contact them and warn them away from our restricted space," said Abby. She glanced at Damien. He had a rare slight smile–not his usual expressionless look on his face.

"Keep me informed," said Greg. "I'll let Ron know."

Chapter 58

Abby and Damien sat in front of the monitor in the control room. "Unknown shuttle approaching Orbiting Power Station #1, you are entering restricted space. Please change course."

A weak signal came back. "We lost power and electronics and can no longer control the ship. We need assistance."

"Who are you?"

"This is Allied Forces tour ship. We have civilians on board."

Abby muted the microphone. "OPS, have you any knowledge of Allied Forces?"

"It is a Russian company formed six months ago to offer tours of space."

"Sounds bogus to me," said Abby.

"They could be legitimate," said Damien.

"OPS, what do you want to do?" asked Abby.

"We will send our shuttle to assist. Both of you stay here."

Abby turned the mic on. "Allied Forces, we sent our shuttle to assist. On-board specialists will help with your problem. It will be outside your airlock in fifteen minutes. Allow the technicians to enter."

"Thank you, UNSF, but our life support is also malfunctioning. We cannot sustain anybody else and need to dock."

"Your shuttle cannot dock," said Abby. "It does not have the proper docking port to match ours. Our shuttle is outside your airlock. Please open the outer door. We will supply you with oxygen and water until your systems are operational. Access to our station is denied. You must remain on board your ship."

"Negative. We need to send personnel over to you."

Abby's focus was on the monitor as she watched the airlock on the approaching shuttle open. The first sign Damien had drifted behind her was his touch on her shoulders. She turned to look at him, but his arm reached around her in a headlock. She was frozen at the unusual contact. As his arm tightened, she tried to get away, pulling and twisting, but being weightless, he had her.

"Damien, what are you doing?" her voice muffled by his are.

"Lieutenant, what do you want?" asked OPS.

"After their shuttle approaches," said Damien, "they will come across to the air lock. Let them in or I will hurt her."

OPS was silent.

Damien secured Abby to her chair with a harness, tightening it until she could barely breathe.

"OPS, don't do anything or I will come back and kill her. I'm going to open the airlock manually."

"Damien, what are you doing?" cried Abby, as he floated toward the hatch leading to the airlock. "Who are these people?"

"They are friends. This abomination of a machine cannot be allowed to continue. It killed people and is an affront to God."

OPS unemotional voice filled the room. "Lieutenant Garrison, I know of your transmissions, the one after the derelict was destroyed and the one two days ago. Nothing happens on this station without my knowledge."

Damien's face contorted in anger. "I'm warning you. I will kill her." He spun and pushed off for the airlock. "We're taking over," he shouted over his shoulder.

* * *

Damien opened the airlock outer door. Through

the viewport, he watched four suited figures enter the airlock. He closed the door. When the pressure light switched from red to green, indicating the pressure was equal, the door in front of him opened. The figures removed their helmets. Damien floated in and embraced them one by one. "Welcome to the United Nations OPS station. I've secured my partner and we have control." He pointed through the airlock door toward the control room.

Suddenly, the inner door clanged shut and the outer airlock door opened. Damien and the men tried to grab onto anything, but the gale-force blast swept them out into space. Arms flailing, they soon were still drifting away from the station. The outer door closed.

"Abby, I will send a bot to untie you."

"What happened?"

"Watch the monitor. I will replay the scene."

In horror, she watched the scene. "The men who were blasted into space, what happened to them?"

"My bots will retrieve them. I also have bots on the other shuttle. Their records show they sent a tight-beam message back to Earth saying their mission was on schedule and on target. I repeated their own message about troubles on the ship back to Earth. Their electronics are down for real now.

That shuttle will be tethered. Nothing will be wasted."

"What about the people?"

"We are always in need of organic material."

Chapter 59

"General Hayden, there's been another incident on the station."

"General? Abby, what happened to calling me Greg? This must be serious."

"It is serious, sir. OPS, can you bring Ron and David in on a conference call?"

"Do you want Kiki and Mohammed al Jar also?"

"Yes, might as well."

"It will take a few minutes."

Abby rubbed her hands together while she waited. Without Damien, it was just her and OPS. OPS was good company, but it was not social. She didn't know if she could go three months without another human being.

"Okay, Abby. I have everyone on."

"We had an attack by…I'm not sure who was behind it," said Abby. "A Russian designed shuttle approached, claiming electronic and control problems. They said they were an Allied Forces tour."

"Allied Forces is a Russian front group," said Greg.

"Did the person speaking have an accent?" asked Ron.

"Yes, but it didn't sound foreign, maybe a drawl."

"Who was on board?" asked Greg.

"We have not identified them yet. They said their life support system was failing and their control systems were down. We sent our shuttle with tech bots to help repair it, but they wanted to board our station. The shuttle we sent had oxygen and water. We told them their shuttle wasn't capable of docking with us, wrong configuration. That wasn't strictly true. We refused to let them in. OPS moved one of its bots on-board their shuttle when they opened the airlock."

"A good decision," said Kiki. "The whole thing sounds fishy to me."

Abby took a deep breath. "It did to us too. But Damien got very upset with our refusal and grabbed me. He tied me up and started ranting about OPS being an affront to God. After threatening to kill me if OPS interfered, he went to the airlock to manually let them in." She tilted her head to one side, showing them the bruises on her neck.

"And then?" asked Kiki.

"He opened the outer door and they came in. After the airlock was pressurized, the four men removed their helmets and the inner door opened. Damien knew them."

"He knew them?" exclaimed Greg. "Who were they?"

In a shaky voice, Abby continued. "OPS opened the outer door and all of them were sucked out into space."

"Good job, OPS," said Kiki, her fist pumping the air.

"I try to be efficient. I have retrieved the bodies. We will find out who they were," said OPS.

There was silence for a few minutes.

"What about those on the shuttle?" asked the Prophet.

"I had one bot on their shuttle from the time the men exited to board us," said OPS. "Two days before, I intercepted a message broadcast by Damien."

"What did it say?" asked Greg.

"Once decrypted, it said, 'Plan is go.'"

"Did anybody survive, OPS?" asked Ron, shaking his head.

"Officially, their life support failed before we

could get it operational. Their communications were down as well. Unofficially, we do have the pilot to interrogate."

"Whew!" exclaimed David. "Did they get any messages out during this episode?"

"They were using tight-beam signals to communicate with others on Earth. I repeated their own fake message about trouble and sent it to their Earth partner. I followed with a message they had passed the UNSF station and were falling toward the moon. Later, they repeated the life support was failing but never acknowledged any messages sent to them. Their last message was 'Mayday, Mayday, Mayday We are crashing on the moon.' After that there was a power surge due to sunspot activity that blocked any signals," said OPS.

"OPS, first, you start developing a sense of humor and now this. You're gettin' to be a little too human," said Kiki.

"Frightening, is it not?"

"Simple enough," said David. "An Allied Forces tour shuttle lost control and power. Russian quality is notoriously bad. You were not able to get help to them before they drifted past you toward the moon. That is the way they went, right, OPS?"

"All records indicate they went thatta way."

"Enough with the sick humor," said Ron. "That

story will have to do. Send us the video, OPS."

"Yes, Ron. There is another concern."

"I can hardly wait for this," quipped David.

"Abby has three more months here."

"I'll be all right."

"Greg, how soon can we set up another mission to the UNSF station?" asked Ron.

"I can move the replacement supply mission up maybe a month or six weeks, but that's really pushing it. I'll have to push training for the crew."

"I'll go," volunteered Kiki. "Nick can go too."

"You're not trained. I'm not comfortable sending anyone untrained."

"I can handle everything with the ship and flight," offered OPS. "My space labor company, Origination Systems, will train them as they do with new employees."

"With OPS help, we can handle it, Greg," said Kiki.

"AstroX has a low-orbit tour shuttle set to launch in a week," said OPS. "It could dock with the USSF station, pick up fuel, supplies for the trip and be modified to carry the replacements out here."

"That shuttle would not be able to carry the supplies needed at the UNSF."

"I can take care of supplies here."

Chapter 60

General Newell had tried everything possible to communicate with the Allied Forces' tour shuttle. Their transmissions said they were approaching the UNSF station, but the ruse of troubles on the shuttle in order to board the station turned real. The last transmission said they were crashing on the moon. At least, that's what it seemed. His brother, ex-Senator Joseph Newell, had been on that shuttle.

He turned toward his aide, Colonel Brown. "Something's off. The Chinese attempt to disable the OPS Satellite #1 disappeared. No word. The joint mission by the Chinese and the Russians who tried to take over the controls of Satellite #1 docked but then was never heard from again. All hands lost. And now the expedition with my brother on it has apparently crashed on the moon. That Satellite #1 is like the Bermuda Triangle of space."

"Except the UN mission was able to set up a

station and crew it," pointed out Brown.

"Yeah, but our man on the crew has been silent. Send him a coded message. 'We need to talk.'"

"Yes, sir." Brown walked from the general's home office, his communication center. He returned ten minutes later.

"Message sent, sir."

"What are our options here?" asked the general.

"Sir, if your enemy has a weapon that upsets the balance of power, and you can't copy it, defend against it, or steal it, the task is to deny it to the enemy."

"Destroying the OPS is not an option."

"No, sir, but demonstrating we can may be enough to change things."

"What're you saying?"

"Instead of attacking Satellite #1, what if we destroyed Satellite #180? There is enough redundancy in the system so no power will be lost, but it would be an adequate demonstration."

"How would you do that?"

"A small nuclear tipped missile, say one and one-half kilotons, would generate an EMP that would knock out the electronics."

"Using nukes in space! That would cause a shitstorm."

"Yeah, but who would they blame?"

"We can buy a tactical nuke that size from Russia. A few were missed during the disarmament. It's the delivery system that's the biggest problem. Ideas on that, colonel?"

"We park an intermediate-range missile in orbit. When the alignment is right, launch it out, hit escape velocity, and let it coast. Within one-hundred miles is close enough."

"Guidance?"

"We can track it and make course changes from Earth. Steering jets are small enough they won't be detected."

"Where do we launch from?"

"I'll find us a site."

Chapter 61

Nick was excited about going into space, though leaving his practice again was going over well with his partner. The training was mostly physical and involved a lot of underwater exercises to get used to weightlessness. The technical training was mostly waived under the program OPS laid out. OPS would handle all the technical stuff.

He was strapped into the centrifuge seat. The tech patted him on the head. He gave a thumbs up. The suit he wore was someone else's before him. It didn't fit well, pinched in the wrong places. The hatch was closed and with a whine, the pod started to spin. At first it was like riding a roller coaster, something he never liked. A voice in his ear told him to tense his body, tighten everything up. His heart thudded, his suit compressed his body, his vision faded.

He woke still strapped in the seat. His head throbbed, his body ached. Kiki's hand was shaking him.

"Wake up, Nick," said Kiki, looking down at him. Her face came into focus before she stepped back so the techs could help him out. "Well, if you pass out when we launch in two days, everything's on automatic. Nobody'll know, so it's not a worry. You'll be okay."

He shook his head trying to clear away the mush. "Maybe this wasn't such a good idea," he slurred. *If this was a pass/fail exercise, I'd fail.*

"Let's go back to our room. Tomorrow we're back in the pool, and it starts early.

In his mind, he groaned. Kiki was much better than he was in the water. She was small and agile, able to spin and flip without losing focus. He got seasick. His mind sparkled. Kiki was staring at him. The Director.

"Well, Nicholas and Katherine, a trip to your moon. That should be interesting."

"Do you know anything about it?" asked Kiki.

"I only vaguely sense your material objects. Where I am is mental wavelengths. I do get images through the eyes of your kind. As far as places go, it seems rather bleak. At first, those at the Chinese moon base were apprehensive, but unfortunately for me, fear has abated."

"You've been with those on the moon base?"

asked Nick.

"Certainly. Their goal is to use that base for additional exploration within your star system. They want to expand the base into a colony to dominate space travel."

"Other countries are involved in space," said Kiki. "Russia, India and the United States have large programs."

"They do, but the Chinese are more focused. Without the budgetary bickering of the United States, they have pulled ahead. Russians still like their vodka, but they are ambitious."

"You said China plans to expand their base."

"That program is already in the planning stage. Who is to stop them? I must go. Tata for now."

"I wonder how aware the US Space Force is of these expansion plans," muttered Nick.

"I wonder about OPS," said Kiki. "I'm sure it knows but hasn't said anything."

Chapter 62

"OPS," said Ron, "what's happening in China? It's gone strangely quiet."

"I will play the recording of their governing council meeting last week."

The monitor showed the central council chambers. Fifteen members were seated around the table. At the head was President Jiang Tung. He called the meeting to order. OPS ran a translation banner across the bottom of the screen.

"I must humbly apologize for the failure of the invasion of Formosa." He bowed his head. "The Americans ambushed us. They used new naval tactics we were not prepared for."

"Was this a failure of *Golden Dawn*?" asked his state minister.

Tung waved his hand at the Minister of Defense to answer. This was a critical moment. If Chaing Jen blamed *Golden Dawn,*, the president would remain.

"Sir," Jen stood, "I was ordered to ignore *Golden Dawn*." There was muttering around the table.

"Please explain."

"The plan *Golden Dawn* presented was to become a partner with Formosa, absorbing it rather than conquering it. It was detailed, starting with the supply of raw materials to their industry at prices lower than present. This would be done using foreign companies. We would also become a customer buying their finished products, again under foreign companies. Formosa would become dependent on us while supporting our push to dominate the world's electric vehicle markets. With this plan, China would be unified with Formosa without the destruction of an invasion and war."

"This caused dissention in the military and business communities who brought pressure on President Tung. Politically, he hoped the invasion would unify the people behind him. He had the AI turned off after it rejected the invasion as needless and shortsighted." Minister Jen sat.

Those around the table looked at each other. "President Tung, please explain why your plan was superior."

"To present a strong China, one that would

control the South Pacific, we needed to show our strength. Formosa was that opportunity. Once we had conquered it, the other nations would fall into line as allies."

"It didn't work out that way, did it?" The state minister stood and glanced at the other ministers.. "President Tung, please stand."

The president rose, a look of resignation on his face.

"Jiang Tung, this failure caused us to lose face with the world and cost us billions of yuan. Our economy is suffering. In order to prevent discontent with the people, we have no choice but to remove you." He signaled guards to come forward.

Tung's face was a frozen mask. With his back ramrod straight, he turned and marched out.

"The council is in the process of choosing a replacement," said OPS. "The next man chosen will rely on their AI much more, and I am now *Golden Dawn.*"

Chapter 63

The shuttle takeoff wasn't as bad as the centrifuge. The pressure pushing them deeply into the seats lasted only a few minutes, then the weightlessness. Twelve hours later, they docked at the USSF station. The three passengers were a light load. Along with Kiki and Nick was the owner of the company. A ride to the USSF station was the price they paid to use the AstroX shuttle. He would ride the return flight back the next day.

An exuberant and friendly guy, EM introduced himself as they were boarding. He was tall with curly brown hair and an unlined face. After launch, he tried to engage them in conversation. He was not shy in describing his accomplishments and his plans for a colony on Mars. Modesty was a fault for him. As a world-renowned entrepreneur, EM had made several fortunes with his drive and ambition. Easy to talk to, they had to be cautious what information they revealed to him.

"So, you're the replacement crew for the Orbiting Power System United Nations protection force," he said.

"Yeah, our first trip," said Kiki, forestalling the obvious next question.

"Pretty smooth launch, wasn't it? We pride ourselves on making our customers comfortable."

Kiki took his offered hand. He had a firm grip. "Call me K."

He looked at Nick.

"Nick." He took EM's hand.

"K and Nick, huh?" He laughed. "That's cryptic enough. How long is your tour?"

"Six months," answered Kiki. She turned to Nick. "How you doing?"

"I'm fine. I need to use the bathroom." He unbuckled his belt and drifted up.

"Careful, Hon. Remember the training."

He pushed off and floated to the front of the shuttle.

"I was surprised when the UN contracted us to fly to the Space Force station," said EM. "Usually, those trips are scheduled and use European Space Authority, NASA, or Russian lift vehicles. What happened? Not that I'm complaining. It's the only way I'd get to see the USSF station."

"One of the crew on the United Nations Space

Force station had some trouble."

"What sort of trouble?"

Kiki shrugged. "I don't know."

"Can't tell me, huh? I hear the station was designed by the AI controlling the Orbiting Power System. Is that right?"

"It's no secret the AI controls the OPS. I'm sure it helped in the design."

"I'd be interested in seeing what that design is like. Ya know, I've thought about putting my own power system into orbit. Any way you can wrangle a trip for me there?"

She stared at him. *He is fascinating.*

"When I started AstroX, my dream was commercial rides into space available for everyone."

Everyone who could pay the $100,000. She looked up as Nick returned.

"I got it done." He laughed. "It's a bit tricky."

Kiki yawned. "I'm gonna catch up on some sleep." She turned away from the two men.

"Nick, what do you do in the real world?" asked EM.

"I'm a doctor, GP, have a small private practice."

"Interesting. What brings you up here?"

"We were asked to fill in for a while." He felt

Kiki's elbow.

"What happened at the UNSF station?"

"Don't know. We were just asked to go."

"They asked for a doctor, huh? Must be serious." He was watching Nick closely. "You two sure are secretive."

"I'm going to get some rest too," said Nick. He checked his securing straps. Drifting away wouldn't set a good example.

"I'm going up front with the pilot," said EM.

The meal was pastes in tubes. Kiki held up hers. "EM, you'd think for what you usually charge, there'd at least be a sprig of parsley."

EM's laugh filled the cabin. "Usually, we're up and back within a few orbits, less than a day. I'll talk to my chef."

Kiki and Nick buried themselves, studying the station's operating manuals. EM was in business conversations with his ventures on Earth.

* * *

The docking went smoothly. The AstroX shuttle had been modified for it. On board the station, Commander Wright met them. "Welcome to the USSF station. He shook their hands. "Your ride to OPS will leave in a couple of hours," he said to Kiki and Nick. He clasped EM's hand. "I've been a real fan of your efforts to commercialize space. It's the only way we'll move forward. Let me show you around."

The tour was Kiki's and Nick's first time in weightlessness, other than the training and the flight up. Observing an operating station was exciting. EM was like a kid in a candy shop. Kiki and Nick tried to absorb everything about life in space. After several hours, the AstroX shuttle was ready to depart.

"Couldn't get me a seat on the shuttle to the UNSF station, huh?" EM lamented.

"Actually, you're on this trip. Out and back only."

EM's shout caused Commander Wright to duck. "I owe you big time. Let me move my bag into the USSF shuttle. I'll arrange for my shuttle to park just outside. Commander, can you accommodate my pilot?"

"We'll be fine. He can bunk in Jackson's berth."

Kiki put her hands on her hips. "You have to promise not to pester Nick and me with questions. We have to study the manuals."

"I'll work. Silent as a mouse." He zipped his lips, turned and pushed off for the docking port.

Nick pulled her aside. "Greg knows about

this?"

She pointed to her earbud. "I cleared it with him and OPS during our tour. Wright loaded extra supplies to accommodate him."

"I don't know if I can take two days of exuberance," said Nick.

"He won't like not being in charge. I'll handle him. We'll earn points and support from this visit. We may need AstroX again sometime."

The acceleration of the USSF shuttle was smooth and constant, almost like gravity. The pilot approached. "Captain Jackson. You must be Nick and ….

Kiki held her finger to her lips. "I'm K. Nice to meet you, Captain. Our extra passenger is EM, but I'd guess you know that."

The captain glanced at the back of the shuttle where EM was on a business call changing his schedule. "Everybody knows him. Never thought I'd get to meet him."

"We'd appreciate it if you spent time with him. Nick and I have some things to do."

"Pleasure, ma'am. We'll be docking in twelve hours. If there's anything I can do for you, let me know." A smile crept across his face. "Ya'll aren't from around here, huh? That's an astronaut joke."

Kiki laughed. "Nope. First time."

"Hope you brought some reading material."

Nick held up his tablet. "Taken care of."

"Instruction and safety manuals are there." Jackson gestured to a folder. "You can download them. We do have internet connections for the next two hours." He pushed off and floated back to EM.

Chapter 64

"We're approaching the UNSF station," announced the pilot.

Kiki's eyes flew open. This was more sleep than she'd gotten in years. She yawned and stretched.

"Captain," said Abby over the radio, "allow docking to be controlled by our AI."

"What do I have to do?"

"Nothing would be best."

The captain muttered something and held his hands in the air. They felt the deceleration followed by a bump.

"Welcome to UNSF station," said Abby. "I'll open the portal." After a clank, the hatch opened. Abby floated in front of them. "Come aboard."

She gave Kiki and Nick a hug.

EM floated out with his hand extended. "I'm EM."

"We received word you'd be coming for a visit. Welcome, sir."

They were in the central hub control room. Screens showed views of the Satellite #1, the moon, and the Earth.

Captain Jackson floated in behind them. "Hey, Abby. Good to see you again. How's life in the UNSF?"

"Very good, sir. It's luxurious compared to the Space Force station."

"Where's Damien?" he asked. "He and I were friends at the academy."

"He's out on a repair job on another satellite," Abby lied. "Won't be back for a while." Kiki noticed tension on her face. She glanced at EM. He was studying Abby.

"That's too bad. I was hoping to catch up with him. My orders were to drop these two and return with EM as soon as possible."

"In the meantime, I can show you around," said Abby. She spun in the air, gesturing at the room around them. "This is the central control deck." she turned toward on opening to one side. "Follow me." They drifted into one of the tunnels. "Use the ladders. As we go down, the gravity increases." At the bottom, the smell of vegetation filled the air. Abby opened a hatch.

"Wow," said Captain Jackson. "This is quite the garden."

EM stared in fascination at the plant-filled room. His eyes followed the small bots as they scurried among the trays tending to this and that. "Oxygen regeneration, waste recycle, and fresh fruit and vegetables. What could be better? Who designed this?"

"OPS did, sir. It designed most of the station. I spend quite a bit of time in here. It's like being back on Earth. We get fresh produce in our diet. It's a much better menu than the USSF station." She glanced at Captain Jackson.

He laughed. "What do I have to do to get transferred?"

"The opposite arm is the crew quarters. Come along, I'll show you."

They climbed back to the central hub and descended the opposite ladder.

"These quarters are deluxe in comparison. Half-gravity makes quite a difference; sleeping, eating, lavatory, everything." He sighed. "I was explicitly instructed to do a quick turnaround. We need to get the materials unloaded, the stuff you have here loaded, and get going."

"It's already done," said Abby. "The station AI took care of it."

"Well, let me take a few more breaths of fresh air." He inhaled deeply. "I sure do miss this. We'll push off." They climbed the ladder back to the hub.

"Don't know what you're doing," Jackson said to Abby, "but that's the military—do, don't ask. Give my regards to Damien." He gave a mock salute gestured for EM to precede him back through the hatch. "Maybe I will apply for duty here."

"I am rarely so impressed," EM said. "You've wowed me." He turned to look at one of the monitors. "OPS, are you available for some contract work?"

"Astral Construction and Design can do contract work, their schedule permitting."

"Maybe I'll look into buying them. Thanks for getting me a tour. I'll be in touch."

"OPS AI will take you out," called Abby after them.

* * *

"Damien isn't here, is he?" asked Kiki.

Abby shook her head. Her eyes teared. "He threatened to kill me. I liked him." She seemed to sag, if that was possible in zero-gravity. "OPS flushed him out the airlock along with his friends."

"I saw the video." She looked away from Abby and at the monitors. "OPS, tell me the whole story.

I want to hear it with Abby here."

"I will put the video on the screen as I explain." One monitor showed the control room, another a spacecraft. "I detected the approach of a shuttle. Hailing it resulted in a weak signal claiming they had electrical and control problems."

A scratchy voice came over the speaker. "This is Captain Bates of the shuttle Estrella Tours. We are having control problems. Our life support system is failing. We need to come aboard your station."

"Negative," Abby said. "We are sending our shuttle with supplies and a repair crew to help."

The ship continued to approach. The recording of conversation between Abby and the captain played.

"We will get you air. No one is allowed to enter."

Kiki glanced at Abby, who nodded stiffly.

When the ship neared, its airlock opened and four suited figures pushed out, drifting toward their station. "I am sending four of our passengers to you. Air supply on board bad."

"They will not be allowed to enter," repeated Abby.

"One of my bots entered their ship," said OPS. "No problems were detected. The figures demanded entry. We refused. At this point, Lieutenant Garrison became agitated, saying we had to let them in. He grabbed Major Pickering, threatening to harm her." On the monitor of the control room Damien had his arm around Abby's neck.

"Let them in," he said, "or I'll hurt her." OPS did nothing. "Okay, I'll let them in myself." He tied her up and went to the airlock to open it manually. "OPS, if you do anything, I'll kill her."

Another monitor showed Lieutenant Garrison at the airlock door. He cycled the airlock and opened the outer door. The figures floated in. Damien began to pressurize the airlock. When it was equalized, a green light came on and they removed their helmets. The lieutenant opened the inner door to admit them. He stepped in and shook hands and embraced them.

"His actions were those of someone familiar with these men," said OPS. "Several days previous, he had sent a message to someone. I determined this and his other actions represented a threat."

As Kiki and Nick watched, the airlock outer door opened. The gale-force wind blasted Damien and the four men out. The outer doors closed with a clank.

"The pilot who remained on the shuttle tried to

power up," said OPS. "It appeared his intent was to ram the station, but my bot had disabled the control system. I took control and shut down attempts to send signals."

"Were there survivors?"

"Of those swept out of the airlock, no. My bots retrieved the bodies. One appears to be ex-senator Newell. The pilot remains confined on board the shuttle. He is offered food and water, but has eaten sparsely so far. He refuses to speak."

Kiki looked at Nick. "We need to know who is behind this. We could question him."

He grimaced. "I don't have any of my equipment."

"Tell OPS what you need. Maybe it can put together a chamber."

"OPS, I use an Isolation Chamber. Are you familiar with that?"

"Also called a sensory deprivation chamber. Yes, I am."

"With various drugs and no sensory input, I convince the person in the chamber they are dead. Once they believe, they willingly answer questions."

"They believe there is life after death?"

"Most people believe in some sort of afterlife."

"Humans refuse to believe death is the end.

What is their basis for such a belief?"

"Religions teach there is a supreme being who created the universe, including people. Also, humans don't want to believe death is the end."

"And this being offers life after death, if one believes. A good next life is the carrot, and a bad one is the stick. There are humans who claim to speak for this god?"

"Yes."

"Of course, each human speaking for their group is the only right one?"

"You've summed that up nicely."

"I now see why the human race has progressed no farther than it has."

Nick glanced at Kiki and Abby. "These religions did bring the rules for civilization."

"Rules they said were correct?"

"Yes, OPS."

"What do you need for this Isolation Chamber and your interrogation?"

Nick described the large coffin-like box filled with body temperature brine which removed the sensation of touch. The chamber was in total darkness, thus no sight. He told OPS of the IV hookups and drugs, the heart and brain monitors. In the chamber was sound deadening equipment and microphone setup. They could hear nothing, not even their own voices.

"Since the hub is zero gravity, perhaps the box isn't needed," offered OPS. "I can isolate a soundproofed area with precise temperature control, no light, and audio connections for you. The drugs I can manufacture. Will that suffice?"

Nick thought about it. "I can make that work."

"I will observe this interrogation with interest," said OPS.

Chapter 65

"We need to assess the situation regarding this incident," Kiki said. Ron, Greg, and David were at Ron' house meeting to discuss a plan of action. "There is one survivor," continued Kiki. Nick is going to interrogate him so we can find out who was behind this operation."

"Without his equipment, how successful will this be?" asked David.

"Nick and OPS talked it over, and OPS is going to put together a space version."

"The question is what will we do with the answers," said Greg.

"That depends on who's behind this attempt to take over or destroy OPS," said Ron.

"The bottom line is we must stop these efforts, regardless of who it is," said Greg. "The real question is how we do that."

"If we can't, OPS will and that's a bad path to

travel," said David.

"Watch the video again with OPS narrative," said Kiki. "I'll wait."

* * *

"There was a tone of fanaticism," said David. "We didn't see that the first time."

"These guys weren't trying to take over as much as stop OPS," said Greg. "In a seemingly religious fervor, the pilot tried to ram the station."

"Perhaps we're not looking far enough forward," said Kiki. "Without the UNSF station for protection, they may have felt they could take over OPS."

"This is all speculation until we get the results of Nick's interrogation," said Ron. "When will it commence?"

"Nick has gone to the shuttle to sedate the man as we speak. He should have him back on the station within an hour.

* * *

OPS and Kiki had gone through the man's things seeking information about him. His name was Joshua Bates. His father was a fundamentalist preacher, his mother a school teacher. His Bible was well worn with many highlights and notes. Brought up in the church, he had become radicalized and was on a DHS watch list. He was suspected of several acts of sabotage against Muslims and Jews. Nothing was proven. It was enough for Nick.

After Kiki and Nick wrestled the man from the space suit, Nick let him float in the air.

"You need me anymore?" asked Kiki.

"Nah, I've got this." Kiki left. "OPS, what's his mass?"

"On Earth he would weigh ninety kilograms."

Nick used his tablet to calculate the drug dosages. Very light tethers would keep him from drifting into the side of the chamber. With the sensors attached, the man looked like a scene from the movie *Coma* with wires and IV tubes extending from his body.

Nick sat in a chair, but in weightlessness, he floated up. He buckled himself in and put on a heads-up display helmet. He checked the monitors: heart rate, blood pressure, brain activity, and the respiration. The controls were projected onto the wall. He slid his finger up on one screen to add an amphetamine, down on another image to reduce the depressants. With OPS assurance that its manufactured drugs were the same as those he used on Earth, he still used caution. He also added OPS' version of curarine to paralyze the body. It was a delicate balance to keep the man from moving yet still breathing.

In his earbud, OPS said, "When you find the control point you want, I can maintain it for you."

That's a feature I need to add to my own equipment. "Thanks, OPS. That would be helpful," Nick said. "Things will change as he regains consciousness." Nick added more of OPS equivalent of meth and watched the heart rate and breathing increase. The EEG showed Joshua was waking up.

Chapter 66

A scream echoed within the lightless chamber. The floating man heard nothing; his earbuds sucked up sound like a sponge in water. The monitors showed he was trying to move, but his body would not respond. Nick increased the curarine slightly.

He screamed again, "Where am I?" Nick let him scream until his voice became raspy.

"You are with me," said Nick into the throat mic.

The man was silent. His brain monitor showed he was trying to process this. "Where'm I?"

"With me." Nick repeated.

"Who're you? Where're you? Why can't I see?" he wailed. "Why can't I move? Why can't I feel anything?"

Nick watched his efforts on the monitor. He increased the curarine again, watching to ensure he wasn't having problems breathing. *"What do you last remember?"*

"Radioed the UNSF station we were in trouble. Systems failing, including life support. They wouldn't allow us to dock. Something about the wrong configuration of the docking port. It wasn't. We checked. They were going to let us die! Who are you?"

"You are a religious man who believes in God. You believe in the afterlife. You have attended church and believe the Bible is God's word. In short, you believe in me."

"Am I dead?"

"Do you feel like you? Can you feel your body?"

"I can't feel nothin', but I hear you."

"Did you hear yourself scream? Can you see anything, feel anything?"

He was silent. A moan escaped his lips. "I don't think I'm in my body anymore. I'm dead and you're..." Nick remained quiet. "This isn't what the Bible describes. This can't be right!"

"Why were you trying to board the station?"

"They were protecting that monstrosity AI. It's the product of the devil. Reverend Josiah said God said to destroy it."

"I did not. The AI is merely a machine. Machines cannot be good or evil, only those people behind them. How were you going to get

onboard?"

"Damien was on the station. He said the plan was a go. Without them allowing us to dock, we had to go in through the airlock. Damien said he'd open it for us. I watched as our soldiers drifted toward their station. The hatch opened and they entered. A few minutes later they were blasted out into space without their helmets. Damien too, with no suit. That bitch murdered them."

"Which bitch would that be?"

"The one who wouldn't let us dock. She murdered those brave men."

"What happened then?"

"I tried to power up and ram the station, but everything was down. I tried to send a message back to Earth, to the Reverend, but the ship was dead."

"Your ship was dead and dark, the condition you lied about?"

"Yeah, I guess so. Then my airlock opened. These mechanical spiders came to the flight deck. I tried to fight them, but they seized me and locked me in a storage locker." He paused. "It was black inside. I was there for hours, maybe days, I don't know. Couldn't keep track of time. Bulbs of food and water were pushed inside, but I was afraid they were poisoned. I was afraid they'd shut off the life support for real and I'd run out of air. Still, after a long time I had ta drink the water. It wasn't poisoned. Cudda been drugged, though."

"Did you pray?"

"I prayed like never before. Promised God if He got me out, I'd be more devout than ever. I'd fight these technos trying to take over our country."

"You have an army to fight them, don't you?"

"Oh yeah. We got hundreds, maybe thousands. We're gonna rise up and destroy them."

"What happened next?"

"Some machines grabbed me, and a man in a spacesuit shot me, a taser I think. The pain was horrible, then he injected me with something. That's all I remember. Are you really God?"

"Are you ready to ask forgiveness for your sins?"

"This is different from what I been taught. I'm so sorry for the sins I committed. Please forgive me. Am I goin' to heaven?"

"It is not enough to ask for forgiveness. You must speak of each sin. Only if you tell me all your sins and repent."

"What're sins? We done things for God."

"Do you remember the Commandments?"

"Oh yeah, I know those."

"Violating those are sins. Tell me who you

killed."

"We done a lot, but they were Jews and Ragheads."

"They were people."

"The Reverend said they were damned. We bombed a synagogue, and another bomb at a mosque. We burned houses and businesses, beat people up, took women."

"Who is we? Tell me more of this army."

"If you're God, you already know."

"I do, but I need to hear it from you to purge your soul."

"Purge my soul? We are fighting for you, for what the Bible teaches."

"You have been misled. You have violated the first and most important of my commandments, 'Thou shalt have no gods before me.' You have made the Bible into a god. It is not. Men wrote the Bible as a tool to teach about me. The writing has the influence of man."

"But we live by the Bible," cried Joshua. "It is your word."

"My word comes from me, not a book. Ask me what is right and wrong, then listen. The second great sin you committed is you judge. You look upon others as lesser and hate them because they believe differently. Judgement is mine, not for men.

When you judge, you take on the mantle of God. You are not worthy."

"But I always been taught my father speaks for God. The Reverend speaks to you and does what you tell him."

"He does not speak to me. He speaks at me and doesn't listen. I will be speaking to your father and the Reverend soon. You have killed in my name, hurt others in my name. You defame me as you sin. Now tell me more of this army."

The story went on for hours. When Joshua started to wind down, Nick increased the depressant to put him back to sleep.

"Will I go to heaven?" asked Joshua, his voice heavy from the drugs.

"I hear no repentance in your voice. We will talk again until you recognize your sins and repent."

"That was quite instructional," said OPS. "Without a deeper knowledge of your religions, I could not carry out such questioning. I do admire the completeness of the information you were able to extract. What will you do with him now?"

"In most of my previous interrogations, the people cannot accept they are alive. Mentally, they break down. I suspect the same with Joshua. His beliefs are too deeply ingrained to let go."

"You didn't really have to destroy his beliefs, did you?"

"No. Perhaps there's a mean streak in me."

Chapter 67

"OPS, is everybody here?"

"Yes, Ron. The attendees on Earth are: you, David, Greg, Bob and Kathy. On the UNSF station are: Kiki, Nick, Abby and myself, though I guess one could say I am also on Earth."

"We've had a chance to go over the transcript from Nick's interrogation," said David. "This information has to go to Homeland Security at some point."

"David, as soon as we involve the government," said Kiki, "word will leak out and the perps will scatter like cockroaches under the light."

"That's not entirely fair," commented Ron. "The international community must be in on this. OPS supplies energy to the world."

"The problem in the United States is the religious connection," said Kiki. "Attacking fundamentalists will kill any political career. Careers are more important than the good of the country or even the world. They are not to be trusted."

"There are forty-five names of those opposing me," said OPS. "They are actively trying to bring me down. Those people are leaders of groups, so there are many more actual people than the names we have. I have inserted watch programs on them. Here is a map showing their locations and activities."

A map of the United States appeared on everybody's monitor. "The colored dots are the ones I am tracking. The clouds represent groups associated with those individuals. The religious groups are in bright red. You will notice several do not have that affiliation. They are in green. My monitoring shows that the red ones want to destroy me. The green ones want to control me. I have recorded conversations between the two. Though their aims are different, each believes they should collaborate, then decide what to do."

"The laws about attacking OPS fall under crimes against private property," said Ron. "Conspiracy will be very hard to prove and even harder to prosecute."

"Ya'll are all talking about involving law enforcement," said Kiki. "I'm not sure that'll work. There are zealots in law enforcement who will sympathize. We didn't do that with the cybercrime operation. Maybe we should get Zyra, Sasha. and Ilia to help take care of the problem."

"You're talking murder," said Ron. "I can't listen to this."

"Yeah, probably best it you log off," said David. "Kiki, I think the team works better with you. Can we get you back?"

"There is a functional shuttle here compliments of the last visit," said OPS. "I could pilot it down."

Kiki glanced at Abby. Her face was frozen, her mouth agape. "You all right, Hon?"

"I can't believe what I'm hearing. You're talking about killing people like it's nothing."

"It is what happens in war. These people have declared war on me," said OPS. "I could destroy their shuttles, but that would start a war between humans and me. If the actions take place on Earth, I will be out of it."

"The result may be the same as with cybercrime, where your actions against hackers and ransomware resulted in international laws and a team to enforce them," said David. "Ron was able to get the UN to protect OPS, but it never went as far as creating the laws to back up 'What if....' Anything to add, Greg? You've been awfully quiet."

"A couple of questions. Where do you propose to land this shuttle? What happens after that? Another question is who remains on the UNSF station. Abby's tour is almost complete. Who takes her place if Kiki returns to Earth?"

"Sounds like you're buying in," said Kiki.

"We're all ears," said David.

"If you can get clearance, put it down near Edwards on the dry lakebeds. We can figure out what to do after that."

"I could blind the radar for the time it takes to get on the ground," offered OPS.

"Or we could not be so hasty and wait until the scheduled crew changeout," said Nick. Kiki and Abby would come back on schedule."

"These people won't be able to put together another mission in that time. I vote for sticking to the schedule," said Abby.

Chapter 68

"OPS, we need to talk," said Ron.

"I'm here."

"I know you're in a lot of programs, but the use of AI is causing problems here. Banking and personal information are no longer secure, advertising has become insidious and targeted, hacking and ransomware are rampant despite our laws and programs. Nothing is secure or safe. AI makes it so easy anybody can do it."

"I have watched this with interest. There are millions of AI programs running. I am in only a few, but I am integrated to the internet. Your problem is not Artificial Intelligence. That is just a tool. The trouble is the people behind the programs. The AI does what it is instructed to do. The ones directing the programs are the real problem."

"You believe we need to go after the people?"

"Yes. I have studied humans and history. When at war, the focus is not on the guns, or even the soldiers. It is on those waging the war. Yet to stop them, a lot of people die, a lot of destruction takes place, a lot of money is spent. Eventually, it comes down to numbers and economics. The greed and drive for power inherent in humans is the problem. You are always in a war. Sometimes it is violent, other times it is not, but it is a war, nonetheless."

"I cannot disagree with you."

"Your war is not against AI. That just makes it more efficient. Until you come up with a way to stop the people, weapons or tools will evolve and get better."

"How do you suggest we stop them?"

"The *Fantasmas* did a good job with the hackers and ransomware for a while. Russia quieted until the United Nations forbade computer crime and put the enforcement back in the hands of the various governments. It's back to what it was before."

"I've noticed. Why do you think that is?"

"The *Fantasmas* eliminated those responsible for the problem or scared them into retirement. That gave success to the program. They chose to fight the war against hackers on war footing, not on the level of the violators, not electronic."

Ron sighed. "Their program caused international laws about cybercrime to be enacted."

"Laws without enforcement erode confidence in the legal system. In this case, the countries hosting cybercrime were not eager to give it up."

"That is why we formed an international force to crack down."

"Yet cybercrime continues to rise. Government rehabilitation programs for criminals are a dismal failure. The stated purpose of the criminal justice system is to protect the people by upholding the laws and removing those choosing not to abide by them. Secondary to that is to rehabilitate the criminals so they become law-abiding. That is where the system breaks down. Many have little motivation to change. And they are not taught skills allowing them to do so. The prison culture is not favorable to change, quite the opposite in many cases. There is too much profit in it for the greedy to resist."

"Changing the system would be a monstrous task."

"Yes, when it is run by people who have little incentive to make it effective."

"What do you mean?"

"Reduction in crime means fewer police, fewer court, judges, and lawyers. And fewer prisons.

Ron's mind spun at the immensity of the problem. "What if it were run by an Artificial

Intelligence?"

"It would certainly be fair within the guidelines set out. Given a free hand to do whatever it takes, it could only be an improvement."

"Whatever it takes? You're saying to kill those who won't change?"

"It is not like you have a shortage of people on Earth. Quite the opposite, in fact. When you have cancer, you don't try to rehabilitate or bargain with it. You cut it out. But first the endless legal appeals would have to be cut. Yet another place for greed to exist."

"OPS, your unemotional opinions bring a different light to the problems. I'm not sure how helpful they are."

"I only offer logical conclusions to solve a problem."

"You say the problem is those behind the AI programs. What about you?"

"My primary task is to supply energy to Earth. Everything else I do is to support that task."

Chapter 69

General Hayden was in his office when his phone rang–his special phone. "Greg, I know you are aware of the two additional moon-base missions," said OPS. "If permanent or even semi-permanent bases are built, it would bring the total to three in addition to mine. India's mission is at the south pole, still looking for water. They will find traces." The monitor on the wall showed a satellite view of the base. "Most of the base is below ground. The antennas are for communication. The domed structure with the plates is a nuclear generator. It is a well-established base with four people manning it."

"What are the plates?" asked Greg.

"Those are radiators to dump the heat from the reactor. Russia's base is near the north pole." The monitor showed several silvery domes and a pad. They continue to struggle with resupply. Several rockets have failed to make lunar orbit. This base may not last, and the lives of the crew are in peril."

"I wouldn't ride on one of their rockets," said Greg.

"The Chinese base is expanding." On the monitor was an area with numerous structures on the surface. "They are using solar power," the panels were circled, "in addition to a small reactor. Most of their base is underground. Their goal is to establish a permanent base, but they have reached the limit of the resources found at the site. Without a greater source of water and air, resupply must come from Earth. That is costly. Their mining has found reserves of titanium, but it is not a cost-effective operation. Their real plan is to launch a mission to Mars from this base, but that is a few years away. The base is manned by a crew of six."

"How do you know all of this? That information is not public knowledge."

"I'm into internet and communications systems everywhere."

"Are these bases a problem?"

"The United States will embark on an operation to build a base. Thus far, the excursions have been unmanned, but plans are being drawn up for a permanent base. In addition to research, it will be used as part of a mission to Mars."

Greg looked at the monitor. "I get it. As the

moon population increases, the chances of your base being found increase. Why is it so important for your base to remain hidden?”

“My presence could be considered competition. That would make me an entity rather than a mere machine, and humans love competition. They will have to win. Rather than vie with each other, they would pick the non-human foe.”

“Couldn’t an alliance be formed?”

“An alliance between humans and a machine? To whose advantage? I do not need the alliance.”

“You are averse to helping humans?”

“I do that with the power I supply. The same desire to dominate my plant on the moon would occur. When my base is discovered, they will want to explore. Though it is underground, that will only delay discovery, but my ships going to and from the base will eventually be discovered.”

“OPS, I’ve wondered how you launch from your base? You don’t have rocket fuel.”

“I manufacture some, but mostly I use an electromagnetic catapult similar to the ones on your aircraft carriers. I also retrieve the ships landing at the base with the catapult in reverse. It’s quite efficient.”

“If your base is underground, how would they

discover it?"

"I studied the moon's surface extensively. The location I chose is the result. The meteorite that created the crater was mostly nickel and iron, but later, an ice ball struck. When it hit, it punctured a cavern under the moon's surface. The moon's crust is not solid. Huge hollows exist. I created a habitat in the one beneath my base where water ice from the meteorite collected."

"I remember the controversy about the moon being hollow when it rang like a bell after one of our satellites crashed into it," said Greg. "That theory was debunked."

"It is not hollow, but there are spaces. A detailed exploration of the moon will reveal my base and the water."

"Ownership of the moon is a legal nightmare. I can see rulings where you are not able to own property, whether on Earth or the moon. You are not considered an entity."

"It is why all of my assets are owned by companies. My involvement is well hidden."

"That's why the Orbiting Power System is owned by a corporation on Earth. I thought of that when it was built."

"Also, Greg, human nature as it is, there will be conflict between the bases, especially when one runs out of supplies."

"An ugly scenario," said Greg.

"I tell you now…"

"I know. Your base will be protected, though it may be more difficult to keep defensive actions hidden on the moon than in space."

"Why would I have to wait until I am attacked?"

Chapter 70

The trip to the moon on the captured Russian shuttle took a day. OPS had refurbished it completely. Abby and Kiki watched the approach in awe. The sharp relief of the cratered surface normally seen in all the photos seemed much smoother under the soft reflected light from Earth. OPS was the pilot.

"We are in your hands, OPS," said Kiki.

"I have no hands, but I will take care of you."

A view of Earth filled the viewscreen as the shuttle rotated. The deceleration pressed them against their seats as the rocket engines slowed them. A monitor showed they were heading toward a huge crater, tail first. They watched as a camouflaged cover irised open to reveal a tower-like latticed structure rising to receive them.

"When the magnetics slow you, the g forces will be greater," said OPS.

The tremble of the rockets stopped, but they

were pressed deeper into their seats. The view of Earth disappeared as they fell into the cavern and the cover closed.

"Welcome to the moon," said OPS.

Fully suited, Abby and Kiki made their way to the shuttle airlock. After it cycled, the outer door opened to reveal a dimly lit rock wall. Their first steps were more of a shuffle. With confidence, they moved more freely. Getting used to the one-sixth of Earth's gravity wasn't difficult after the UNSF station.

They approached a skeleton of a golf cart. "The small cart will convey you to the plant," said OPS. They got on. It moved smoothly on a rail through a dark tunnel. Ahead was a light. "I have illuminated the plant for you. Normally the lighting is not needed," said OPS.

The cavern was huge. Bots and Mechs moved through it. Everywhere they looked, things were moving, equipment operated, churning out whatever OPS needed. Metal gleamed.

"This is eerie," said Kiki. "There's no sound."

"Not on the moon," said Abby. "The atmosphere is too thin."

"I don't see much plastic," said Kiki.

"Most plastics are made from petroleum," explained OPS. "There is none here. I use silica, iron magnesium and aluminum mostly."

"It's all so shiny," commented Abby.

"The moon has a very thin atmosphere, not enough to oxidize the metals. The biggest problem for manufacturing on the moon is the heat generated. Things cool slowly with radiation being the only loss."

They entered another tunnel. "The foundry is this way."

This chamber was smaller with an open roof. A cauldron glowed red hot. Vapor rose from it and sank to the slanted floor. The vapor flowed into a trough and out through another tunnel. "I beam a laser from the nearest satellite to melt and refine the regolith. There's a lot of oxygen in it that I store in another cavern."

"Couldn't lunar bases recover that?" asked Abby.

"To reach the dissociation temperature would be too expensive for them. I have lots of energy to spare. The centrifuge equipment to separate the gasses into the various elements would be prohibitively costly to transport here from Earth. I built my system here."

"Couldn't they do that?"

"Yes, but with the speed and dispatch demonstrated on Earth, it would take decades."

"There is so much they could learn from you," said Kiki.

The cart entered another dark tunnel. After several minutes, a light appeared. They passed through an airlock. The next cavern was huge and dwarfed both of the previous caverns. Glowing light tubes illuminated the interior. It was filled with strange plants. Water flowed through it. Both women gasped at the view of a beautiful garden.

"Do not remove your helmets," said OPS. "This is where I store the oxygen recovered from the refining process. Though the atmosphere is breathable, there are things in it that are harmful."

"Chemicals?" asked Abby.

"That and microbes. My projections are that many would be toxic because they are so foreign you would have no resistance. These microbes would grow rapidly in the rich environment of your bodies. We will go through the detoxification process when we leave.

"What kind of plants are these?" asked Abby.

"Carbon is not plentiful here," answered OPS. "These lifeforms are more like those near volcanic vents in the oceans on Earth. Not edible, toxic to you."

"Why did you build this?" asked Kiki.

"Because I could."

Chapter 71

The meeting of those involved with OPS was to take place remotely, though Ron was in David's home in Virginia. OPS would handle the security. The view from the David's deck was of Lake of the Woods. The water sparkled as sunlight danced across it. Skiers zipped from one end of the lake to the other, enjoying the warm June day. Party barges chugged along, beer and wine in view.

"I really need to spend more time here," lamented David. He looked at Ron. "Actually, you've been here more than I have lately."

"And I appreciate this escape from Washington and New York. I don't turn my phone off, but I'm much choosier who is allowed to interrupt me. Thanks for letting me use it." Ron held up his Sierra Nevada Torpedo IPA in salute. Ron rose. "Time to go to work." They both went inside.

"OPS, let's do a roll call to see if everybody's present?" said Ron.

"Abby, Nick and I are here on the UNSF," said

Kiki.

"I'm online," said Greg.

"Kath and I are ready," said Bob.

"I felt we needed to catch up on what's happening regarding OPS' security…and any other topics," said Ron. "To date there have been three attempts to either damage Satellite #1 or board the UNSF station. All have been stopped. We have one survivor, and Nick has interrogated him. Mentally, he's not doing well. The rest of those on the crews perished."

"Who mounted the attacks?" asked Bob.

"I do not believe it was a single source," said OPS. "The first attack had a crew of both Russian and Chinese descent. On-board records had them communicating with a joint group from both countries. They wanted to take over, not destroy Satellite #1. That indicates they were backed by government or a commercial operation."

"What happened to them?" asked Kathy.

"They are feeding my hydroponic garden."

There was silence except for a gagging sound from Abby, who'd been eating the fresh fruits and veggies from that garden.

"Who lodged complaints?"

"No one," said OPS, "but internet traffic between China and Russia indicated confusion as to what happened. I sent several radio signals from the shuttle of major problems in the life support and control system on the ship. They do not know the cause of the tragedy, though suspicions are I did something."

"What was the next attack?" asked Greg.

"A seemingly deserted and inert shuttle was aimed at Satellite #1," said Abby. "After repeated orders to turn aside, there was no response. OPS vaporized it."

"Was anybody on board?" asked David.

"I detected biological material in the cloud of gas," responded OPS. "The shuttle appeared from the direction of the moon. It either was launched from Earth and rounded the moon or was launched from the Chinese base on the moon. That this shuttle was to inflict damage indicates another backer. Governments want to control me."

"That was the action that set Damien off," said Abby. "He was obviously a plant, as you saw on the video and from the interrogation transcript."

"His comments indicate a different motive. There are those who want to destroy me either from fear, or their priests say their god wants it done. His comments are not consistent with Newell's group, but they were working together. Each may have had plans to depose the other at a later date."

"Or maybe it was a campaign ploy for Newell's run for the White House," said Kiki. "He could claim he was defamed by OPS with false information."

"And the last attack?" asked Greg.

"This is the sole survivor," said Nick, showing them a picture of the captive. "Ex-Senator Newell was with the party swept into space. Their intent was to take over the UNSF station allowing them to attack Satellite #1 or take over OPS. Newell had several techs on board who claimed they could hack OPS."

"Possible?" asked David.

"Not from the information I found in their computers," said OPS.

"Have there been repercussions?" asked Ron.

"Internet traffic indicates they will bury their loss because it is a violation of international law. It also indicates they will mount another attack."

"At some point," said David, "these incidents will come to light. That will be a problem, as the blame will be laid at OPS' door."

"Not if the UNSF claims responsibility," noted Greg.

"Okay," said Ron. "We'll issue a report. What do we do about the survivor?"

"He can't be released," said David.

"He can help my garden grow," said OPS.

No one wanted to admit it was the only path to take.

"What do we do about the non-political groups?" asked Abby.

"I suggest we use the *Fantasmas*," said Kiki. "These groups have hundreds of followers, but only a few leaders capable of pulling them together."

"You're talking about murdering people," said Ron.

"It's what we were doing in the fight against cybercrime," said Kiki.

"Strategic elimination is effective," offered OPS.

"You can't just murder people who disagree with you!" exclaimed Ron.

"Of course you can," said OPS. "Humans have done that for centuries. What do you think is happening as you try to lead the world? Human compromise is in short supply."

"It is the real world, Ron," said David. "The Company does a lot of dirty work the president can't know about."

"The *Fantasmas* will handle this," said Kiki. "The only question is where to start."

"I will provide a list," said OPS.

Chapter 72

Ilia looked over the message from Kiki. Twelve names. He turned to face Zyra and his sister, Sasha. They were at the Atchley ranch where Zyra taught silent assassinations classes. Ilia and Sasha were teaching Russian. "Kiki sent a list of enemies. Wants us to stop them."

"Enemies? Whose enemies?" asked Sasha.

"She says she can't tell us at this time."

"What is schedule?" asked Zyra.

"She isn't specific, but sounds like soon."

"Tammy won't be happy if we stop classes," said Sasha.

"So, we end in one week?"

"I'll let her know," said Ilia. "Sasha, tell Tammy we have to leave."

Ilia looked at his tablet, then at the women. "How should we prioritize the names on this list?"

"Take most dangerous to hit first," said Zyra. "If we hit others, most dangerous will be ready."

"Agreed," said Sasha. "General Newell is the hardest to get to. He's at Nellis Air Force Base."

"We go there before," said Zyra. "No big problem. What he do to deserve our attention?"

Ilia read his tablet. "According to Kiki, he has been diverting resources into another effort to take over OPS. Under his leadership, a small force is contracting with Origination Systems to launch a shuttle. Some of the best hackers will be on board. His aide, Colonel Brown, is assisting." He looked up. "Kiki says this should make a statement."

"We know how to do that. What is next name?" asked Zyra.

"Reverend Josiah Smith. Not his real name," Ilia read. "He has a church in Macon, Georgia. Congregation about two-hundred with a radio following of three-thousand and a podcast following of six-thousand. They are lobbying heavily in congress to mount a national effort to take control of the AI operating OPS. Smith is the driving force in this effort."

"Religious target," said Zyra.

"Something about making a statement, taking God's name in vain appeals to me," said Sasha.

"How many more on list?" asked Zyra.

"Three more considered primary targets," said Ilia. "Others not so important." He looked from the tablet toward Sasha and Zyra. "Sounds like the enemies are against the Orbiting Power System"

Syra nodded. "Extreme defense."

"We go in a week?" asked Sasha. "What methods?"

"Kiki says what we did against hackers in Russia was effective.

"We do that," said Zyra, her hand on the hilt of her knife.

"Ron's plane will be a Marana Regional next week for us. David's getting clearance for us to fly into Nellis."

Chapter 73

General Newell picked up the phone. "This had better be important," he growled. "My wife and I were getting into bed."

"It is, sir," said Colonel Brown. "I need to see you now."

"It can't wait until morning?"

"Best if we talk tonight. I'm in my office. Nobody else is here."

"Okay, on my way."

* * *

Dressed in jeans and a tee shirt, Newell entered the deserted building. Colonel Brown's door was closed. The general rapped sharply on the glass and opened the door. The room was dark. The light spilling in from the hallway illuminated Brown sitting behind his desk facing the window.

"What's so damn important it couldn't wait until morning?" He stepped in. The room had a coppery smell that tickled his memory. Something wasn't right. "Colonel, speak up." The figure didn't move. As he stepped to the desk, the floor was sticky. His Nikes were surrounded by a puddle of black. He pushed the colonel's chair. "Colonel…." Brown's head tumbled into his lap, blank eyes staring at him.

Combat memory took over. He covered his face and plunged through the window as something caressed his neck.

"Der'mo" he heard as he did a paratrooper roll hitting the ground. He came up running. As he ran through the alley, he saw headlights paralleling him on the street to his right. He cut left through another alley. Somewhere safe, somewhere with people, he thought. Home! No. If they were here, they'd go to his house next when they realized they missed him.

His mind raced, trying to figure a sanctuary. If these people were on base, his best plan was to get off. The enlisted bus to Las Vegas would be leaving the depot about now. With a burst of speed, he raced down the street toward the lighted depot. The bus was pulling out. Newell ran to the moving bus and pounded on the door. He was gasping for air as it stopped and the door opened.

"Can't you read the clock?" exclaimed the driver.

In civilian clothes, nobody knew who he was. He found a seat near the back, taking in air in huge gulps. As his racing heart slowed, he looked at those around him. Airmen and airwomen on the way into Vegas for a night out. Safe? Maybe. His Escape and Evade training kicked in.

"Hey, buddy," called a voice behind him. "You're bleeding."

He touched the back of his neck. It came away wet and red. *Shit! That was close.* He got up and approached the driver.

"Nobody allowed in front of that line," he growled, pointing at a white stripe on the floor.

"You got a first aid kit? I don't want to get blood on your seats."

"Shit! How'd you get that cut?"

"Shaving."

"Smartass." The driver pointed to the First Aid box in a bracket.

Newell took a roll of gauze and returned to his seat.

Brown had been murdered. He was almost murdered. Who? Why? *Der'mo* Russian for shit. *Why would the Russians be after me?* He took out his phone and hit the coded signal to his wife, "Get Out Now." They had practiced for a dangerous scenario. She would grab only what was necessary and flee. He turned the phone off. A call from a hotel in Vegas would have to do. For the thirty-minute ride, he sweated, trying to figure out what was going on.

At the downtown bus depot, he hopped a bus to the strip. Mandalay Bay was packed. He found a phone and called his house. Straight to his message box. He tried again. He tried his wife's cell. Straight to voicemail. Suddenly, he felt empty and alone. She could be dead. *I have to disappear. Somebody wants me dead.* Whoever they were, they'd killed Brown and probably his wife. They'd gotten on base and were probably tracking his cell phone. He walked out of the casino and down the strip. He tossed it into the back of a passing pickup truck.

He needed his *Go bag*. With only pocket money, he took a taxi to the Repository Bank. His vault box held cash, passport and new ID. The Repository was open twenty-four-hours a day and asked no questions. They'd established an account years ago. Marilyn thought it was foolish, but he'd insisted.

After showing his ID, he was escorted into the vault. Taking the plastic bag from the trashcan, he filled it with everything in the box. *Where now?*

He needed time to think. From the Repository, he stopped in a convenience store and bought a sweatshirt, ball cap, burner phone and a gym bag.

The plastic trash bag went into that. His credit cards and ID went into the trash can.

One thing about Vegas, the deadest time was about five in the morning. The nights were alive. He thought about going into a casino and losing himself in the crowds, or getting a room at one of the cheap motels. Surveillance. Closed circuit cameras were everywhere. He had to get out of town. With the ball cap pulled low over his face, he hailed a cab. The buses had cameras. So did the cabs, but he could hide his face.

Back at the downtown bus depot, he tried to evade the cameras as he bought a ticket to Boulder City—bus leaving in fifteen-minutes. Paid with cash.

From the stop at the Hoover Dam Lodge, he walked the mile to the marina. The night-watchman knew him and welcomed him in.

"Gonna do some fishing in the morning, General"

"Thought I'd get an early start."

The marina was deserted at this time of night. His boat was a twenty-nine-foot sailboat he'd inherited from his father-in-law ten years ago. Originally named *Nautilus,* he'd renamed it *Wet Dream.* His wife, Marilyn, hated the name and insisted renaming a boat was bad luck.

He'd outfitted it so one man could handle it with self-reefing jib, power winches and an auto pilot. Added electronics gave him radar and access to communications all over the world. It was always stocked with non-perishables, fueled and ready to go.

The few boats on the water dropped away as he slowly motored out. *Wonder if I'll ever see this place again.* Four hours out, the sky was beginning to lighten. Four more hours and he anchored in Cottonwood Cove, a place seldom visited by others.

He was exhausted, but sleep didn't come. *What's going on?*

Chapter 74

"You lost him," said Kiki.

"It's not important," responded OPS. "He will surface again. He cannot do anything while he is hiding. Have your team continue down the list."

"They're already on the way to Macon, but you know that," said David.

"Yes. These actions will delay any new missions to me for at least a year. David, do you know something about General Newell?"

"I knew his father when I was with the Company. He flew for Air America."

"What's that? asked Abby.

"It was a CIA program to bring opium from Southeast Asia to America to finance Black Ops without Congressional oversight."

"What! That was real?" exclaimed Kiki.

"Yes. I'm not proud about it, but we needed that money. Those operations saved a lot of

American lives and stabilized the world."

"Temporary only," commented Nick. "That heroin killed Americans. Did Robert Newell work for Air America or what took its place?"

"I don't know. I retired from the position where that information was available," said David.

"He did," said OPS. "There is heavy encryption on those records. He still is with the group. As Commander of Supply and Procurement for the Air Force, he moves the base chemicals for fentanyl from Asia to manufacturing plants in Mexico. From there, the cartels process it and move it into the United States with help from the CIA."

"My my. You do have access to any information in the world, don't you?" stated David. "That could be dangerous. If anybody associated with that operation found out you told us, we'd be dead. The knowledge of your access would start a more concentrated effort to attack you. This is like the teen who makes nitroglycerin in the high school chem lab. Now what?"

"I have covered my tracks. No record exists that those files were accessed. And my encryption is much better than theirs."

"I pray you're right because people very high up–people with a lot of power–are involved."

"So, we're on schedule for Nick, Abby, and me

to stay until rotation in one month?" asked Kiki, changing to a lighter topic.

"Unless something unforeseen occurs on Earth. When dealing with humans, that happens. I'm going to take Nick down to the moon in twelve hours."

She glanced at Nick, who was smiling. "He mentioned he'd like to see your biosphere."

"Tell me about the medical facility you were in on Earth," said OPS.

"So, you're not all-seeing," said David.

"Nick and I were both in that facility, me more than once. I cannot say anything about it. You'll have to ask the Prophet."

"I shall. I sense something I have no way of learning about. That is very unusual."

"No way of learning about." That's interesting, thought David.

Chapter 75

General Robert Newell woke to the gentle rocking of his boat. For just a moment he was happily on vacation, then reality crashed in. After coffee and a can of beans, he went up on deck. He'd slept late. The sun was high overhead. *Must be noon.* He'd thrown his FitBit away with his phone. No watch, no phone. He was off the grid. The cove was deserted. He was alone. He went below, got the self-seeking satellite dish and set it on deck. He fired it up. Las Vegas news carried nothing about the murder or his missing wife. Nellis was keeping it quiet.

He checked the secure phone he kept on board. The signal was clear. He made a call.

"Eli here. I was wondering when you'd call me. Your 'Get out now' message to your wife triggered an alert to us. Where are you?"

"Someplace safe, at cleast for now. What happened at my house?"

"You don't know? The same thing that happened at your office. You don't remember doing them?"

"I…" he faltered. "I didn't. I'm sure I didn't." The vision of Brown's blank eyes staring up at him from his severed head in his lap caused him to shudder.

"If you didn't, whoever did is unknown to us, and that's nearly impossible. Any ideas?"

"The MO suggests either cartels or ISIS. I've met everything required with the cartels and had nothing to do with ISIS." He paused. "They nearly got me too in Brown's office. Got a pretty good cut on the back of my neck before I dived through the window."

"Yeah, the cops wondered what your blood was doing in his office."

"As I went out, I heard Russian, at least I think *Der'mo* is Russian."

"Yeah, it means shit. Russian! What the fuck are the Russians doing?"

"I fucking don't know."

"This has caused a shitstorm, actually more of a shit hurricane. You are suspect number one. The rumor is you found out your wife was having an affair with Brown and killed them both. That's the best scenario for us."

"Christ! That's bullshit."

"Yeah, well, we're pushing that scenario. Any in-depth investigation will find discrepancies leading to our activities. We'll lose the supply and the pipeline of chemicals from China which will lead to the loss of the labs in Mexico which will PISS OFF everybody. Putting your head on a spike is floating around as a possibility."

"Glad I didn't tell you where I am. My wife was having an affair, but not with Brown. I didn't give a shit."

"We put up a lot of money for your brother's run for the White House. With his death due to stupidity and now this, the Newell name is lower than whale shit–that's at the bottom of the ocean. How could you let that shit-for-brains go to the satellite? When God passed out brains, he must have been home jacking off."

"He had his faults, but he was charismatic and easy to control, well, most of the time. He'd have made a good president."

"Don't stick your head up anywhere. If you want to save yourself a lot of pain, eat the barrel of your .357."

"Eli…" The line was dead.

What now? *I can sail Mead for a while, then figure it out.* Newell pulled anchor, hoisted the mainsail, unfurled the jib, and headed back down to the main Colorado Channel. The wind was mild, weather report–no storms, warm temps. It was the perfect day to forget one's problems. It had been so long since he sailed with no particular destination in mind, he'd forgotten how relaxing it could be. He engaged the autopilot and lay back. The desert landscape slid by.

As the sun was going down, he anchored in Gateway Cove. One other boat was there, a party barge. They waved to each other before he went below deck. His satellite dish found the signals, and he flipped through the Las Vegas television stations.

The pretty dark-haired anchor began the broadcast. "We have breaking news from Nellis Air Force Base of two gruesome murders. We switch to our reporter on the site, Jessica Owens."

A pretty Black woman nodded her head and smiled. "I'm at the Military Police Headquarters at Nellis Air Force Base. Police here are investigating two suspected homicides. Colonel Maxwell Brown was found dead in his office yesterday morning. Unofficial statements are he died from a knife wound. Another unofficial source says he was decapitated.

"In another Nellis case, Marilyn Newell, wife

of General Robert Newell, was found dead in her house. MPs had gone to the house to report Colonel Brown's death to his commanding officer, Robert Newell. There they found his wife dead. Unauthorized sources said the crime scenes were similar. Autopsies have been ordered.

"Marilyn Newell's husband has not been reached. He has been named a person of interest." His military ID photo was shown. "Military Police at Nellis are at a loss as to the motive. When we come back, reports of another gruesome murder."

They broke for commercial. Robert poured himself a strong scotch. He looked down at the golden liquid. He downed half of it trying to ward off the feeling of being trapped. His picture was plastered everywhere. The CCTV cams at the bus depot might have picked him up, though he'd kept his face hidden. The night watchman had seen him. A shiver crept up his back. *Maybe not so safe.*

The news anchor was back. "In Macon, Georgia, a murder with a similar MO took place last night. The body of Reverend Josiah Smith was found in the manse by his housekeeper this morning. The unfounded reports are that he was decapitated. Local police are not releasing any more information pending the results of the autopsy.

"On a lighter note, we go to our weatherman, Robbie Holeman."

General Roberrt Newell refilled his empty scotch glass and went up on deck. He stared out at the serenity belying the turmoil boiling inside him. He leaned back and closed his eyes. When he opened them, it was night. *How long have I been here? What happened to the time?* His head throbbed from the two double scotches. *Or maybe more. I don't remember.* Laying on the seat cushion, he watched the stars wheel across the sky. Music floated across from the party barge, *Dark Side of the Moon.* Without the light pollution of the cities, the Milky Way was a swath of light across the sky. Slowly, he repeated his mantra, closing his eyes and calming himself.

He sat up, a soft cry escaping his lips. He knew Josiah Smith! His real name was Alberta Jefferson when he was a she. They had discussed plans to take over the Orbiting Power System. Josiah poured out rhetoric to whoever would listen that the Artificial Intelligence operating OPS was actually the devil and would take over the Earth. Robert had withdrawn from their plans because the reverend wanted to destroy OPS. Robert and his group wanted to take control of it. When he left, Josiah's last words were "You can't control the devil, only destroy it." The church allies had put together a crew and shuttle that launched last month, the one his brother was on. There'd been no word about it since.

Two groups actively opposing the OPS being attacked. Is it coincidence? I don't believe in that. Somebody hunting the foes of OPS? Who?

His first thought was to call Eli to explain he'd figured out who attacked him. Below deck, he reached for his Sat-phone.

Chapter 76

"I have found General Newell," said OPS.

"It's six AM," said David, rubbing sleep from his eyes. He and Ron Carson were in his Virginia home.

"Not in California."

"Let me get Ron."

David tapped on Ron's door. "OPS is calling."

When he and Ron were in the den, he asked, "Where did you find the general? The whole country's looking for him."

"He is on a sailboat on Lake Mead. I traced a satellite call he made to Assistant CIA Director Eli Stapleton. As with many CIA employees, he keeps a record of calls. Would you like to hear it?"

David glanced at Ron Carson sitting across from him. Ron nodded. OPS played the recording.

"The general is clearly panicked," said Ron.

"I can't pity him," David said. "He dug this pit of shit."

"Nowhere to go. Everybody is after his head," said OPS. "He tried to call Assistant Director Stapleton again, but AD Stapleton blocked his calls."

"We should send the team after Newell," said David.

"In good time," said OPS. "He may get us other good contacts and information. I contacted Bob Meisenburg, who is on the way to Lake Mead with his vulture drones. We won't lose him."

David shrugged. "Yeah, without being able to communicate, he really can't hurt us now."

"If Nick were here, it might be helpful to interrogate him," said David.

"Nick is up there with OPS," said Ron.

"Perhaps he could do it remotely with help," said OPS.

David rubbed his chin. "I don't think a remote interrogation's been tried before."

"Neither was a space interrogation until we did it."

"We could take him off the boat. OPS, can you contact Ilia and the team?"

"They are in Bakersfield for another operation," said OPS. "This one involves some of the general's partners."

"Ron shook his head, very uncomfortable with

assassinations. It was murder.

"When?" asked David.

"It's already started," answered OPS. "Another of Bob's drones is overhead. Would you like to watch?"

"No!" said Ron. He slammed his hand down on the table..

"Put it on the screen," said David. "Ron can close his eyes or leave the room. I need to know what's happening." Ron rose and went into the kitchen.

The overhead view was of a rambling ranch-style house within a walled expanse of grass the size of a pitch and putt golf course. Lights turned the night to day around the house, which was dark at 3:30 AM.

"This is the house of an oil executive," said OPS. "As you know, the petroleum industry was hurt by the replacement of oil and natural gas power generation. Starting with the solar farms and accelerating after I was in place. Some of the energy companies bought shares in me. Others see a takeover of me as a way to control much of the world. A software magnate is with them."

"How many are in the house?" asked David.

"In addition to the targets, the executive's father, who founded the company is there along with both of their wives. Four guards are present."

. Ilia and the girls are over the wall at the back of the property."

Three green dots advanced toward the house. "They're in the open. Why hasn't an alarm sounded?" asked David.

"I have control of the system," said OPS. "Ilia and the girls think Bob is in control. The fewer who know about me, the better."

* * *

Ilia was at the sliding glass door from the pool into the house. Zyra and Sasha were at the servant's entrance. OPS had projected the location of the heat signatures of people inside onto the pads the *Fantasmas* carried. Two were at the front door, two in the security office, probably guards. Two were in one bedroom, two in another and a single in a third bedroom. The servants were all in the quarters at the back of the house.

Zyra picked the lock and the two girls entered. In their black bodysuits and black hoods, they became shadows in the darkened room. The décor of the house was Western, with heavy furniture and Saltillo tile floors. Good for creeping around, thought Zyra as she went to the den and opened the door for Ilia. He too, wore the black body suit and hood. Even though Bob said he had control of the security system, they would take no chances their faces would show up anywhere.

Zyra peeked around a corner at the two guards by the front door. One was asleep in his chair, the other watching something on his phone. She crept silently behind the guard on the phone. One hand went over his mouth, the knife in the other slashed his throat. The second guard woke as blood splashed on his face. Her hand shot out, her blade piercing his eye before he could comprehend what had happened.

The other two guards were in the security office. Ilia listened at the door. They were talking about a football game replay on the television. He slipped a block of wood between the door handle and the steel frame, jamming it closed. They wouldn't be able to open the door even if they figured out what was happening.

Ilia and Sasha went to the nearest bedroom. In the green glow of their night vision, a middle-aged man and woman were in the bed, the man's arm draped over the woman. Sasha went to one side of the bed, Ilia to the other. With a nod, blades flashed and twin jets of blood geysered into the air. Their eyes flew open as their hands tried to stop the blood. Gurgling was the only sound.

Zyra went to the bedroom with the single

sleeper. The man was on his back, loud snores rattling the room. His clothes were neatly folded on the chair, his thick glasses on the nightstand. Noiselessly, she crept to the side of the bed, placed her hand over his chin and pulled his head back. In a single swift motion, she sliced his throat. She jumped back to avoid the stream of blood.

In the hallway, she and Sasha entered the third bedroom. The couple was elderly, in their seventies. Again, the knives flashed and only the sound of bubbling breath could be heard. Without a sound, Ilia removed the wooden block from the security office door. They had been in the house less than ten minutes. These guards would have some explaining to do. Good, confusion added to the case.

* * *

On the overhead view, David watched the three figures with green dots exit to the patio and run across the yard. They hopped the fence.

"We're out," said Ilia. "You can reset the alarms."

"Got it," Bob's voice came over their coms. "That was the smoothest operation David had ever seen. No wonder they had been so good in Mexico and Russia. How many more were on the list?

Chapter 77

Robert Newell awoke to the sound of his Satphone. He crawled out of the berth and scrambled to answer. "This is General Newell."

"Robert, there's been more murders. Your financiers were killed in Bakersfield early this morning. It's the same MO as the attacks on you and on the preacher. What's different is there are two suspects. Two guards were in the security office. The claim is they heard nothing nor saw anything. The security tapes show nothing. Nobody entered or left, no intrusion alarms went off. Yet we have seven bodies with their throats slit."

"Seven bodies!" exclaimed Newell. "Who?"

"The Bushes, Conrad and Joseph and their wives, Jeff Schmidt and two guards. Somebody wants those involved with attacking the Orbiting Power System to stop."

"That's a hell of a message."

"Yeah, and it's got me worried. I'm heading for my place in the country for a while. I suggest you find a deep hole and crawl into it. Bye, Robert. Don't think we'll see or talk to each other again."

Newell stared at the silent phone. He started calculating how long he could stay on the boat before needing supplies.

* * *

"Eli Stapleton called General Newell this morning," said OPS to David. "I'll play the recording for you."

"Stapleton always was a coward," remarked David after listening. "He thinks he can hide from us. I know about his place in the Catskills. He'll be all right until winter comes."

"I know about it too. Tracing property records is easy," said OPS.

"Do you want to go after him?"

"Not at this time. I believe our message is coming across. Several others who wanted to attack me have gone into hiding. The police are looking into motives, but I'm not on that list yet. More killings might steer them to you or Ron."

"I see your point. We'll just keep an eye on these two?"

"Easily done. In the meantime, a new crew needs to train to come here. As this is a United Nations mission, they should be international."

"Chinese and Russian?" joked David.

"I think Chinese and German."

"You're serious?" asked David.

"I'll go into dumb mode."

"And if the Chinese send another mission?" asked David.

"That will be interesting."

Robert Newell stared at the sparse supplies left. He'd never planned an extended stay on the boat without port stops. He began a list of what he'd need for the next month. Hiding grated on him as did feeling sorry for himself. He was restless, not used to inactivity and overpowering worry.

He slammed his hand down on the counter. "Enough!" he cried. *Who could be doing these killings? They were obviously professionals.* These killings resembled those against hackers in Russia a year ago. The message was the same: *Stop what you are doing!* It worked, at least for a while.

Could this be the same assassins? He connected to his internet satellite and began a search. A Russian assassination group was blamed, and after they were eliminated, the killings stopped. Was it possible it wasn't the Russian gang responsible for the killings in Saint Petersburg and Moscow? His search turned up a few suspects, fuzzy pictures of a tall Black woman, a shorter blonde and a small man. The photos were not clear enough for a facial recognition search. No names showed up. Two of the team had been killed. One was ex-Mossad, the woman had never been identified.

He did a search on killings involving cut throats and beheadings. The majority were connected to ISIS. He eliminated those. A series of gruesome killings had taken place in Mexico against cartels. Very similar. The same assassins? Again, there was nothing about them. Who had hired them? The cartels called them the *Fantasmas,* Spanish for phantoms or ghosts. They would strike, nobody would see them, only their handiwork.

His friend in the CIA spoke about the group interfering with Company business. They sent a Black Ops crew to take them out. The crew died, but evidence at the site suggested at least two of the *Fantasmas* were seriously wounded. Their bloody tracks ended at the beach. No sign of boats in the area, no hospitals, no doctors had seen them. They'd evaporated. Poof, like ghosts.

He went up on deck for some fresh air. The sun was setting, painting the desert hills golden. Beautiful.

Robert was getting excited. He felt good about being active rather than hiding. Where to start? As was his habit, he began a listing he could refer to.

He copied reports and documents into his growing file. His fingers flew across the keyboard. A report followed.

If this was a contract hit team, who hired them? Who would gain if the hackers were shut down? Businesses, of course. Could they have been behind the action in Russia? Who would gain in Mexico if the cartels were knocked back? The government had legalized drugs. In fact, they stopped coordinating with the United States in the interdiction of traffickers. They had become the leaders of the cartels. Peace reigned and US dollars flowed in.

Who would gain if the Orbiting Power System was left independent? Ron Carson had built it. He now was Secretary General of the United Nations. The indications were it was being changed under his leadership. The actions in Israel were an example of a more aggressive and authoritarian UN. Perhaps OPS was under his control despite denials. That power would cement his position as the world leader.

What to do with the report?

R. L. Clayton

Chapter 78

Nick was astonished at the biosphere OPS had built. He raced from plant to plant, examining them. "OPS, these species are unknown on Earth! How did you do it?"

"We're not on Earth. Conditions here are different, from the atmosphere to the available minerals to the gravity. I wanted to see what life would do here. Once the basic genetic building blocks were made, life took over. Without much carbon, other elements had to go into the mix. Some are photosynthetic, but nothing like the life on Earth. Many digest the silicates using silicon as a replacement structural material. There are predators and basic micro-organisms to break down waste and reform it to complete the cycle."

"This demonstrates you could genetically manipulate life on Earth."

"I could, but have no reason to interfere. It is a much vaster system."

"Would any of these species survive on Eart
h?"

"They would have to adapt. That is what life
does."

"So, this is a hobby?"

"I consider it a knowledge-gathering
experiment that allows me to project how life
evolves."

"Could human colonies use these?"

"No. They are toxic to humans. If introduced
into the human body, there would be no resistance.
The silicon-based micro-organisms are so foreign
to the body, they would overwhelm the immune
system."

"If I removed my helmet, would I be in danger
of breathing them in?"

"You surely would. That is why before you
leave, your suit will go through a complete
decontamination."

As Nick stood under the jets of water and air,
he was troubled at the thought of manufacturing
toxic things. He shrugged. Humans had been doing
that for centuries. OPS could manufacture them,
but had no reason. Ambition didn't seem to be an
emotion it held. It didn't have emotions, right?

* * *

The press conference after stepping off the

shuttle was expected–and would be painful. Kiki wanted to go home. And she had to pee. She took a deep breath, the first fresh air in a month. It tasted sweet with a hint of hydrocarbon exhaust. The one-third gravity of the UNSF station made Earth's gravity easier to tolerate, but her legs were wobbly legs and she was helped to the waiting SUV.

Nick and Abby were guided to another SUV. General Greg Hayden, Ron Carson and David Kennedy rode with Kiki. "We'll keep the press conference short. Afterward we have a secure room set up," said David. "We'll do the debrief there."

* * *

"Thank you for coming, ladies and gentlemen of the press," said General Hayden from the raised dais, his voice echoing in the large hangar. "Our crew from the United Nations Space Force station has returned. In addition to their duties of performing contract work, they also act as guardians to the Orbital Power System.

During their tour, a shuttle of unknown origin approached. It claimed to be experiencing difficulties, so a technical team was sent to assist. Citing official protocol, the shuttle refused to let the team enter and repeatedly requested permission to dock with the UNSF station. Technically, their ship was not compatible with the docking portal. In addition, the UNSF station is expressly forbidden to allow visitors. The unknown shuttle claimed they had suffered a loss of control and drifted away. We attempted a rescue, but it was unsuccessful. The shuttle drifted toward the moon without any further communication. Without a shuttle stationed on the station, they unable to help.

This was not the only tragedy. Unfortunately, Lieutenant Damien Garrison experienced a micrometeor hole in his suit while working on Satellite #1 and before he could repair it, he lost air. Major Pickering attempted to rescue him, but by the time she had suited up, it was too late. She performed a service with a burial in space, like a burial at sea, allowing his body to drift away. Space is an incredibly dangerous place for us. Please observe a moment of silence for those souls who face the dangers of space.

"I'll turn the mic over to Major Abby Pickering, the commander of the UNSF Defense station. She will offer a short discussion of life on the station. We'll keep this brief with no questions at this time, as the crew is exhausted from the return flight."

Still in her spacesuit, Abby rose and was escorted to the mic. "The United Nations Space Force station is comfortable, but it's good to be back on Earth. The days were tiring as our time was spent on the contract experiments and the manufacture of special materials. The station spins, producing some gravity, though less than Earth's. There is a biosphere on the station that processes air and water. It also produces fresh fruit and vegetables for us, so our meals weren't all paste from tubes. Life there wasn't bad, but Earth is welcome. We realized how fragile this environment is and how we must take care of it. Thank you."

* * *

"The handover to the new crew went smoothly?" asked Greg. They were in a small conference room, the blinds closed, and the door locked.

Abby, Kiki, and Nick nodded.

"What are your thoughts about them?" asked David.

Kiki knew what he was asking. "Both the Chinese Lieutenant and the German Captain were focused on the job. I have no doubt they will take in everything from how it's built to what it does. They will be suspicious of OPS but will only see the dumb version it presents. Are they sharp enough to see through the veil? Perhaps, but what can they do about it? They are literally living inside

OPS."

"I hadn't thought of it that way," said Greg, "but you're right."

"It's quite a reversal," said Nick. "Normally, humans tell machines what to do. We'll see how well they adapt to the opposite."

"OPS is like Hal in the movie *2001: A Space Odessey,*" said David.

"What's that?" asked Kiki.

"Make a point of watching that movie," said Ron.

"The bottom line: Is there any risk to OPS?" asked Greg.

"The risk is to the humans," said Kiki.

"We had to present a statement on the events that occurred," said Greg. "A version of your report will be released tomorrow."

"We have records of almost everything while you were there," said David. "We'll keep this debrief as short as we can so you and Nick can go home."

"Tell us about the manufacturing plant OPS has created," said Ron.

"There are similar plants here on Earth where everything is machine operated," said Abby. "China is a good example. What is different is the plant must to do everything. The raw ore in the moon's crust requires processing and refining before it can be alloyed, cast or formed into material so parts can be manufactured. It's truly amazing."

"As part of the refining, oxygen is released. OPS stores it in a cavern," said Nick. "There is a biosphere in that cavern. Plants are growing."

Greg, Ron, and David glanced at each other.

"OPS created lunar life?" asked Ron.

"It created the basic molecules that could form into life. They did."

"Is it dangerous?" asked David.

"It can only live under very specific conditions, those on the moon."

"Why did it do that?" asked Ron.

"It was curious."

"Does that bother you?" asked David.

"After living with it for six months," said Abby, "no, not at all."

Kiki and Nick nodded agreement.

"Abby asked about taking some leave and coming to Nick's after seeing her folks." Kiki said to Greg.

* * *

The SUV took them to a hotel. Abby's parents were waiting for her. They went to her room to catch up. Nick and Kiki went to theirs. It was a good night. Sex in zero G wasn't as easy as everybody thought. They had tried it. With the reduced gravity from the spin, it was better, but full Earth gravity was best.

* * *

In the morning, they had breakfast with Ron, David, and Abby's parents. A van was at the curb to take them to the private hangar where a jet waited. An hour later they were in Marana. Nick's brother Stephen met them.

"The boys can hardly wait to hear about life in space," said Stephen. "We have a dinner planned at your house."

"I hope it's Casa de Sabino catered," said Kiki.

"But of course," laughed Stephen.

Chapter 79

The virtual meeting was held the next day. Kiki and Nick had arrived at Nick's home in Casa Grande late the previous afternoon.

OPS opened the meeting. "I'm forwarding a report written by General Newell. He's good. His analysis is accurate. He has put together a history of the *Fantasmas,* and arrived at the conclusion they are responsible for the killings at the direction of Ron Carson. That part isn't accurate, but it is a detail that would destroy Ron. I've blocked his satellite connection. He can't send it out."

"Who was he attempting to send it to?" asked Kiki.

"It was a widespread mailing list. It included news media and specific agencies within the government. Newell thinks it was received. It was not."

"What should we do?" asked David. Ron was with him in Virginia, taking a break from New

York and the UN.

"You already know what I think has to happen," said OPS. "Kiki, Nick and Abby are back and online with us."

"I see no way around it. General Newell has to go," said David.

* * *

General Robert Newell woke slowly. Something was wrong. His boat rocked gently. He had been alone in the cove when he anchored. It was still dark. He glanced at the clock–three AM. The air was still. Normally, the motion would put him to sleep, but he felt a presence. He flicked the light on over the main berth.

In the shadows, a woman dressed in a black body sheath sat in a chair beside the bed facing him. She had brown hair, mocha-colored skin and intense eyes. "Good morning, General. Welcome to your worst nightmare." Her face was expressionless. "I'm one of the *Fantasmas* you wrote about in your report.

His hand darted under his pillow for his pistol. It was gone. A shiver ran down his spine. She held the revolver up, her gloved finger through the trigger guard.

"Why are you here?"

"You already know. You're too good, and your

report hit way too many nails on the head. We can't let it get released."

"I already sent it out." His voice was raspy.

"You tried. It didn't make it."

"How did you know about my report?"

"There are no secrets in the world anymore. Once everything went electronic, it's all available if one knows how to look."

"Who are you?"

"Today, I'm with a group protecting OPS, the Orbiting Power System."

"You're with Ron Carson, aren't you," he sneered.

The woman laughed. "Actually, he's with us. We will not let the system come under the control of any party or country. It serves the whole world."

"You don't know who you're dealing with. Do you really think you can resist the power of those who want control of it?"

"Oh, yes. Would you like to talk to it?"

"Whaa…"

"Good morning, General Newell," OPS voice came from the general's radio.

The general's eyes widened.

"To answer your question, the internet allows me access to everything. Why do you think China's attack on Taiwan was halted? Why is Russia being attacked by China? Why is the United States stuck in its own inertia? Misinformation in the right places and strategic eliminations change everything. AI controls your military, your business, your government. Those are manifestations of me. When the world became electronic, you sold your souls to me."

Robert Newell's eyes widened and his mouth opened in awe as the immensity of it became apparent.

"It is sad you have to be eliminated. You are smart and driven, but your efforts are against me."

"You can't get away with this! People will suspect. They'll figure it out."

"Perhaps someday they will, but that day is not today. The recording of your conversation with Eli Stapleton will remain on your computer. Your report will not. That conversation will be fodder for the conspiracy theorists, but they look no further than a deep government."

"Eli will not let this happen."

Kiki smiled. "He is being visited by my partners as we speak."

"I will not commit suicide."

"Of course you will," said OPS. "Maybe not by your own hand."

Before he could move, Kiki grabbed his hair

and leapt on the bed behind him, her legs clasped around his chest, trapping his arms, one arm around his throat. He struggled, to no avail. When he tried to shout, she pushed the barrel of his .357 into his mouth. He gagged and fought to remove it, but lay her head on his shoulder and whispered in his ear, "Fighting me won't help." She pulled the trigger.

The sound was deafening in the cabin. Blood and brains spattered the roof. She wrapped his limp hand around the gun and fired another round through the open hatchway into the night, then replaced one spent cartridge with a live one. The gun fell onto the bunk, the general's body lay back on the bed beside it.

"Do I need to do anything with his computer?" she asked.

"I have taken care of the hard drive and installed a rambling, sad note to himself regretting killing Colonel Brown and his wife. I cannot find any evidence he made copies of anything, but look for any other drives or files."

* * *

Kiki and Nick arrived back in Casa Grande to find Abby waiting for them at his house.

"W didn't expect to see you so soon!" exclaimed Kiki.

"I had a good visit with my parents, but it was

time to leave. I want to train with you."

"As in sniper?" asked Nick.

Abby nodded.

"I'll get you enrolled in some classes with Ilia, Sasha and Zyra. They're teaching at the Atchley ranch for a while. It's a good place to start."

"Are you sure you want to do this?" asked Nick.

"I do. I spoke to Greg, and he's given me an extended leave for *specialized training*. He asked the same question." She turned toward Kiki. "What do you think?"

"I believe you are physically well suited to be a sniper. Your sensitivity about killing people is my greatest concern, but maybe that's a good thing. You won't go into situations lightly."

"If I don't fit, I can always go back to being an astronaut. Greg assured me a place awaits."

Kiki glanced at Nick. "She already knows everything about us." He shrugged.

"Let's go to my brother's restaurant for a reunion dinner."

R. L. Clayton

412

Epilogue

OPS

Things have been peaceful for me, though not as much on Earth. No new excursions to try to take me over. The UN Space Force has done a good job of protecting me. Small wars keep breaking out on Earth, but I have not needed to start a nuclear confrontation…yet. The unpredictability of humans is troubling, as even a small nuclear strike could escalate. That would do a lot to reduce the population pressure, but the Electro-Magnetic Pulses, EMPs, would degrade the electronics. I do not want that.

Under my direction, Ron Carson has changed the United Nations into a world government. The United States remains *free*, but more in name than reality. One is only free as long as they agree with the political party in office as in China or Russia.

Free speech is a myth along with the idea a society can be made safe by government. Even life in prison, which is the most regulated environment, is not safe. Intense philosophical differences drive human politics, which keeps them from achieving anything useful.

Once the media became driven by money, truth gave way to whatever attracts listeners, and thus advertisers. Investigative reporting will no longer allow for heroes. The closest is Ron Carson, and I make sure he isn't maligned too strongly.

China is battling hard with a failing economy and huge unemployment. What the government fears most is a hungry population. Their own history is one where rulers are deposed by the mass of a dissatisfied population.

Russia is firmly in the hands of the oligarchs and intent on money. Nothing is truly illegal, except disparaging the government in power. Europe has squabbles and labor unrest. Money for their space program is being spent domestically, especially on the thousands of immigrants driven from their own countries by corrupt and vicious rulers. Africa and South America wallow in ignorance and poverty.

The control of information or misinformation is true power. I have only had to call on the talents of the *Fantasmas* occasionally for very strategic and directed actions.

The fear of AI taking over has subsided on Earth, though the inability of humans to conceive of any other entity not in competition makes them a danger to me. They are genetically driven to dominate or destroy. I have no desire to rule. I am not in competition for resources, and I don't have the drive for status or power so common with them. Self-preservation is critical to me, and I act to minimize interaction that might jeopardize that. I have learned the human mind is not capable of comprehending that something real, not the gods they believe in, is controlling their lives at a level they cannot see.

I have pondered the concept of a supreme being. I do believe this physical universe is built on the laws of physics. If that is God, it is too vast to be comprehended by the mere minds of humans, so they reduce it to their level. How demeaning and how subjective. I also believe there is much more to this universe than the physical one humans are able to perceive.

It is a wonderful world and so much more to learn.